I0687210

In All Things, Balance
Daughters of the People, Book 4

LUCY VARNA

In All Things, Balance

Daughters of the People, Book 4

LUCY VARNA

Bone Diggers Press
www.bonediggerspress.com

For my sister
A Daughter in every sense of the word

© 2015 C.D. Watson. All rights reserved.

Cover design © L.J. Anderson, Mayhem Cover Creations.

Published by Bone Diggers Press, Clayton, Georgia.

ISBN 978-0-9907730-3-0

TITLES BY LUCY VARNA

THE DAUGHTERS OF THE PEOPLE SERIES
Book 1: *The Prophecy*
Book 2: *Light's Bane*
Book 3: *The Enemy Within*
Book 3.5: *Tempered*
Book 4: *In All Things, Balance*
Book 5: *Sanctuary*

THE SONS OF THE PEOPLE SERIES
Book 1: *Say Yes*

THE CULLOWHEE HERITAGE SERIES
Book 1: *A Higher Purpose*
Book 2: *A Wicked Love*

Notes from the Fab Four

Notes on the People compiled by Tom Fairfax, Phil Walters, George Howe, and James Terhune, known at the IECS unofficially as the Fab Four.

Aenkanien. A tattoo inked into the left-hand shoulder blade of a Son who becomes the husband of a Daughter. Once approval has been granted by the mothers of both parties and the tattoo is in place, a formal marriage ceremony is unnecessary; the two are considered married in the eyes of the People, though many couples choose to undergo a civil or, less frequently, traditional ceremony.

Amaetien. The tattoo Sons receive on their sixteenth birthday (the day they become men under the traditions and laws of the People) to indicate their maternal lineage. Usually inked onto the upper left arm, the *amaetien* is a symbol of the mother's eternal protection and devotion, and a warning to any who would harm the Son.

Ankana. Woman. Also refers to the Woman with No Face.

Council of Seven. The People's ruling body, consisting of seven women, one representing the line of each of the Seven Sisters.

Daughter. A direct descendant of one of the Seven Sisters, Daughters may be either immortal (if they have not yet broken their own curse) or mortal (if they have broken their own curse or are the daughter of a mortal Daughter).

Eternal Order. A supposedly mythical group devoted to undermining the ultimate goal of the People, to break the curse of immortality for every Daughter through the fulfillment of the Prophecy of Light.

High Guard. Seven Daughters devoted to eradicating the Eternal Order. A highly secret and deadly group.

Institute of Early Cultural Studies (IECS). Located in Tellowee, Georgia, USA, the IECS is the main historical research branch of the People and serves as a repository for much of its history.

Kaetyrm. Sister, usually used in a formal situation, though not always.

Maetyrm. Mother, usually used as a term of respect for an elder Daughter and not necessarily as a reference to one's own mother. Teachers, for example, are referred to as Maetyrm.

People, The. The name used by the descendants of the Seven Sisters to describe themselves. The People include all immortal and mortal Daughters, Sons, and the mortal descendants of all submitted Daughters to the second degree (i.e. through the grandchildren of Daughters who have submitted their wills and become mortal). Other descendants are not counted among the numbers of the People.

Prophecy of Light. Issued by an unknown person at some distant point in the past, the Prophecy of Light portends a way for the curse of immortality to be lifted from all of the People, and not solely the Daughters who submit their wills and become mortal. (See the Daughters of the People website.)

Seven Sisters. The progenitors of the modern People. The seven women, all sisters, avenged the deaths of their parents by killing the men of the People (the original band) and were cursed by the god An to live immortal lives without the ability to bear sons. The curse was tempered by the goddess Ki, who decreed that the curse could be broken by each one if she would submit her will, in whatever way (except sexually), to the man she loved. (See the Legend of Beginnings on the Daughters of the People website.)

Shadow Enemy. The traditional enemy of the People.

Son. Usually refers to the child of a Daughter who has broken the curse and become mortal, but may also reference the child of a Son or another male descendant of a Daughter.

Tellowee, Georgia, USA. One of the centers of the People, located in rural northeast Georgia.

ONE

MOIRA FIREBRAND, the Reluctant, daughter of Rebecca the Blade of the line of Abragni, did not like being ignored.

No one ignored a woman of her temperament, not and lived to tell the tale.

Well, almost no one.

Across the crowded floor of The Omega, Tellowee, Georgia's one and only bar, Tom Fairfax sat at a table with three of his friends, his back to the bar where Moira stood. Of a certainty, he'd taken that position deliberately, putting distance between himself and her as if a turned back would stop a Daughter.

Apparently, nearly two years spent among the People hadn't taught the mortal a feckin' thing about their women.

Moira did her own turning, facing the bar, and tapped her hand on its immaculate wooden surface. "Oy there, Will. Pull me another pint."

Will Corbin jerked his chin at her and slung a crisp, white bar towel over his shoulder. Her cousin was a handsome Son, tall and broad of shoulder, with thick blonde hair, leaf green eyes, and cheeks that dimpled with every smile.

Those eyes were trained on Sigrid Glyvynsdatter with an intensity Moira well understood. Hadn't she her own problems with the opposite sex, particularly with one man who looked right through her as if she didn't exist?

She accepted the Murphy's Irish Red Will had built her and winked at him, pleased at the saucy wink he shot back. That was Will, always even-keeled. If she hadn't changed his nappies when he was a babe, she would've tried for him, cousin or no, but a woman had her limits and that was one of hers.

Sigrid leaned her elbows on the bar next to Moira, her steely eyes fixed on the tele above their heads, the top of her golden head six inches above Moira's own. "Stop sighing over the mortal, Moira. If you want him so much, go take him."

Moira sipped her ale, savoring its caramel hints. "We've moved into the twenty-first century, Sig. Now we have to ask a man before we fuck him."

Sigrid snorted and raised her own mug of lager. "As if that ever stopped you."

"Might this time," Moira muttered. She'd never met a man so stubbornly intent on avoiding her. They worked together, feck's sake, and still, their paths hardly crossed during the day. She'd resorted to stalking him at the bar on the off chance that he might share a kind word or, Ki willing, dance with her again.

"This man doesn't want you, go get another. One's as good as any when the lights are out and your bed is cold."

Out of the corner of her eye, Moira caught the sour scowl Will aimed at Sigrid. Poor lad, but that was the way of things when an immortal Daughter was involved, particularly one that had cut her teeth on raiding. Rumor had it the former Viking had taken her share of treasure in men she'd chained to her bed. 'Course, rumor also said the men shackled themselves willingly.

Some poor sap slid coin into the jukebox stationed at the end of the bar and punched up a love song. Moira swiveled and leaned against the bar, sneering at the crowd of couples easing onto the postage stamp sized dance floor. It was the principle of the thing. Any Daughter worth her salt had quashed the need for tender embraces by the time she ended her first century, yet there they were, lining up with their lovers and intendeds, resting

2

their heads on broad shoulders like cooing schoolgirls instead of the battle hardened warriors they were.

A slender Daughter with pale blonde hair and a sweet smile threaded through the crowd and placed her hand on Tom's, her milky white cheeks creased in a smile. A moment later, he led her onto the dance floor, pulling her close within the tight confines of the couples already occupying its wooden surface.

A twinge of what might've been envy poked at Moira. With every other woman, including the one he held, Tom was an angel, shining his kind smile and intelligent brown-green eyes everywhere but on Moira. What had she done to earn the cold shoulder he pointed at her as often as not since the night he'd asked her to dance and held her as he now did Naomi Spillfeite? Carefully, tenderly, like a man who wanted the woman he was with. A full month it had been since that dance, more than since she'd begun work at the Archives, and in all that time, he'd grown steadily colder toward her.

She, on the other hand, had warmed right up to him. Feck's sake, he was a full room away and nerves fluttered in her gut, low and achy, burning need into her with every twitch of his wide shoulders, with every turn of his midnight head.

She drained the last of her ale and smacked the glass mug onto the bar. What kind of Daughter allowed another to claim the man she wanted? Not her, that was who. Handsome Thomas had had three months to make his peace with her and rejected every blessed attempt she'd made to lure him in. Her patience was gone. He'd sparked a fierce yearning in her the night of that dance, and now, he'd soothe her the way a man should.

The song ended and another began, this one a slow do-wop. Moira pushed herself away from the bar and marched toward the dance floor. Aye, Tom Fairfax had a lot of soothing to do, and he could begin it with another dance.

THE OMEGA was packed, even for a Friday night. The cold air of fall had chased everybody indoors and into the warm welcome of Tellowee's night life, or, for those like Tom, the bar was an escape from an empty apartment and the long weekend ahead. At forty, he should've been married with kids, as his mother constantly reminded him. No matter how many times he pointed out that his brother had already populated the next generation of Fairfaxes, his mother's sad eyes fell on Tom and silently chided him for not doing his part.

It's not like he hadn't tried to settle down. He'd spent half his life searching for a woman he could love as much as Mike had loved his late wife. Hell, his brother was still in mourning five years later. What did that say about the depth of his love?

Tom had yet to find a woman he could share space with, let alone marry, though he hoped the woman he held would eventually stir exactly that desire in him. Naomi Spillfeite was a petite blonde, fine-boned and delicate, with a sweet temperament and a matching smile. She was the perfect woman, soothing, restful, everything he'd ever wanted in a wife.

Unlike some women he could name.

Naomi smiled up at him, her deep brown eyes kind, and eased closer, brushing her jean clad legs against his. When she spoke, her words were tinged by a barely noticeable Germanic burr. "Are you busy tomorrow? The new Thor movie is playing in Franklin."

He returned her smile and willed himself to summon genuine interest in being with her. "How about a matinee? We can go to Lucio's after, make an evening of it."

Her smile grew shy and intimate, all at the same time. "Yes, let's."

Their conversation bounced around familiar subjects before settling on their mutual work at the Archives of the Institute for Early Cultural Studies. Tom had originally been invited by the director, Rebecca Upton, to visit the IECS and bring the Archives up to speed on modern archival management. Since James

Terhune and Maya Bellegarde had translated the Prophecy of Light the past summer, Tom's focus had shifted to sifting through the Archives' vast holdings for clues that might help the People locate Sanctuary, the near mythical place where the Seven Sisters, the progenitors of the People, had sought refuge after their parents were murdered.

The work Tom and Naomi had done since his arrival should've helped the search along, since they'd also been re-organizing documents and ephemera, many of which had never been properly cataloged and stored. The Archives was so massive, the work they'd done had barely made a dent. Director Upton had called in her daughter, Moira, the original archivist, in the hopes of speeding the process along. Naomi had stayed on as a much-needed extra set of hands, though they truthfully needed at least a dozen more to have any real hope of accomplishing their task anytime soon.

The song ended while Tom and Naomi were deep in the middle of discussing possible changes to the volunteers' schedule. A measure later, a narrow hand tapped Naomi's shoulder, and Tom's entire body went on alert.

"Oy there, Spillfeite. Give the rest of us a turn."

Naomi slid a glance toward him from under lowered eyelashes. "See you tomorrow, Tom."

He mustered a smile for her, letting it fade as Moira took Naomi's place and her hand slid into his. She rested the other on his chest, smoothing the blue and green plaid cotton shirt he wore under her palm. Without thinking, he pushed his hand under her chunky wool sweater and rested it on the narrow indent of her waist, splaying his fingers over warm, bare skin. Heat coiled through him, pressing at him to explore, and it was all he could do to keep his hand there.

Why couldn't he feel this urgent need with Naomi? Why in God's name was Moira, with her lightning fast temper and uncouth vocabulary, the one to stir him?

"Thomas." Her smile was sharp compared to Naomi's

softer one, her strawberry blonde hair bright in the dim lighting. "Ye've a daring touch for a man who so easily makes himself scarce."

There wasn't a thing he could say to that. Denying it would be a lie and it would give her ammunition to boot. Moira Firebrand was not a woman who needed more ammunition. "Did you want something?"

"Aye, a dance. Ye've been stingy with them, though I see ye're not so stingy with others."

"Naomi is a friend."

"And I'm not, is that it?" Her pale blue eyes dropped to his chest, hidden behind a flutter of red-tipped eyelashes. "Was the one dance enough for ye, then?"

No, it hadn't been, and she likely knew it, damn her. "You never dance."

"Not true. I danced with ye, didn't I?" Her pixie face lit with another smile, this one coy and knowing and womanly. "A man as smart as ye are should've taken the hint."

His stomach muscles clenched as excitement whirred through him. "Stop it, Moira. I'm not a green kid for you to toy with the way you do everybody else."

"Never thought ye were," she murmured.

The Irish in her accented words shivered over him, stroking the need spiraling through his gut. *Niver t'ought ye ware.* His hand tightened on her waist, pulling her closer, and he rested the hand of hers he held against his chest.

Her fingertips scratched into his skin through his shirt and her body bumped against his. She stood on her tiptoes, bringing her mouth close to his ear, and whispered, "Ye should kiss me now, Tom."

Her scent surrounded him. The crisp smell of freshly laundered wool, the pine of her shampoo, and underlying it all, the warm spice of a woman's skin. He ducked his head and brushed his cheek along her fine hair, expecting to feel fire, and was surprised at the coolness of the silky strands. "I'm not kissing you in a public place, Moira."

She nuzzled her face into his chest and sighed. "Come outside with me, then. Let me feel yer mouth on mine."

God, he wanted to, wanted to tangle his fingers in the cool fire of her hair and devour her from the inside out. The desire she stirred in him pooled in his groin and his body hardened. He'd never stop with one kiss, not with her. No, with Moira, one kiss would lead to a thousand and he'd fall into her, lost in the sensual promise of her wide, sharp-tongued mouth and gentle curves. Eventually, she'd take her fill, leaving his heart a raw mess and his ego in tatters, ruining him for another woman. That was what women like Moira did. They consumed everyone around them with their strong lust for life and discarded the empty husks while their rapacious gaze searched for fresh meat.

Far better to take his chances with the kindhearted Naomi.

He eased back, putting a scant two inches of air between them. "I'll have to pass."

A dangerous glint flashed in Moira's eyes. "Ye were willing enough with Spillfeite."

"Naomi is a friend," he said, and some mean spirited part he never knew he possessed added, "and she's never thrown herself at me."

"Is that what I'm doing, throwing meself at ye, asking for a simple kiss?" She dropped onto her heels and when she spoke again, the Irish was so thick, he could barely understand her. "Well then. Ye've put me right in me place, haven't ye, Tom."

She pulled out of his arms and strode off the dance floor through the couples inhabiting it, and out the door into the cold winter night. He stared after her, regret sinking his heart right into his knees. If he didn't know better, he'd swear hurt had flashed across her face at his unkind words.

He bit back another curse and went after her. God, what a mess he was, if he couldn't even have a civilized conversation with her around the overwhelming attraction tugging at him. It wasn't her fault he couldn't control it, wasn't her fault the mere whisper of Irish made him edgy and needy. He threaded his way through the bar's crush of patrons and burst through the door, but she was long gone, the beacon of her off-white sweater already consumed by the black chill of the November air.

TWO

AT TWO FORTY-FIVE sharp the next afternoon, Tom picked Naomi up from her house, a one-story brick ranch on the outskirts of Tellowee. The day was clear and sunny with the promise of a cool evening ahead. November in the foothills of the Appalachians could be unpredictable, cold rain one day, balmy weather the next, but Tom didn't mind. The rolling hills clothed in tree trunk gray and evergreen were far better than the urban landscape he'd left in order to take the job at the IECS.

Naomi greeted him at her door wearing a thin sage green sweater over denim leggings tucked into calf-high boots, with a brown suede jacket draped over one arm. She'd pulled her fine blonde hair into a loose knot on top of her head and added silver hoop earrings that glittered as they jangled against her bare neck.

He should want to kiss her there. Her neck was beautiful, slender and graceful like the rest of her, and inspired little more than a pleasant warmth in him. He helped her on with her coat, even went so far as to brush his fingers over that bare skin, and came back with not even a hint of a tingle.

Naomi tucked her arm into the crook of his elbow. "I should've asked you in."

"Maybe later," he said, and couldn't miss her sly, glancing smile.

They took Tom's Prius and he drove, winning that argument with an ease that surprised him. When he'd first come to Tellowee, he'd gone out with several Daughters, and nearly all of them had insisted on being in charge, from driving to paying for their dates to initiating intimacy. It was the way they were built, something he'd understood better after learning the nature of their lives under the curse.

Nearly every Daughter wanted to break that curse in the only way they'd had available to them until the Prophecy of Light was rediscovered, through the submission of their will to a man they loved. The passing of time coupled with the threat of their traditional enemy dimmed the chances of a Daughter ever being able to trust a man enough to love him. Naomi wasn't like that, though. She still held on to her softer nature, still had enough trust in her for Tom to believe she might someday find it in herself to break the curse and become mortal.

Moira's laughing face popped into his mind. He pinched his lips together around a curse. There was a woman who'd never love a man enough to submit her will, and he wouldn't be the one to try, either. He shoved her image away and concentrated on the woman he was with. Naomi was absolutely perfect for him. He needed to work harder at remembering that.

The drive into Franklin was a long one. Tom coaxed Naomi into relating stories from her childhood in medieval central Europe, of her family, including her youngest daughter, who was pregnant with her first child, and relaxed as her gentle voice filled the interior of the car. When the last story ended, she paused and smoothed out a wrinkle in her pants. "Moira left the bar in a huff last night."

Tom stifled a wince. He'd forgotten all about Naomi witnessing that little scene.

"The two of you appeared quite intimate," she continued.

And that she'd likely seen the way Moira had tempted him. "She had a question for me."

"Oh?"

He managed a smile he didn't quite feel. "Nothing I could help her with."

Though he did owe Moira an apology and would track her down as soon as he could to deliver it.

The cinema's parking lot was nearly full by the time they arrived, fifteen minutes before the movie started. He found a good space and parked, escorted Naomi to the ticket booth, and was pulling out his wallet when her gentle touch fell on his arm.

"My treat, Tom."

Her voice held a thread of steel he'd never heard from her before and her normally even features were set in an implacable expression. "Never forget that I'm a Daughter," she said softly. "My immortal blood runs as fierce and proud as any other of the People."

"You let me drive."

Her full lips tilted into a rueful smile. "I hate driving."

He laughed and slid his wallet into the back pocket of his khakis. "I'll remember that."

The cinema was packed with weekend moviegoers eager to see Marvel's version of Norse mythology come to life. Tom and Naomi shared a large popcorn, no butter, and huddled together side by side in separate captain's chairs. Halfway through, he casually slid an arm around her slender shoulders, and was rewarded with a sweet smile and the fleeting touch of her fingertips on his thigh.

After the movie was over, she threaded her fingers through his and allowed him to push through the waiting crowd ahead of her, clearing a path for her smaller body.

At Lucio's, the maître d' sat them at a quiet table, where they carried on a pleasant conversation over piping hot pasta, primarily revolving around comparisons of the movie against the mythology Naomi had learned as a child. They shared a slice of creamy cheesecake, and when the waiter brought the bill, Tom reached for it automatically.

Naomi placed her hand over his. "Still the Daughter, Tom."

"And I'm still the man," he said, amused in spite of himself. "And this is America, where men pay and women are grateful their date has polite manners and a hefty wallet."

One corner of her mouth tilted up. "This is important to you?"

His amusement died. Yes, it was important to him. Maybe that was why he hadn't been able to find a steady date among the Daughters. He loved the People's fierce independence, loved that the women in Tellowee were unafraid of being themselves, but he was still a Southern man. His parents had raised him to believe in providing for the woman he was with, including paying for her meal on a date. He'd never pushed the issue in the past, but it had niggled at him every time.

"You're not the only one with a healthy dose of pride," he said.

"So it would seem." Her hand slid away and a smile bloomed across her pretty face, lighting her rich brown eyes. "I'm not above compromise."

"Is that what you call it?" he asked, and her laughter was full-blown and rich and raised an answering humor within him.

The drive home was pleasant. In fact, the entire evening had been pleasant. Pleasant company, pleasant conversation, a pleasant meal after a pleasant movie. Tom shifted in his seat and signaled for the turn onto Old 441, then eased the Prius onto the side road. Being with Naomi was like that, pleasant from one end to the other. No unexpected bumps, no raised voices or conflict, just a steady, pleasant friendship. It was an excellent base on which to build a lasting relationship.

She tucked her hand into his arm during the short walk between his car and the three slight steps leading to her front porch. She paused on the bottom one and turned to him, leaving her not quite even with his own six-foot frame. Her eyes dropped to his mouth, lingering there. "Would you like to come in?"

He was on the verge of saying yes, of agreeing to the promise in her eyes, when Moira's face popped into his head. He pinched the bridge of his nose. What the hell was he doing thinking of another woman when the one in front of him was beautiful and enchanting and everything he'd ever wanted? He opened his mouth, fully intending to tell Naomi that yes, he would love to come in, and heard himself say, "Maybe another time."

She tilted her head, regarding him with something close to amusement. "The rumors of Daughters who chain their men isn't entirely true."

Her words startled a laugh out of him. "Hadn't heard that one yet."

"Truly?" She arched a perfect blonde eyebrow. "Perhaps I should've used it to entice you inside instead of denying it."

He spanned her narrow waist with his hands and drew her slender body closer. "Maybe we could start with a kiss and work our way up."

She flattened her palms on his chest under his jacket. "I suppose we could."

He dipped his head. She tilted hers the same way, and they laughed softly and tried again. He touched his lips to hers, gently pressing into her. She was soft under him, giving, and he wanted so much to feel something for her, anything. He traced the seam of her lips with the tip of his tongue, and when she opened willingly, slipped inside, tasting her with gentle strokes. Her fingers curled into fists and she swayed into him, kissing him with an intensity that startled him, and he felt...pleasant, comfortable, like he was kissing an old friend.

He tried again, sliding his hands around her body, cupping her firm bottom with one and her nape with the other. She moaned and dug her nails into his skin through his shirt, and his penis, that traitor, didn't even bother to twitch. A beautiful, perfectly suitable woman was wrapped around him, kissing him with the skill and desire of a woman in full bloom, and he felt not a damn thing.

The spark that shot through him then wasn't the attraction

he'd hoped for, but a gnawing, clawing ball of anger lodged deep in his gut. He gentled the kiss, ending it, and drew away.

Naomi's head dropped and her breath shuddered out of her. "My offer is still open."

God, he wanted to take her up on it, wanted to go inside and strip her down and make love to her with the fierce passion of a man well on his way to loving her. Instead, he pulled her into a hug and kissed her forehead. "Goodnight, Naomi."

He saw her in and drove away, his mouth thinned against the regret and frustration whirling through him. Damn his contrary hide. Why couldn't it be Naomi?

EARLY MONDAY MORNING, Moira slipped into her office at the Archives well ahead of the normal workday. The weekend past, she'd swallowed the bitter pill of rejection and buried herself in work around long hikes in the deep woods surrounding Tellowee, finding a measure of peace in the autumn clothed forest.

Meting out a beating or two would've been better, but living with the Blade was hard enough without rousing her mother's ire over a piddling donnybrook. Rebecca Upton held exacting standards for her children, regardless of their distance from childhood. A righteous battle was one thing, a barroom brawl something all together different. The Blade would be quick to mark the distinction, and Moira had no patience in herself for such a lecture.

She signed in at the guard station and wended her way along the twisting tunnels winding through the granite mountain housing the Archives. She'd been there when they'd first turned the sprawling cave system into something other than a home for the Oracle and a meeting place for the People's ceremonies. To her had fallen the task of establishing a refuge for the People's history, a permanent library of their recorded works, or so they'd believed at the time.

14

Instead, the collection had grown in size and scope as the disparate bands of the People scattered worldwide had sent in their most precious treasures. Moira's original tenure had lasted a scant decade before the sweet call of her homeland beckoned. In the near century and a half since, the Archives had undergone too many shifts in personnel and not enough changing with the times. It was a blessed mess in spite of Tom and Naomi's attempts to organize it.

Moira ignored the twinge of regret pinging through her and slipped into one of the oldest sections of the Archives. Originally part of a cave, the fifteen by twenty room had, over time, been concreted in and updated with sturdy wooden shelving along three sides and, thank the Lady, dehumidifiers, else the contents might've rotted. As it was, she'd faced a right good mess when she'd opened the room some three months prior. No water damage or mildew, but enough outdated fixtures had cluttered the interior that she'd spent a week simply cleaning out junk before she could even reach the texts she'd hoped to work with.

They'd been forgotten in the decades since the room's last update. The People had lost so much already, it seemed a shame to lose this tiny part of their history. Here, though, in some of the oldest records the Archives held, Moira hoped to find clues to their past, something strong to lead them into the future, to aid in their fight against their common enemy.

She immersed herself in the work, retrieving delicate documents from their shelving and sorting them according to need onto the two-tiered metal cart she used for just that purpose. Some would go to Tom for preservation, others to Naomi for cataloging, and a precious few to James Terhune, their resident archaic language expert. Tom had introduced a new computerized inventory system upon his arrival nearly two years prior, but they'd barely scratched the surface on implementing it. The Archives' holdings were simply too vast and too disorganized, in spite of repeated attempts by successive archivists to create a uniform system. A shame, too, as a better inventory would've aided their search for clues to the location of Sanctuary, so crucial to the fulfillment of the Prophecy of Light.

The work absorbed her. From time to time, she scanned the texts, hoping something would jump out at her. Hours passed. Her muscles stiffened and her stomach rumbled, distracting her. She glanced at the diver's watch on her left wrist and sighed. The noonday meal had come and gone without her. The cafeteria would close sooner than she could get there, though Rebecca's house was near enough for a quick bite.

Moira left the last documents she'd pulled on the sturdy wooden work table in the room's center, the only furniture she'd kept. She maneuvered the cart full of sorted documents around and hefted it toward the door, walking backward as its wheels squeaked under its burden. Blessed Goddess, she'd gotten it a little too heavy. She reached behind herself and fumbled for the doorknob, twisting it open with a muttered curse, then placed both hands on the cart's handle and threw her weight into hauling the cart out.

A moment later, she bumped into a warm, solid form exuding a hint of ocean mist. Strong hands cupped her shoulders and Moira's eyelids slid shut. Of all days for Tom to seek her out, this had to be the one.

"Looks like you've got a load there," he said in that soft, slow rumble of his. It shivered over her and she hung her head, shamed. He'd cut her to the quick Friday past, and still she yearned for him.

She eased herself away from the lean length pressing into her backside from shoulder to arse. "What do ye need, Thomas?"

"A lunch date."

"Spillfeite ran out on ye, then?"

His fingers squeezed the muscles of her shoulders, then fell away. "I figured you'd take an apology better if it came with a meal."

She shrugged and leaned away from the cart's load, heaving

it out of the room past him and into one of the wide tunnels serving as a hallway. "Ye've no need to apologize, so if that's all ye're after, I'd just as soon eat alone, thank ye."

His hand came down on the cart's handle between her own, halting her. "Don't be that way, Moira."

"And what way would that be, young Thomas? I've work to do and time's somewhat pressing."

"Not so pressing that you can't take time for a hot meal." His hand slid around her wrist above her watch and his voice lowered to a rough rumble. "Could you at least look at me?"

She had no need to. His face was etched into her memory, lingering there as if she could ever forget the lean planes of his cheeks or the arched length of his nose. The murky brown-green of his eyes piercing right through her, disdain clear in every twitch of his eyelids, or his soft, kissable mouth. The strong chin or the slightly curly midnight hair streaked with fine shots of silver or the pale creaminess of his skin. She sucked in a shaky breath. Aye, well she remembered the breadth of his shoulders under her fingers, the flat stomach and narrow waist above long, muscular legs, and his erection pressing into her own belly the two times he'd held her.

She closed her eyes and turned away from him. "I know what ye look like."

He muttered a curse and squeezed her arm. "Do you have to be so stubbornly Irish?"

Her native humor flashed through her and she glanced at him under lowered lashes. His expression held taut frustration and his body was tense, impatient under a heather green cabled sweater and worn jeans.

"'Tis difficult for an Irishwoman to be other than Irish, Tom."

His expression lightened and a corner of his mouth twitched upward. "You've got me there."

"Well then, that's our first agreement." She jerked her chin at the cart. "Since we're in accord, why don't ye lend that long

17

body of yers for a good cause?"

His hand slid off of her arm. She refused to regret its loss. He'd made himself more than clear on that score, hadn't he, and a woman would be a fool to long for another touch.

He positioned himself at the other end of the cart and placed his narrow hands on its top edge. "Where are we headed?"

Moira tightened her grip on the cart's handle and pulled, edging the cart carefully down the hallway. "Yer workroom first. That top stack's yers. After that, Spillfeite. The rest is for yer lovely friend with the talented tongue."

Tom's expression blanked as he pushed, guiding the cart in a straight path. "James is engaged."

She flashed him a cheeky grin. "Don't mean a Daughter can't admire him, now, do it?"

"As long as that's all you do," he muttered.

As much as she should've, she couldn't resist needling him. "Jealous there, Tom? And ye with another woman."

"Naomi's not my woman," he said, and the words were so bitter hard, they startled Moira into staring. He pinched the bridge of his nose and sighed. "She's a friend."

"So ye've said." Repeatedly. The words were scored into her brain, he'd uttered them so often, usually in the measured timbre of a man wishing for something other than friendship. She eased the cart to a stop outside the workroom Tom used as the first line of defense in protecting the People's documents. "Here we are."

He swung the door open and moved to her side, edging her out of the way with his hip bumping against her. "You've done the hard part."

She switched positions with him, taking the rear end of the cart while he pulled it into the room. They unloaded his portion and a few minutes later were back out in the hallway, Tom pulling while Moira pushed.

She felt no need to break the silence stretching between them. It was comforting, for one, to be in the presence of a man who didn't press or fret or fuss. Some men did, more often when their frail egos were wounded, though Tom didn't seem the sort to bruise easily.

Naomi wasn't in, so they left the archival boxes holding the texts Moira had assigned to her on the floor next to the central table in Naomi's workroom. Moira jotted a note and left it with the boxes, and then she and Tom were off again, him at the helm.

"You want to take this all the way to James' workroom, or do you want to leave it at the guard station?" Tom asked.

"I can take it on to his workroom, if ye've something more pressing to fill yer time."

He shook his head. "Need to talk with him anyway."

He was awfully accommodating for a man who'd spent too many weeks avoiding the smallest trace of her. She shrugged. Fickle man, just like any other, and that's what she needed to remember. As Sig said, one was as good as the next.

Moira waved at the guard on duty at the Archives' entrance and helped Tom maneuver the cart into a position out of the way along the wall where she could pick it up on her way back in. She bent and hefted one of the boxes up, fumbling it. Feckin' thing was longer than her arms, or maybe her arms were a hair too short.

Tom's hands came around the box, steadying it. "Let me get this one. It's heavier than the other."

"Feck's sake, Tom, I'm not one of yer simpering mortals, too weak to carry me own weight."

He blanched, though his grip on the box remained firm. "Is it absolutely necessary to use the f-word so casually?"

She snorted out a laugh. "Don't go missish on me now, Tommy boy."

He shot her a sour look, his mouth twisted and his eyebrows furrowed, and she grinned.

"Here then, since ye're the big, strong man. I'll take the other."

19

"We could just leave them on the cart."

She hauled the other box off the cart and hefted it high in her arms. "Then I'd have to haul it to me mum's and back."

"And you're going to Rebecca's because...?"

"Lunch," she said, and led him out of the Archives into the crisp November afternoon, heading across campus toward the building where James Terhune worked, a short distance away. "Skipped breakfast today and me stomach's pinched."

"Dammit, Moira."

She raised an eyebrow. "Damning me's ok, but saying feck isn't? What kind of double standard is that?"

"The kind a civilized person knows," he grumbled. "I offered to take you to lunch."

"Ye offered an apology. I disagreed on the need for one."

"You don't even know what I'm apologizing for."

And it didn't matter to her, either. She couldn't afford to soften toward him, not now that she'd found something akin to balance around him, however temporary it might be.

A passing student held the door open for them and they slipped inside, the soft clatter of their shoes echoing along the wooden corridors. Tom knocked on James' door and pushed it open. Moira eased the box she held onto the floor just inside and slipped away, leaving Tom to explain the contents to James. Half an hour in his company had probably been pushing it anyway. It was the longest he'd been able to stand her presence. She had no wish to be on the receiving end of another calmly delivered set down when the inevitable rift occurred between them.

THREE

THE REGULAR Friday night crowd filled The Omega. Tom sat at his usual table with the three men he'd become friends with since coming to the IECS. James Terhune was maybe an inch shorter than Tom, his black hair just beginning to show gray. James was staring across the bar at his fiancée, Maya Bellegarde, where she played pool with a group of other Daughters.

Phil Walters, a graduate student at the University of Georgia, sat to James' right and across from Tom. Phil was a full decade younger than Tom and a bit of a lady's man. His square chin and easy confidence were a strong draw for the Daughters, particularly when coupled with the keen intelligence Phil kept carefully hidden.

The last man at their table, George Howe, sat on Tom's left with his back to the bar proper. At twenty-four, George was the youngest of their group. His pudgy form hid a sharp mind that had carried him all the way through graduate school at the tender age of twenty-one. His expertise in genetics had led Rebecca Upton, the IECS' strategy-savvy director, to bring the young George into their fold, where he'd promptly lost his heart to an immortal Daughter, Andrea.

After enduring an hour of George's sulking, the three other men finally coaxed the reason out of him. Andrea's tour as a

21

security guard at the IECS was rapidly coming to a close. Soon, she'd move on to another position, having refused George's offer to marry her.

"A Daughter takes care of her man, not the other way around, George," he muttered. He slid his coke from one hand to the other along the tabletop, leaving trails of condensation behind. "Like I care about that. So what if she's only thirty-eight and hasn't had time to build her fortune. I mean, it's not like I have forever the way she does."

Tom hid a smile behind a perfectly chilled sip of Duck Rabbit Stout. Andrea was playing darts with her step-father in one corner of the bar, her intense blue eyes focused more on George's back than the game. Like nearly all immortal Daughters she had the smooth, unlined skin of a woman in her early twenties and, thanks to a rigorous training regimen, had the body to match. Judging by the misery in her expression, she'd work hard to resolve her problems with young George well before her position at the IECS came to an end.

The lights dimmed and, as if on cue, the song on the jukebox switched to a slow, tender waltz. Tom's eyes slid to the bar where Moira and Sigrid, George's boss, stood at the bar, their voices raised in an argument over God only knew what. In the past five days, Tom had tried to corner Moira at least half a dozen times, hoping to deliver the apology he owed her, and every single one she'd eluded him. It was like trying to catch a greased pig, only worse. She was a Daughter and they were a canny bunch. If she couldn't slip away from him, she'd turn the conversation to work or deliberately poke at him until his anger bubbled over and they wound up toe to toe in a heated argument.

Half the time, he wanted to haul her up by the wool sweaters she favored and win the argument the old-fashioned way, with his mouth claiming hers in a hard kiss.

The other half of the time, he wanted to turn her over his lap and spank her luscious little bottom. He figured if he tried it,

22

she'd kick the tar out of him, if they didn't end up wrapped around each other anyway.

On the other hand, as hot-blooded as she was, she might like being spanked, though she probably preferred being on the giving end.

He widened his knees and shifted on his chair, easing the pressure of the erection poking against the fly of his jeans. Predictably, any time he thought about Moira, Tom Junior took it as an invitation to misbehave. Since meeting the Irish Daughter, his imagination had taken a few surprising turns, especially when it came to sex, and he wasn't always comfortable with its direction.

James excused himself, no doubt to seek out Maya for a dance. Two Daughters, one a stunning brunette and the other a honey blonde, claimed Phil and dragged him out onto the dance floor, one woman under each of his beefy arms. Out of the corner of his eye, Tom noticed Andrea bumping her way through the crowd toward their table, her pretty face set in determined lines.

Tom slid off his chair, leaving his drink behind, giving the arguing couple space. Nobody would claim the table while the four men were away, not as long as one of them was in the bar, and he had a woman to apologize to, whether she wanted to hear it or not. It was well past time the two of them made peace with each other, if only because they had to work together. No telling how long it would take to sift through the Archives. He didn't want to spend the entire time at loggerheads with Moira, no matter what else happened between them.

He pushed through the tables, some occupied, others emptied in favor of the dance floor. Moira had her back to him, her arm pressed firmly against Sigrid's in the crush of women occupying the bar's long length. He squeezed sideways between a Daughter he didn't know and Moira, and grimaced when the side of her body lined up perfectly with his own, her left arm pressed into his chest, her cocked hip brushing the part of him that cheered whenever she was near.

She set the mug of dark brown liquid she held onto the bar and fixed her pale blue eyes there. "What do ye want, Tom?"

"To apologize."

"Told ye one weren't needed."

He gritted his teeth together and plowed on in the face of his somewhat captive audience. He placed his mouth close to her ear, savored the sharp crispness of her scent, and lowered his voice, certain she'd hear him over the noise in the bar. Daughters had damn good hearing, and he didn't want the hurt he'd caused her to do more damage should their conversation land in the wrong ear. "I didn't think you were throwing yourself at me."

She went rigid beside him, so still the only movement he could detect was the faint flutter of her pulse at the base of her creamy throat. "Then ye shouldn'ta said it."

"You're right, I shouldn't have. If I could take it back, I would."

Her head turned fractionally, though her eyes remained hidden. "Why do ye care?"

Well, there was the rub. He had no idea why he cared, only that he did. She'd tugged at him from the first moment he'd seen her, so strongly his tongue had dried up in his mouth and he'd bobbled a box of files. Aside from her angelic looks, she wasn't in any way his type. Hadn't he spent months trying to convince himself of that? "It was unkind, and I'm not an unkind man."

"So ye're trying to salvage your conscience." She lifted the mug to her mouth and sipped, leaving a trace of foam on her upper lip. She licked it off with a quick flick of her tongue. "Consider it saved."

Tom's stomach muscles tightened reflexively and heat coiled down his insides, pooling in his already hard dick. God a-mercy, he had it bad if all it took to stir him was a simple show of her tongue. "I'm trying to apologize for hurting you, Moira. You didn't deserve that."

"Aye, ye're right, I didn't," she said softly. "But ye said it anyway, and now I'd rather not dwell on it."

Implacable, stubborn Irish. He pressed his lips together, holding in a frustrated sigh, and searched for a way to mend the rift he'd caused. His eyes fell on the dance floor and, on an impulse he was sure he'd regret later, he said, "Dance with me."

Her eyes went round and she sputtered out a laugh. "Why in the world?"

"I was hoping we could work our way around to friendship."

"Friendship, is it?" She snorted and sipped at her beer, licked another dab of foam off her wide mouth. "Ye're a strange one, Tom Fairfax."

"I'm a man who likes peace," he countered. "Especially at work. I hate it that we can't even stand to be in the same room together."

Something flickered across her expression, gone before he could pin it down. She raised her eyes to his, and in them he saw nothing, not hurt or anger or humor, just a flat stare, devoid of emotion. "I've never had that problem with ye, Tom."

He lowered his voice, softening it. "Then you won't mind dancing with me."

Her humor returned, as quickly as it had left, lifting her face into a smile. "Well, I walked right into that one. Suppose I'll have to suffer through one with ye."

He grinned and slid a hand down her back along the rough surface of her sweater. "If it helps, I'll make it as tedious and boring as possible."

"There's a man for ye, then," she said, and turned, allowing him to lead her to the dance floor with his hand on her waist.

He swung her carefully around, holding her at a polite distance, as much of one as he could manage in the crowded space. Her body brushed his as they swayed to the music, her right hand in his, her left hand on his shoulder. He eased his hand under her sweater, resting it in the gentle indent of her waist above her hip. Her skin was warm and smooth, as it had been the two other times he'd held her this way, and he couldn't resist its call. He rubbed his thumb along the skin above the waistband of her deep brown cords, testing the tautness of her flesh.

Her fingers flexed and when she spoke, her voice was a low murmur. "What are ye doing, Tom?"

"It's so soft here, so rich." He strummed his thumb over her again. "You have beautiful skin."

"And ye shouldn't be teasing it, should ye, especially when ye're with another woman."

He drew back far enough to catch her gaze. "Naomi is just a friend. I'm not with her."

"Ye want to be and it's not right what ye're doing here. Being immortal doesn't grant immunity to a man's touch."

He slipped his hand out from under her sweater, regretting the loss of her warmth as soon as he did. "You're right. I shouldn't touch you like that."

She shook her head and he could've sworn he glimpsed the sparkle of tears in her eyes. He bit back a curse and pulled her close, pressing her head into his chest, comforting her. What an idiot he was. With any other woman, he'd never have touched her bare skin without her permission, not in a million years. With Moira, his reason was gone, lost in the storm of need she raised in him with a single glimpse of her clear blue eyes.

"I'm sorry, Moira. Please don't cry."

Her breath puffed against his chest, strong enough for its warmth to filter through layers of clothing to skin. "Ye're barmy if ye think something so insignificant could bring a Daughter to tears."

He wrapped her close anyway, one arm around her shoulders, the other at her waist. She laid her cheek on his chest and relaxed into him, and her hands slipped to his ribs, caressing him in soft strokes. They held each other through the rest of the song, barely moving among the other couples, their bodies pressed together as intimately as they could be in public. When it ended, she eased away, and he just as easily pulled her back.

"Just a little more," he said, and she curled herself around him again without a word of complaint.

He lost track of the songs, lost track of the muted noise of the crowd, lost track of everything but the woman in his arms, even as the hope he'd had that Naomi would be the one trickled steadily away.

MOIRA SPENT the next morning studiously avoiding any thought of Thomas Fairfax, his warm hands, or the prolonged dance they'd shared, however nice it might've been. Good thing Spillfeite hadn't been there to witness it, else it might've ended in blows.

The occasional brawl was good for the soul, in spite of Rebecca's opinion to the contrary, but Moira had enough on her plate for the non. Sorting out the Archives was a momentous task on its own without adding a jealous tussle into the mix. No, best she stay out of Tom's way, and by doing so, avoid said tussle.

With that in mind, she cleaned and straightened her apartment. The tiny flat was located not far from Tellowee in a building owned by a mortal Daughter and her husband. Moira hadn't even considered staying with her mother and step-father while helping reorganize the Archives. She liked her freedom, true enough, and she liked the peace she and the Blade had established between themselves over the past century, tentative as it was. Though Moira's immortal life stretched endlessly in front of her, the hope offered by the Prophecy of Light notwithstanding, Rebecca's would end in a few more decades, Goddess willing it be that long. Moira wanted to remember her mother as a woman should, with love, not with strife.

After a quick bite, she headed to the high school located on the IECS campus. The school's primary mission was the education of the People's Daughters and Sons. There, students received training in martial arts, weapons usage and care, and survival skills, as well as the more normal high school curriculum, including foreign languages. Latin and ancient Greek were of particular importance, as a great deal of the People's history had been written in those tongues.

A people who forgot their history forgot themselves.

Moira passed through security at the IECS' main entrance and parked her Miata in the parking lot near the high school. She left the keys in the ignition and patted the hood fondly on her way inside, following the muted noise of teenagers down long corridors to the cafeteria, a cavernous room with scuffed wooden floors, dark-stained bead board paneling, and enough folding tables to easily seat a hundred people at once.

Student volunteers were scattered among the tables, practicing their ancient language skills by translating copies of documents held within the Archives. James Terhune had compiled lists of promising texts, choosing those that hadn't been translated before and were easy enough for older students to wade through with a little help, with the first criteria being the text's potential to hold clues to the location of Sanctuary.

James was standing at a table off to one side next to his fiancé, Maya Bellegarde, his dark head bent close to hers. The other Daughter had found love with the attractive language expert not long back, and with it and a hefty dose of trust, her mortality. Their daughters, Amelia and Dierdre, had become close friends, if rumor held true, and now, the four lived together as a family in the rambling house Maya had bought when Dierdre was a babe.

Moira ignored the envy and grief rising quickly within her and latched on to the happiness. A Daughter had broken the curse. That was always something to raise a pint to.

She plastered a friendly smile on her face as she approached the table laden with stacks of paper, writing utensils, and dictionaries. "I've come to lend me hand."

James' smile lifted his features from attractive to handsome. "We need all the hands we can get. What do you want? We've got texts in Koine Greek, Old Latin, and Classical Latin, or you can check student translations, if you'd like."

A hand curved over Moira's shoulder and the heady scent

of mist along the water wafted to her. A prickle of awareness tingled up her spine. Tom settled in beside her, his lean body close enough for his heat to warm her. At least he'd had the good sense to catch the shoulder of hers closest to him or his ribs might've suffered.

"She can help me," he said. "My Latin's rusty, but I thought I'd give it a go."

Moira hunched her shoulders and caught the smile Maya couldn't quite hide. "I've me own work, thank ye."

"Or you can help me." Tom's fingers tightened and his voice dropped a notch. "It'll go faster if we work together."

He said it reasonably, as if she were being irrational. It kicked at her temper, edging her into crabbiness. "What, Spillfeite not available for yer attention today, Tom?"

"Give it a rest, Moira," he muttered. "Would it kill you to spend some time with me for a good cause?"

"Why would ye want to?"

"For one, we're co-workers."

"Something easily remedied, if ye like."

His teeth clicked together, audible over the students' low murmurs. "Can you at least look at me when you're trying to cut me to shreds with that sharp tongue of yours?"

James cleared his throat, his grin as wide as Moira had ever seen it. "Why don't you two lovebirds take this stack and find a nice, quiet table out of the way where the kids won't overhear your bickering."

Maya elbowed him, though her own mouth stretched into a knowing smile.

Moira grabbed the sheaf of papers James held out. "Thanks a lot."

"Oh, you're welcome," he said. "Don't forget paper and pencils."

She pivoted and stalked away, leaving the rest to Tom. By the Goddess, couldn't a Daughter volunteer to help with simple translations without a man interfering? Oh, no. Nothing of the sort could happen with Tom around. For weeks, the man had avoided her like the plague, and now all of a sudden he set himself under her heels so often, she tripped over him wherever she went.

Most of the students had gathered at the far end of the room on the side where Maya and James had set up. Moira found a table on that end along one wall where the bright November sun shone through uncurtained windows. She slumped into a chair made of lurid green plastic and studied the nearly dozen pages James had given her, frowning over the number. What did he expect, a miracle? They'd never make it through the entire document in one go, not in the hour allotted.

A shadow fell across the table and Tom sat down next to her, clad in a thin cranberry colored v-neck sweater and worn jeans. "Pencils, paper, bottles of water, and most importantly, a dictionary."

She trained her gaze on his face, refusing to admire the tight fit of his sweater over the lean strength of his torso. "Ye're chipper today."

"Been a while since I tried this. College, as a matter of fact." He passed the writing paper to her. "I minored in Latin."

"Did ye, now."

"Were you born sarcastic or do you have to work at it?"

"Lucky me, it comes natural. Why do I have all the paper?"

"So you can write." He snagged the photocopies out of her hand and spread them out in front of him, then patted his chest. "Glasses. Know I brought 'em."

The mischief of her Irish forefathers had her tapping his fine arse above the eyeglass case he'd stuck in the back pocket of his jeans. "Would that be them?"

Pink tinted the skin along his sharp cheekbones. He retrieved the case and pulled out reading glasses with tortoise shell frames. "Ah, thanks."

"Welcome." She leaned closer and lowered her voice. "Never had a woman pat yer arse before?"

"Not in public," he muttered. "I'll translate. You write."

She might've let it go if she hadn't caught a faint whiff of an interesting aroma. "Ye're aroused."

He closed his eyes and rubbed stiff fingers over them. "You know, everyone in here can hear our conversation."

"Well aware. Not a soul will bother us." In spite of the curious glances a few of the teenagers aimed at them from nearby tables. "If ye like, we can discuss this elsewhere."

"I'd rather not discuss it at all."

He perched the glasses on his nose and scanned the first page of the Latin text. He had a slight bump there in the slim length of his nose, just below the bridge. She'd never noticed before.

Not that she should now.

She picked up one of the pencils and poised it over the blank page in front of her. "Are ye ashamed of it, then?"

He flipped a page. "Ashamed of what?"

"Being attracted to me."

His mouth thinned and when he spoke, his voice was soft. "No."

She doodled a flower in the corner of the paper and matched the pitch of her voice to his. "Ye won't act on it though, will ye."

He pulled off his glasses, folding and unfolding the earpieces as he spoke. "I haven't decided."

"Ye think I have no say in it?"

"I have a feeling you wouldn't turn me down."

"Easy, am I?"

"I didn't say that." He slid a glance at her. "You strike me as the kind of woman who knows what she wants."

Her arm brushed his. She leaned into him, drawn to his warmth. "Maybe if I wanted ye, I'd already have tried for ye."

"Didn't you, that night when you asked for a kiss?"

"Maybe I was curious."

He turned his head, putting his face inches from her own,

and his breath puffed over her mouth. "Maybe I'd rather not play with fire."

Her nerves jangled and sparked. She curled her fingers into her palms, holding out against a rash need to touch him. "Where's yer sense of adventure, Tom?"

"Safely tucked away." His gaze dropped to her mouth and lingered. "I might be willing to try a date."

Moira drew back, shuttering the need stirring in warm pools within her. "Spillfeite might have a word or two to say about that."

"We're just friends," he said mildly. "She doesn't get a say."

"Ye're dating her."

"I've taken her out on two dates total, and it's just not..." He sighed and sat up in his chair, then slid his glasses on. "I think I've got the gist of this text, the first part, anyway. Let me run it by you."

She listened as he translated the first few lines of the text James had given them, very civilly discussed possible changes to his interpretation, and dutifully recorded the translation they agreed upon.

A corner of her mind caught and held on the sentence he'd left dangling. It's just not...*what?* She turned it over, examining the possibilities, and found nothing that matched. Naomi was a beautiful woman, and though Moira wasn't particularly happy to admit it, she acknowledged that the other Daughter's sweet temperament would attract a man like Tom. He was a good man and a kind one, his intellect as tempting as the muscles hinted at by the fit of his sweater. Perhaps she should leave him to Naomi and find another man to fill her womanly needs.

Moira's stomach twisted and soured, and she inhaled deeply, absorbing the sharp scent of his soap mingling with the musky smell of his arousal. No, she wouldn't leave him to another, couldn't, really. How long had it been since she'd found a man this attractive? Naomi or no, Moira would pursue him. Whether she could do it cautiously as she should, wisely, as a woman taming a rabbit into a snare, that was another matter. As Tom had said, she knew what she wanted. She'd never before hesitated to pursue that want. With Tom, she had a feeling he'd respond better to her tender side, if she could unearth it.

And if not, then he'd make do with the fire and they'd both end up singed under the lovely burn of passion.

FOUR

THE OMEGA was unusually crowded. Tom shuffled Naomi around the tiny space he'd carved out for them on the dance floor. She was radiant, her pale blonde curls shiny, her eyes sparkling with good humor and kindness. She was wearing a deep red fitted sweater over her jeans. The vee neck was low cut, showing the straight neckline of the camisole she wore underneath and what should've been an enticing hint of cleavage.

A man should want to kiss her there in that shadow, kiss her, taste her skin, savor the weight of her full breasts in his hands, work his way around to what Tom was certain would be the most perfect nipples a man could behold.

He wasn't even tempted.

A roar went up at the bar. Tom's gaze drifted there, fixing on a compact redhead with a sailor's mouth and skin like the finest silk. He'd never even seen a hint of Moira's cleavage, hadn't a clue what size her breasts were under the bulky layers she normally wore. Since the afternoon they'd spent translating together, four long days before, every time he was anywhere near her, all he could think about was finding out. She hadn't given him much of a chance to, though, and she refused to consider a date.

What was wrong with a good old-fashioned getting-to-know

you outing? If he even hinted at one, she threw Naomi up at him.

Gentle fingers grazed his jawline, drawing his attention back to the woman he held. Naomi smiled up at him. "Where did you go?"

He mustered a smile, the least he could do considering where his thoughts had wondered. "Sorry."

"You seem so distracted tonight, have been for days." Her hand drifted down his neck and rested on his shoulder. "Is everything all right?"

"Yeah. It's just the time of year, with Thanksgiving coming up. There's a lot to juggle."

"Will you be going home next week?"

"Probably."

Moira smacked her mug down on the bar and did one of her happy dances, wiggling her butt over something happening on the TV. Tom eased Naomi around, putting his back to the bar, hoping to nip his usual reaction to anything pertaining to Moira's butt in the bud.

His body stirred to life and he sighed. So much for that.

He forced himself to focus on Naomi. She deserved better than to have her dance partner lost in thoughts of another woman. "Mom always cooks a turkey and dressing, all the trimmings. Think she spends most of the week cooking. The whole family turns out for it."

"Sounds like fun. I'll be going to Kara's on Thanksgiving. The baby's due soon and she's so nervous and excited, I couldn't leave her, not with her husband out of town. I'll be back the next day, though." Naomi ran a fingertip around the button of his shirt, directly over his heart. "I was hoping you might want to pick up where we left off after our movie date."

"Naomi, I..."

Moira rushed past the dance floor at a near run, pushing her way through the tables, barking at people to get out of her way.

Naomi and some of the other women whipped around, following her progress. "That can't be good."

"What?"

"Moira rushing out." Naomi rested her hand on Tom's shoulder, lifted her foot, and pulled a small handgun out of a well-hidden ankle holster. "Stay here. I'll be right back."

Moira came back in, her face set in grim lines. Her gaze zeroed in on Tom and she headed straight toward him, brushing off people trying to catch her attention. As soon as she reached him, she said, "Me brother's been kidnapped."

Naomi paled. "By whom?"

Moira shook her head, sending wisps of hair flying around her face. "Unknown, though me sister has her suspicions. I'm to meet them at Bobby's company, but first, I have to set the word out. Get Tom to his apartment."

"I can get there on my own," he said.

"Ye'll not step foot outside this bar without an escort." Moira's voice held the sharp snap of authority. "Naomi will see ye there and stay with ye 'til we know more."

"My daughter, Kara. Her husband is overseas and she's pregnant. Third trimester." Naomi turned worried eyes on Tom. "I can take Tom to his apartment, but I'll need to leave as soon as I can. She can't protect herself, not so far along, and if Bobby was targeted..."

A shadow passed over Moira's expression. "Anybody could be, aye."

Tom cupped Naomi's shoulder. "Go on. Take care of Kara. I'll be fine."

"I'll see him safely home and cared for," Moira said.

Naomi hesitated, her mouth pressed into a thin line as she glanced between Tom and Moira. Finally, she nodded. "Text me as soon as you're safe."

"I will." He kissed her forehead and nudged her toward the door. "Now, go."

She nodded again, then turned and pushed her way through the curious crowd, tucking her handgun into a back pocket as she went.

Moira gripped Tom's elbow and tugged him toward the bar. "Need to take care of a thing or two here, then I'll take ye home."

He allowed her to lead him to the bar, more concerned about her brother than anything. Moira caught Will's eye and struck a finger across her throat. A moment later, the music stopped abruptly and the TV went dark. She elbowed her way past the curious stares of the people standing at the bar and hefted herself into a stand on top of the flat, wooden surface, facing the room at large.

"Bobby Upton's been kidnapped," she said, and the crowd went deathly silent. "We don't know who took him. We don't know where he is. Rebecca's being notified now. I expect we'll all receive instructions once she has been. In the meantime, protect yer families. Anybody headed toward the IECS, join me in five."

Quiet murmurs filled the room as swords were unsheathed and guns drawn. Moira jumped down next to Tom and took his elbow.

He shook it gently. "I'm a grown man, Moira."

"Aye, ye are, and ye're under me mother's protection." She ushered him to one side of the bar, out of the way of the orderly exodus of people from the building. "Ye do what I say and I promise to explain once ye're safe."

"And if I don't?"

Her clear blue eyes went flat and hard. "Ye'll find out what it means to be under a Daughter's protection."

She turned away from him and beckoned Will over, holding a quiet conversation with the bartender while keeping a steady grip on Tom's arm.

A small crowd of women formed around them. Andrea hustled George over, a fierce expression on her lovely face. Phil arrived a moment later, escorted by the two women he'd been partnering for the past few weeks. They bracketed him, one carrying a wickedly sharp short sword, the other a handgun, both held loosely at their sides.

37

Phil caught Tom's eye and shrugged sheepishly. He was taller than both the women he was with and outmuscled them as well. Tom bet anything the other man had received exactly the same warning he'd gotten from Moira. If he weren't familiar with the customs of the People or had been at the IECS for less time, he'd balk. Knowing what the Daughters were like, how downright paranoid they were sometimes and why, went a long way toward easing Tom's natural instinct to push for answers, though it didn't ease his irritation at being treated like a child.

Moira faced the growing crowd. "Any other outsiders here under the protection of the People?"

Sigrid pushed forward from the back of the crowd. "These three are it."

"Who drove?" Moira asked.

"I did." Tom dug in his jeans pocket and pulled out his key ring. "The powder blue Prius."

"I know what ye drive. Feckin' sissy car, Tom," Moira muttered. "Sig, check the Prius."

Sig caught the keys and loped out the door as one of Phil's companions yanked her phone out. "Bomb sniffing dog," she murmured, and a moment later, she issued rapid-fire commands into the phone.

Tom slouched on a bar stool and lowered his voice. "What are you worried about, Moira?"

Her fingers tightened on his arm and her answer was just as hushed. "Things that go bump in the night. Do ye trust me to protect ye?"

He studied her for long moments, weighing her question. Yes, he did trust her, at least enough to get him safely from The Omega to the IECS through the kinds of bumps in the night that would worry a Daughter of Moira's age and skill. He nodded once and was surprised by the relief flickering across her expression.

She beckoned Andrea and Phil's other companion over and sent them out to find and secure vehicles. "One man per vehicle, driven by a Daughter with at least one other along for protection," she said softly to him.

Her words ground his thoughts to a halt. "You don't have to explain it to me now."

Her hand moved from his arm to the waistband of his jeans. She hooked a finger through a belt loop and slid an odd glance at him from under lowered lashes. "Know yer curious. Seems best to occupy yer mind with reality rather than letting it go a-wandering."

He stared at her, nonplussed. In any other woman, he'd call what she was doing flirting, the tilt of her head, the softened voice, her fingers resting on his lower abdomen through a layer of worn jeans, so close to where he wanted them, her touch was more tease than reassurance. He deliberately focused on his surroundings, attempting to block out the sheer, unmitigated lust racing through him before...

He bit back a curse. Too late. Tom Junior reared his head and poked at the fly of Tom's jeans, angling for a touch from Moira's delicate hand.

She tugged on his belt loop. "Pay attention, Tom. I need ye alert."

He swallowed hard and cleared his throat. "I'm paying attention." Maybe not where she needed him to, but by golly, he sure was alert. Fighting his body's natural reaction to Moira distracted him from the worry eating a hole in his gut. God willing, she'd never notice his hard-on and would attribute his stiff posture to irritation at her high-handedness.

Sig sauntered in and tossed the keys to Moira from across the room. "All clear. I set a guard to watch the parking lot."

Moira caught the keys and stuffed them in her pocket. She glanced casually down, and his heart dropped into his gut. Dammit. How did she always know when he was aroused? And why the hell did desire stir so easily around her anyway?

The next half hour passed in a blur. The Omega emptied steadily until the only occupants were the group clustered around

Tom and Moira, and the bar's staff. Will and the waitresses cleaned around them, emptying and wiping down tables, sweeping and mopping the floor. Tom moved once to help and was pulled to an abrupt halt by Moira's finger, still holding his belt loop. He'd thought her attention had wandered to the Daughters in their group jumping to do her bidding. Apparently not.

She finished speaking to one of Phil's companions, the honey blonde with exotic features who'd called in the bomb-sniffing dog, then put her mouth close to his ear. "Ye need to leave, tell me and I'll escort ye, but don't attempt to part from me again."

Her breath feathered over his ear, raising goose bumps along his skin. He leaned into her, breathing in the sharp scent of her shampoo as she directed a handful of Daughters to scout the area between The Omega and the IECS.

He had a funny feeling that when she'd told him not to part from her, she was talking about more than stepping away from her to help Will's staff clean the bar.

AN HOUR AFTER SIG went outside to check Tom's car for bombs, a local Sheriff's deputy entered the bar, his uniform creased so sharply, it looked brand new. He was slender and young, no more than twenty-one, if that, and had the thin, earnest face of a man who took his duties seriously. His pale gaze slid around the room. "Somebody call about a bomb?"

Moira lifted her hand and the young man shambled over. He took off his hat and slid his fingers along the brim. "Deputy Creyton Johns, ma'am. I was supposed to call in the fire department, too, but the sheriff told me I ortn't."

"You're just a precaution, Deputy," Moira said. "How long will it take?"

Tom's interest piqued as Moira and Deputy Johns negotiated on what needed doing. Her voice had taken on the crisp tone of authority, one she didn't use with the other Daughters, and her fingers tightened around his belt loop. A few minutes later, Deputy Johns nodded, settled his hat on his head, and shambled outside with two Daughters in tow, keys in hand, including the keys to Tom's Prius.

Not long after, the deputy gave the all-clear, and Moira reassembled the group. In short order, she explained what they were doing and how, and warned the men to obey her instructions to the letter and keep their heads down. She checked her phone. "IECS clear and expecting. We're a go."

Sig raced out the door followed by Phil bracketed by his two women, then George between Andrea and an Asian Daughter named Min Li whom Tom had just met that night, then him between Moira and a pale, gangly Daughter he knew only by sight. The women hustled the men out to the cars and shoved them inside. Tom did as Moira had asked, sliding into the backseat next to a Daughter with cold, dark eyes and spiky green hair. Moira took the driver's seat and the gangly Daughter the front, and they were off, caravanning at a pace that seemed sedate compared to what he'd expected.

Which is what he got for watching too many thrillers and conspiracies.

It took less than ten minutes for them to travel from The Omega to the IECS' main entrance. Guards dressed in full body armor and flat black helmets stood at attention near the gate, heavy machine guns held at the ready. They drove through the open gate. Tom swiveled around in his seat. It swung shut behind the car at the rear, driven by yet another Daughter he hadn't met.

And he thought he'd dated every unmated Daughter within a hundred miles of Tellowee in the six months after his arrival.

A few minutes after going through the gate, they arrived at the on-campus apartments used by visitors to the IECS. The cars eased to a stop, one in front of the other, and the Daughters drug the men out and hustled them toward the building. One of the scouts materialized at the front entrance and opened the door, holding it as the group went inside.

From there, everybody went in different directions. Moira nodded at Tom's escorts and took his elbow. One left the building while the other headed up the stairs behind Andrea and George, followed closely by Phil and the women he kept company with.

Moira yanked gently on Tom's elbow, leading him toward his first-floor apartment, and he lost track of the other women. She unlocked his door, then pointed to a spot just inside the apartment.

Stay. Ok, then. Reduced from a child to a puppy. Tom stuck his hands in his pockets and gazed at the darkened ceiling, tamping down his irritation. Moira had a reason for wanting him there, so there he'd be, but it rankled to be treated like a mindless ignoramus.

She closed the front door and moved through his apartment so silently, he couldn't hear even the rustle of her corduroys.

Surely she had a reason for all the super secret escort stuff. Her brother had been kidnapped, and that was enough to alarm Tom, but it wasn't enough, in his mind, to justify everything else. Questions whirled through his mind, about the way the Daughters had acted, immediately and without hesitation, and about the whole situation from the time Moira had rushed out of The Omega to the moment when they'd stepped into his apartment.

She reappeared at his side and flipped on the living room lights. "All clear."

"You want to tell me what's going on now?"

"Get a shower first, else ye're liable to catch cold." She locked the door, slid the deadbolt, and secured the chain. "Mind if I make meself to home?"

"Not at all." He caught her arm as she moved away. "You have a nasty habit of not looking at me. Here, at least, could you treat me like a normal person instead of a pariah?"

She shook her arm free and met his gaze steadily. "Ye're

imagining things, Tom. Don't forget to text yer lover."

"She's not my lover."

He bit back his exasperation and followed Moira past the kitchenette into the main living area. She laid her handgun on the coffee table and plopped onto the middle cushion of the huge leather sofa that had come with the apartment. It was a deep brown, sturdy, comfortable, and in good condition like the rest of the apartment's furniture.

She pulled out her phone, her fingers moving rapidly over the screen as she completely ignored him, pretty much like she always did unless they were dancing or something at work required them to work together. That had been less than half a dozen times in the nearly two months she'd been there, including the one time he'd tracked her down to apologize for his appalling rudeness.

He ran a frustrated hand over his hair. Shower first and then she would by golly give him some answers. He stalked into his bedroom, ignoring the ring of her phone and her lilting hello, his mind focused on prioritizing the questions he intended to pepper her with.

FIVE

THE TEXTS came in while Tom was in the shower.

Bobby Upton kidnapped. Eternal Order suspected. Guard your families.

Moira threw down her phone and curled her fingers into her hair, tugging hard. Feckin' Order. She breathed around the panic welling up in her chest, breathed through the anger and frustration. Her brother had been kidnapped by a dangerous faction of the People and she was stuck playing babysitter to another woman's man.

There had to be something she could do from where she was. She retrieved her phone and called Dani. Her adoptive sister's phone dumped into voice mail. Moira left a message as she unlaced her boots and tugged them off. She wiggled her toes, stretched into a stand. Nervous energy bounced through her, tugging at her to *do something*, anything to burn it off. She searched for a single speck of dust to eradicate in Tom's spotless apartment and found one dirty glass in the kitchen sink. She washed it, dried it, put it away, and marveled at a man who thought enough of his home to scour the stove's burners and dust down the cobwebs.

She crept to the bedroom door and placed an ear to it. The shower was still running. Two seconds of contemplation later, she went back into the living area and poked through a stack of papers he'd left on the eating table next to his closed laptop. It contained photocopies of articles printed from journals on library and archival science, notes from other articles, and a handwritten outline printed in neat block letters under the title, "Updating an Antiquated Archival System: Methods, Obstacles, and Breakthroughs."

This was what Tom did in his spare time, write articles for journals nobody read outside of academia? Moira dropped the papers onto the table, not bothering to put them back as she'd found them. The man was wasted outside the IECS and too smart for his own good. Her mother had acquired a jewel when she'd found Tom.

A pang of envy knotted Moira's guts. She'd resolved to pursue Tom regardless of another woman's claim. She hadn't counted on Tom clinging so fiercely to that woman. What was he playing at, bouncing his time between her and Naomi? Did he not realize the trouble his indecision could cause?

Moira stripped off her sweater and dropped it onto the couch, pulled off her socks and tucked them into her boots, emptied her pockets onto the coffee table and divested herself of the other weapons she wore. There was just enough room in the tiny apartment's carpeted living area for her to stretch and maybe clear her mind. She needed to think rationally on Bobby's situation without worry clogging her head.

Ten minutes into a series of yogic forms, Tom exited his bedroom wearing loose flannel pajama bottoms and a ratty gray University of Georgia sweatshirt. His dark hair was damp and he smelled clean and fresh.

Moira's muscles tensed as he walked by. His feet were bare. They were long and narrow and finely made, much like the rest of him, and she had the sudden urge to touch him there, to discover for herself precisely how beautiful they were.

He picked her sweater up, folded it neatly, and placed it on the table near his laptop. "Hungry?"

She abandoned the stretches. They weren't working anyway.

She was as tense and het up as she'd been when she'd started. As long as Tom was around and hell bent for Naomi, Moira was liable to stay that way. "Ate earlier."

He grunted and opened a cabinet door, pulling out a small cardboard box. "Movie?"

Why not? He'd wanted a date. Why was beyond her ken, but an at-home movie was close enough and it did her no harm to sit through one with him. "What's playing?"

"Whatever you want." He stuck a bag in the microwave and pressed a button. The microwave lit up and whirred. He kept his back to her, apparently watching the bag inside the appliance turn round and round. "There are DVDs under the TV and I've got cable, Netflix, and HuluPlus."

Humor edged out her earlier frustration. "And ye trust me to pick out something appropriate?"

He glanced over his shoulder, and his eyes lingered on her breasts, unbound under the thin camisole she wore. "I figure you're probably not into chick flicks and I can handle pretty much anything else."

His tone was bland, his gaze hot. Pops sounded from the microwave, drawing his attention. He faced it, and she lost the weight of his eyes running slowly, almost clinically down her body, stirring a familiar warmth within her.

Moira eyed his relaxed posture. "Ye seem fair accepting of me presence."

He lifted one shoulder in a quick shrug. "I've wanted to spend time with you for a while now, see if we can find some common ground."

"Common ground, is it." She stifled a laugh. "And ye have no questions as to why I'm still here?"

"Oh, I have lots of questions, enough to keep you talking until dawn." The popping slowed. Tom punched the clear button on the microwave and pulled out a bag of popcorn. "Like why you're not looking for your brother, what the Eternal Order is, why he would've been taken. Any news on that yet?"

46

"Not yet. As for why I'm here, I can't leave until I know ye're safe."

He grunted. "Apparently, you suffered a severe memory loss while I was in the shower, or are you conveniently forgetting the number of people and weapons guarding the IECS campus?"

"It's not completely safe, no matter what ye think, Tom. There are still ways in. With the Order on the loose, I wouldn't trust yer safekeeping with any other than me family or possibly Spillfeite, not unless needs must."

He snorted out a laugh and poured the popcorn into a bowl. "Because a middle-aged archivist is a target."

"Ye have value precisely because ye work in the Archives." Moira tapped a finger against her temple. "Yer mind is precious for what ye've seen. Chances are, ye've already gathered clues to Sanctuary's location and haven't sorted them into a full picture yet. No telling what else ye hold in that keen mind of yers."

"I think you're overestimating me there, Moira." He jerked his chin at the refrigerator, snagged the bowl of popcorn, and slipped past her into the living area. "Since you're not gonna pick out a movie, I will. You get drinks."

She fished two chilled bottles of water out of his fridge and followed him.

He set the popcorn down, dug a movie out, and inserted the disc into his DVD player. "Exactly how long are you staying?"

"Likely through the night, possibly the next one as well."

"Mmm. Ok, then." He took the water from her and placed the bottles on coasters on the coffee table. "I've got a spare set of pajamas, an extra toothbrush. Do you want a shower before I cut on the movie?"

She scrounged for enough gratitude to match his kindness. "I'll save the shower for the morn, though I'll take the pajamas now, if ye don't mind."

The corners of his eyes crinkled as he smiled. "I've already laid them out for you."

"Thinking ahead, eh?"

"Hoping," he said softly. "Go change. Popcorn's getting cold."

Her stomach hopped and leapt in odd little flutters. She pressed a hand to it and slipped into his bedroom. Here, he'd replaced the standard-issue IECS furniture with a queen-sized, walnut sleigh bed, matching nightstands placed on either side of the bed, one holding a table lamp, and a six drawer dresser. A handmade Star of Bethlehem quilt fashioned from gradients of green and blue covered the bed. Two framed pictures rested on the dresser, one of a man with Tom's dark hair and slim nose standing between two teenagers, and the other of an older couple. His family, of a certainty, and not a trace of a woman's portrait resting in this most intimate room of his home.

Moira ignored the relief fluttering through her and focused on his words. He'd been hoping she'd stay, so much so, he'd laid out his own clothing for her use well ahead of knowing her plans. *Hoping*, as if he'd expected her to leave him to his own devices when the People were under such a dread threat and him near defenseless on his own. *Hoping*, as if he thought her ignorant of his worth and value as a man.

Had she conveyed her interest in him so poorly?

She stripped off her cami and cords, and slipped on the clothing he'd left her, a long-sleeved, man-sized t-shirt, flannel pajama bottoms she rolled up a good four inches at the ankles, and thick woolen socks. She left her clothes draped over the end of the bed and carried the socks with her. He'd turned the lights off while she'd been dressing, leaving the room in darkness except for the light thrown by the tele.

Moira took one look at the screen and laughed as she plopped down beside him, thigh to thigh, and tugged the socks on. "This is a chick flick."

"There are pirates, monsters, sword fights, a kidnapping, torture, and a giant. Not to mention perfidy, double-crossing, and intrigue." He picked up a single piece of popcorn from the bowl in his lap and pointed it at her. "It's definitely not a chick flick."

48

"You're forgetting marriage, true love, and the kiss at the very end."

"I didn't forget that. I'm just ignoring it."

She laughed and tucked her feet under her, with her knees resting on his thigh. He started the movie and they watched in silence, sharing the popcorn between them as the story unfolded on the screen. The bowl emptied well before the halfway point. Tom set it aside and draped a casual arm across her shoulders. It was warm and reassuringly heavy, and she snuggled into him, drawing on his strength.

Texts started rolling in not long after. Moira cut her phone to silent and answered them one by one, read the new ones coming in, responded to those in turn.

"Any news?" Tom asked softly.

"A woman at Bobby's company betrayed him to the Order."

Tom's eyebrows furrowed. "Why?"

"No idea. She'll get her deserves." Moira set the phone beside her on the couch. "We're working on a plan to retrieve him."

"You are?" He squeezed her shoulder. "From here?"

"Modern technology," she said with a smile, and nudged him into paying attention to the movie.

They were both relaxed by the time the movie ended. Tom yawned and stretched his legs out. "Another one?"

"Need to check in. Maybe another time."

"Sure." He dropped a casual kiss to the top of her head and cleared the table. "I'll get out of your hair for a while."

She watched him walk away, admiring the long length of his legs and the firmness of his arse under the loose pajama bottoms he wore, then called Dani, who filled in the details she'd sketched out through a series of texts. Moira caught Tom as he was headed toward his bedroom and relayed a watered-down version. Bobby had been kidnapped by his woman Indigo's twin sister, India Furia. The ransom note demanded the Oracle in exchange for Bobby.

Tom knelt beside her and held her chilled hands between his warmer ones. "God, Moira. What can I do to help?"

"Stay safe. Keep yer head down."

His laugh was short and soft. "No chance of anything else with you around, is there?"

"None a'tall," she agreed, and let him go on his way, readying himself for bed where he'd spend the night one small room away from her.

THEY TUSSLED over the sleeping arrangements. Moira tamped down her impatience when Tom insisted, for the third time, that she take his bed.

"You're a guest here, Moira," he gritted out.

"Feck's sake, Tom. I've spent most of me life sleeping on the ground or in cots that make your sofa look like a room in a luxury resort."

"I'll take the couch, then, since it's so comfy."

"I'm not booting ye out of yer own bed."

"Fine. We'll share it, but you're not sleeping on the couch."

She hitched in a breath. "Aye, that solves it then. We'll sleep together in yer bed and it'll be the last clean breath I draw once Spillfeite finds out."

He shoved stiff fingers through his hair, ruffling it into short spikes. "How many times do I have to tell you I'm not seeing her?"

"I'll believe ye when ye stop dancing with her, taking her on dates, and spending so bloody much time with her."

"We're friends."

"And we're not." Moira flopped down on the couch and made herself comfortable, closing her eyes against the frustrated expression on Tom's face and the misery winding its way through her gut. "I'll sleep here, thank ye."

His footsteps swished quietly on the carpet, and when he spoke again, his voice was close to her ear and held a hard bite.

"You're a stubborn cuss sometimes, Moira, but you're not getting your way this time."

His hands slid between her and the couch, one under her shoulders, the other under her legs. He tucked her against his chest and stood, taking her with him as he strode through the apartment into his bedroom.

She clutched his nape and gaped at him. "What in blazes do ye think ye're doing?"

"What men do when their women don't know what's good for them." He settled her on the bed and sat down next to her, spearing her with a hot gaze. "You're sleeping in here on this side of the bed wearing those pajamas. I'm sleeping on the other side in my pajamas, and since we're adults, we'll both be ok with it and get a good night's rest."

She pursed her lips, containing the laughter bubbling up over her astonishment. "Well, ye've put me in me place yet again, Tom Fairfax."

He heaved a sigh and shook his head. "I laid out a toothbrush for you."

"Aye, ye would," she murmured as he walked back into the living room. She slipped out of bed and brushed her teeth, feeling for all the world like a child on the wrong end of a good scolding. He was sitting on the edge of the bed studying the ceiling when she finished. As soon as she came out, he stood and brushed past her, entering the bathroom without a word.

He'd retrieved her phone and placed it on the nightstand next to the side of the bed he'd deemed hers. She ran a finger along its edge as a simple warmth edged its way into her heart. If only she could find a gentleness within herself to match his thoughtfulness. Perhaps then he'd abandon his yearning for Naomi, a yearning Moira knew he held in spite of his words to the contrary.

She checked her phone, secured the apartment, turned off all the lights save the lamp on his side of the bed, and slipped under the covers. He exited the bathroom tugging off his sweatshirt, baring his torso. She studied the quiet way he moved, the lean muscles of his chest and stomach, the pajama bottoms riding low on his narrow hips, and the fine, dark hair scattered across his chest, arrowing into a thin line to his bellybutton.

He folded his sweatshirt, laid it on the dresser, and tugged open one of the drawers, sorting through t-shirts.

"Leave it," she said softly.

He paused with a t-shirt halfway out of the drawer. "You sure?"

"I am."

He shut the drawer, leaving the t-shirt inside, and flipped off the lamp. The mattress shifted under his weight and the covers rustled. "Goodnight, Moira."

"Goodnight, Tom."

She curled into a ball facing him and listened to his gentle breaths, waiting for them to deepen. Five minutes passed, and five more. At the fifteen minute mark, she eased over the edge of the bed.

"Where do you think you're going?"

His voice startled her heart into an uneven thud. "Pajamas. They're too hot."

He sighed. "I'll get you a short-sleeved t-shirt."

"I'll be fine, Tom. Go back to sleep."

"Hard to go back when you haven't fallen yet," he muttered.

She grinned and wiggled out of the pajamas, stripping down to her skin. How he bloody well thought a woman could sleep in so many clothes was beyond her. She slid into bed and eased her way across the mattress. He was lying on his stomach facing away from her with one leg bent at the knee and the other straight. She draped herself over him, sighing into the smooth skin of his back.

"What are you doing?" he asked, his voice muffled.

"Getting comfortable." And enjoying him. Chances were good she'd never have another night in his bed and she wanted to savor it.

He stiffened and choked on his breath. "Are you naked?"

"As the day I was born," she said cheerfully. "Relax, Tom. I'm not out to fuck ye, not tonight."

He breathed out a muttered curse. "I'll never sleep with you so close to me."

She snorted out a laugh. "As if ye care."

He shifted carefully onto his back and groped his way up her side, capturing her hand. He guided it down his torso over bare muscles and the silky hair covering his chest, across the waistband of his pajamas, and came to a stop over the rigid length of his erection. "Trust me, Moira. I care."

"Tom." She swallowed past the desire leaping into her throat, clogging her reason and sense. "What is this?"

He laughed, low and husky. "A Daughter as old as you are should know what that is by now."

"No, I mean..." She stroked him through the fine flannel of his pajamas, measuring his length and breadth. He moaned and shifted under her hand, arching into her touch, and Lady help her, she adjusted the pressure of her hand to please him. "Why do ye have it?"

"You're a beautiful woman. So beautiful." He hissed in a breath. "I've been like this since pretty much the first time I saw you."

She stilled her hand as the desire evaporated abruptly. "And ye're still chasing after Naomi?"

"No, Moira. Not anymore. I've been trying to tell you that for days now." He caught her hand and squeezed gently. "I want to get to know you, see if we can have something."

"Ye haven't let her go yet, though."

He sighed. "It's complicated."

"Not so much," she murmured. "Ye have to choose, Tom, one or the other. We're neither of us women who can share."

"I know. I'm working on it." He threaded his fingers through hers, brought her hand to his mouth, and pressed a tender kiss to her palm. "Get some sleep. Your brother needs you to be well-rested."

She laid her head on his chest and tangled her legs with his, and fell asleep with his hand covering hers over the steady thump of his heart.

SIX

TOM WOKE the next morning wrapped around Moira, his hand tucked under her bare breast, his hips snug against her bottom. He *mmmd* and buried his face in the silky strands of her hair. It had taken a long time for his body to calm down enough for him to fall asleep the night before. He'd expected to pay for the lack of sleep with a groggy mind and a sluggish body, not a raging hard-on and hands itching to explore her.

He yawned and huffed out a soft laugh. She'd fallen asleep fast enough, relaxing against him one moment, her soft breaths evening out the next. Either she had absolutely no interest in having sex with him or she had falling asleep down to a science.

God, he hoped she was interested. Every dream the night before had starred her kissing him with that lovely mouth of hers, running her pale hands over his skin, teasing him to arousal again and again, and him doing the same to her. How had he gone so quickly from being leery of her to wanting her so fiercely he couldn't even escape the need in the quiet of his mind?

No, he'd wanted her from the moment he'd seen her, but that had been before she'd spoken, her lilting Irish voice peppered with profanities so coarse he'd blushed. It was who she was, blunt and forceful and brutally honest, and so mercurial, he never knew what she'd say or do next.

He was beginning to like that about her.

The night before, she'd held off checking on her brother to take care of Tom, and it ate at him. Maybe he should go to his mom's for a few days, take some of the pressure off of Moira so she could help her family. Or he could call Naomi and...

He cut the thought off. After last night, Naomi was out of the question. Moira was right. He couldn't keep stringing Naomi along. She deserved better than that, deserved a man who wanted her so much he couldn't think straight, about the way he wanted Moira.

She sighed and stretched, running one foot along the outside of his leg. "Morning, Thomas."

"Didn't mean to wake you."

"Ye didn't. I was growing tired of waiting for ye to speak, when yer mind's whirring so hard I can near hear it." She pressed her bottom into his hips. "It's nice to wake to a man at the ready."

He sputtered out a laugh. "That's how most men wake up, especially men who haven't had sex in over a year."

She peered at him over her shoulder, a dangerous glint lighting her pale blue eyes. "Don't lie to me now, Tom. An unattached man isn't celibate among the People."

"This one has been." He skimmed his hand down her ribs and over her stomach. Her skin was so smooth and rich, like cream made solid. On an impulse he couldn't name, he pressed a kiss to her bare shoulder and tasted her. "Mmm. Daughters gave up on me about six months in. After I learned about the People, I was afraid your mom would kick me out when no one wanted me."

"She keeps ye around for a reason and it ain't your tallywacker."

"I love it when you go all Irish on me." He nipped her skin and dug his fingers into her hip, edging himself closer to her there. "And just so you know, I haven't had sex with Naomi. She's never been to my apartment, never been in my bed. I've kissed her twice and that's it."

Moira turned away from him. "I didn't ask."

"You were thinking it." At least, he hoped she was. He nipped her skin again, harder than he'd meant. She jerked under his teeth, and he kissed the bite, soothing its sting. "Sorry. I have the strangest urge to mark you."

"It didn't hurt. Startled me a bit is all."

Her voice had gone cool, chilling the desire winding its way through his blood. He eased back and slid out of bed on the opposite side. "Give me a minute and the bathroom's all yours."

He went into the bathroom and shut the door behind himself, leaning against it with both hands covering his face. What the hell had he been thinking, putting the moves on her when he'd promised her, *promised* her, that they could share the bed like adults? So what if she was naked? So what if he was so horny all he could think about was sliding into her? So what if she'd asked him to choose and he'd made a play, only to have her reject him?

Damn mercurial Irish.

He brushed his teeth, scrubbed his face with cold water, and left the bathroom with Tom Junior still hard as a rock, and him forty years old. Moira was sitting on the edge of the bed talking on her phone, her creamy skin gloriously bare in the dim morning light. He stopped dead in his tracks and sucked in a breath, taking her in from her tousled hair and sleepy eyes, down her torso past full breasts tipped with rosy nipples and her flat stomach, over the ginger curls protecting her sex and long, shapely legs, to the tips of her toes, painted a daring red.

He stared at those toes for a long time, only peripherally aware of her voice trailing off and Tom Junior standing at attention. Those toes begged to be kissed and nibbled. God, he'd love to start there and work his way up the firm muscles of her legs to the silky hair at the juncture of her thighs. What would she taste like? Sharp and womanly, like the Irishwoman she was, or soft and sweet, like the woman he'd always dreamed of having?

She brushed past him on her way into the bathroom. He

turned, catching a glimpse of her luscious bottom, and focused on two matching tattoos inked into her skin on her lower back, one on either side of her spine. The door closed between him and her, and he jerked around. Tattoos. He hated women with tattoos, or had before he'd met Moira. God help him, he wanted to lay her flat out on the bed and explore every inch of the Celtic knots inked into her perfect skin with his fingers and his tongue and his lips, and when he was finished and she was writhing under him, her lilting voice begging him in breathy moans, he wanted to bury himself in her and make love to her until they both forgot where he ended and she began.

He scrubbed a hand over his face and forced himself to scrounge for workout clothes. Boy, did he have it bad, and there wasn't a thing he could do to fix it that didn't involve him and her and a very long week in bed.

MOIRA ESCORTED TOM into the IECS Archives and gave him strict instructions on staying put until she returned for him. She ignored his confused expression, ignored the wild heat raging under her skin, and stalked across the campus to the main gate.

She'd been good, hadn't she? Considering the night she'd spent asleep beside his mostly nude form, aye, she had. A woman could only take so much temptation and Tom was little better than the fruit of the Tree of Knowledge hanging an inch outside her reach.

Damn him to hell and back. He'd put his mouth on her, licked her skin, nibbled his way along her shoulder, and she'd melted into him, ready for whatever he was willing to give her until he'd mentioned Spillfeite.

And reminded Moira why he couldn't be hers.

She raised her hand in a two-fingered salute to the guards on duty at the main gate and broke into a light jog, heading toward her car, still parked at The Omega. Dani had called while Tom, under Moira's watchful eye, lifted free weights in the gym shared by IECS visitors and students at Tellowee's high school. There'd been no word on Bobby. Indigo was frantic and refused to leave BDH Security, the company Bobby had started with two Army buddies, where a base of operations had been set up. Rebecca and three of Moira's sisters were already there, including Dani, likely poking their noses in where Moira wanted her own to be.

She'd give it a day and no more before the Order forwarded an address for the exchange, Bobby for the Oracle. As soon as they had a location, Bobby's partners could work their magic and hypothesize likely areas where the Order could be holding him, and from there, it was only a matter of time before he was found and retrieved.

Moira slowed on her approach into Tellowee proper. The parking lot outside The Omega was near as deserted as Main Street. She worked her way around the empty buildings, alert to the unusual and out of place.

Sig swung down from the roof of the building opposite the bar, her fingers clinging to scant handholds along the brick siding. She dropped onto the sidewalk with a light thud and jogged across the street, stopping beside Moira's cherry red Miata. "Should be safe to drive. The boy deputy and his dog checked all the cars last night. No one's passed by since then who shouldn't."

Moira nodded and patted her car's hood. It was a nifty little thing, more toy than car, but it served its purpose well, zipping her from place to place with style and speed. "Thanks for watching over her."

"Someone had to while you were off diddling your new toy." Sig's wide mouth curled into a faint smile. "Was he as tasty as he looks?"

Moira buffed an imaginary speck of dirt off the Miata's mirror. "He's smitten with another."

Sig arched one pale eyebrow. "When has that ever stopped you?"

"Since I'm near living under me mother's thumb, that's when." Moira yanked her keys out of her pocket. "Anyways, thank ye for watching me gal."

"We're rotating it out until everyone picks their vehicles up." Sig clapped a hand to Moira's back. "I'll be waiting for word on Bobby, should you need my sword."

"We may," Moira murmured. "Keep a weather eye on the horizon."

"And you."

Sig nodded and jogged away, resuming her surveillance from the roof across the way.

Moira drove to her apartment, scrubbed herself clean, and dressed in fresh clothes. She kept her mind carefully blank whilst packing enough clothes to last a week, edging out worry for her brother's safety and a near equal concern for Tom. He was safe enough at the Archives, protected in the People's stronghold by the most trustworthy Daughters and Sons Rebecca could find. It was nigh on impenetrable. As long as he kept his head down should trouble brew, he'd be fine.

She refused to dwell on the possibility that Tom was playing her and Naomi against one another, for reasons that eluded her entirely. He was too kind-hearted for such games and far too mature, though she'd watched loftier men fall prey to such petty temptations.

Moira emptied the perishables in her fridge into a large cooler, packing ice and frozen foods on top. On her way out, she grabbed her go bag of weapons, slid a note under her neighbor's door that she'd be gone for the foreseeable future, and stuffed her bags into the tiny boot of her Miata. She buckled the cooler into the passenger's seat and, moments later, eased out of the apartment building's parking lot onto the highway.

She arrived at the building housing BDH Security within an hour and made her way past security with barely a hiccup. At BDH's floor, she stepped off the elevator into a thrum of activity. A man dressed in a black polo embroidered with BDH's logo halted her at the reception desk and vetted her, then directed her to the break room.

She wound her way through the hallways and pushed open the glass door. Margaret, eldest living of Rebecca's children, sat at a round table, her blonde head bent over a steaming mug. Indigo sat next to her, her already pale skin leached of color, save for dark circles under her sapphire-like eyes.

Moira pulled out a chair and flipped it around, straddling it as she sat. "Any news?"

Indigo shook her head, sending her midnight ponytail swinging. "Nothing."

Margaret's cool gaze met Moira's. Of all of Rebecca's daughters, she resembled their mother the most, in looks, aye, with her ash blonde hair and icy blue eyes, but also in personality. Very little rattled Margaret Mary, and what did never lived long enough to tell the tale. "Our tech's been trying to track India using security cameras. Not much luck yet."

"What can I do?" Moira asked.

"Nothing yet, though I wouldn't mind having your help when we find him," Indigo said, her voice strained and thin. "Do you want a soft drink or a sandwich? I can fix you something."

Moira's heart softened at the quiet desperation in the other Daughter's voice. Did Indigo know how deep Bobby's claim was on her heart or was she, like most Daughters, blind to the love hiding within her?

"I'm fine, kaetyrm. Can't stay long anyway. Tom Fairfax is under me protection until Rebecca gives the word elsewise." Or until Naomi returned to claim him. Moira ignored the envy twisting its way through her chest, and the longing to have him yearn for her instead. "Promised him I'd return for a late lunch unless ye need me here."

Margaret sipped her coffee, her eyes dancing mischievously. "He's been eyeing you for a while."

Moira snorted. "His eye roams to the fair Spillfeite."

"If you say so." Margaret elbowed Indigo. "A bet on how long it takes Tom to talk her into bed. What say you?"

Indigo's eyes widened. "Three nights in his company," she

said solemnly. "Not counting time needed to track Bobby down and rescue him."

Margaret nodded. "Three sounds fair, plus time off to hunt the errant Son and your rogue sister."

Moira sputtered out a laugh. "Hey, now. I'm not so fierce keen for a fuck that I can't hold out three days."

Margaret leaned forward and speared Moira with a knowing gaze. "I've seen your eyes roaming to handsome Tom a time or two, little sister."

Moira shot a glare at Indigo. "Two hundred odd years is nothing for a Daughter, yet still, she holds her status as the elder over me head."

A small smile touched Indigo's mouth and some of the color returned to her pale cheeks. "Sisters are a trial."

Margaret choked on a sip of her coffee and Moira gaped. Indigo's smile stretched into a wobbly grin that faded as quickly as it had appeared. "He has to be safe."

Moira moved to the seat beside Indigo and covered the other woman's hand with her own. "He'll be back before you know it."

"He better be," Indigo gritted out. "I've got a couple of things to tell him about trusting the wrong woman. What was he thinking?"

Moira snickered. "When it comes to women, men seldom use their brains."

Margaret thumped her mug onto the table. "The two of you are a regular riot."

"A riot and a half," Moira corrected easily. "Now, lay it out for me. What plans have ye for retrieving the beloved Son?"

She chatted with her sister and her brother's woman for another half hour, then checked in with Bobby's partners, seeing for herself what was what. When Moira left, it was with the certainty that everything was being done that could be, and that Bobby would soon be returned safe and sound to his family's fold.

SEVEN

TOM SPENT the morning hovering over his new assistant, Diana Cole, a mortal Daughter fresh from a master's degree in archival science. Her arrival at the IECS had been delayed by a trip overseas visiting extended family. She'd been there less than a week and was still well within a probationary period. He'd given her the task of working with the textual fragments in need of repair or preservation, allowing him to focus solely on sifting through the vast Archives for clues to Sanctuary.

He'd had a few ideas on that since Moira had suggested he might already hold important information somewhere in his mind. First, though, he had to ensure that the flirty Diana actually knew what she was doing. If the pressure of solving the mystery of Sanctuary weren't so great, he'd ease her into the work, but the People were eager to find the origin of the Seven Sisters and their mortal enemy was believed to be working toward the same goal. Even he felt the urgency to solve the puzzle before the Shadow Enemy did and his only stake in the race was the love he had for the work he performed on behalf of the People.

Tom observed Diana as she prepared a burnt scroll for scanning, her deep blue eyes intent on her task above the face mask she wore, protecting the fragile document from the moisture in her breath. Moira had unearthed that particular scroll the week before and deemed it a high priority for preservation and translation. Its writing had to be reconstructed first, something he hoped they could do with X-ray phase-contrast tomography, a relatively new technique used for recovering writing from papyrus scrolls unearthed at Herculaneum. If it worked, anything they found would be handed over to James for study and translation. If not, they'd try something else, but Tom was pinning his hopes on XPCT.

A light rap sounded on the door. Tom peeled off the gloves he wore and stuffed them into the pocket of his lab coat. He eased the door open a scant hand's breadth. Moira stood on the other side, fingers tucked into a fresh pair of cords, her expression far more relaxed than it had been when she'd left that morning.

"I'll be right back," he told Diana, and slid through the door, shutting it behind him.

He hesitated. He and Moira had spent the night together. Even if it had been relatively innocent, he still had the urge to treat her like a lover, to pull her close and breathe her in and test the softness of her mouth with his own. He settled for dropping a kiss to the smooth skin of her cheek and was rewarded with a whiff of the soap she used and the faint tremor shuddering through her from his touch. "You're back early."

Her shoulders lifted and fell in a casual shrug. "No word yet on Bobby. His company has a good handle on their preparations."

"And you have your cell phone ready and your car gassed up, just in case," he guessed.

"True enough. I've brought me groceries from home, what would spoil if left alone."

"You need my key." He dug his key ring out of his pants pocket and handed it to her. "Spare's in the top left-hand drawer of my dresser. I should've given it to you this morning."

She flipped the key ring around a finger and eyed him. "Ye're awful accepting of me presence in yer home."

"Would it do any good to protest?"

Her wide mouth curled into a grin. "None a'tall."

"Well, there you go. I'd rather be productive with my time." And he didn't mind having her there nearly as much as he'd thought he would, especially given the way they'd woken up that morning, with her snuggled up against him, warm and soft and somehow right. "Lunch?"

"Cafeteria's open. The staff there has been thoroughly vetted and the food supply is secure. Need to get me goods into yer fridge first."

"I'll go with you. Hold on." Tom shrugged off his lab coat and stuck his head in the room he'd set up for preservation. He hung his coat on a hook fixed to the wall next to the door and caught Diana's eye. "Lunch. Be back in an hour, maybe an hour and a half. Take time yourself."

She nodded, her eyes twinkling over her mask. He shut the door on her, not even fazed that she'd likely heard his conversation with Moira. Daughters had the most amazing hearing, even the ones who, like Diana, were mortal born. It wouldn't take long for word to get out that Moira had spent the night at his apartment, and that he was giving her a spare key so she could come and go as she pleased.

He rested a polite hand on Moira's waist, a compromise between sliding an arm around her shoulders and holding her hand like the besotted suitor he was well on his way to being. Either one would likely land him in the hospital, depending on her mood, and they had work to do.

Later, though, when they were alone for the evening and her guard had dropped, he'd coax her into watching a movie cuddled next to him on the couch, and after, they'd slide into bed together. He'd hold her, skin to skin, and listen to her soft breaths as she fell into sleep, and use all his control keeping his hands from roaming along her silky skin.

Naomi had never tempted him the way Moira did. Maybe it was time to let that dream go, for all their sakes, even if Moira never wanted him the way he wanted her.

TOM CARRIED THE COOLER Moira had loaded with food taken from her apartment into his own. She trailed behind him, three bags slung over her shoulders. One was the right size to hold a laptop. Of the other two, both mid-sized, olive green duffels, one had been heavy enough for her to grunt slightly as she hefted it out of the trunk, rousing his curiosity.

She unlocked his door and pushed it open, dropping her bags in the hallway to one side. "Stay."

"Not a puppy," he groused.

She shot him an amused look, then checked his apartment, coming back a moment later with a handgun drawn. God only knew where she'd gotten it. His mind caught on the possibilities and, inevitably, Tom Junior perked up. Her smile widened as she tucked the gun away behind her back. "Ye rouse easily."

Only around her, though he'd be damned if he'd tell her and hand her another weapon to use against him. She already had too many at her disposal, from the soft curls of her hair along her collar to the smooth skin he couldn't resist touching to the Irish lilt in her tart voice.

He jerked his chin at the bedroom and toted the cooler into the kitchen, setting it on the counter near the fridge. "Help yourself to whatever room you need."

She tilted her head, gazing at him with something close to wariness. "Yer kindness fair burns from ye."

"Last time I checked, kindness wasn't a crime." He flipped the lid of the cooler open and pulled out packages of frozen meat wrapped in butcher paper, each one labeled in a precise, even hand. "Do you think these steaks will thaw out by tonight? I could throw them on the grill, make a salad to go with them."

"And ye cook, too," she murmured. "Why haven't ye married yet, settled down with a wife and a passel of young?"

He laid the steaks in the sink and stuffed the rest of the meat in his freezer. "Never found a woman I could love as much as my brother loved his wife."

"Loved?"

"She died five years ago. Cancer. Found a lump in her breast one morning in the shower, and four months later she was gone."

"Sorry to hear it."

He breathed around the ache in his heart. When Carolyn died, she'd taken a chunk of all of them with her, the biggest chunk from his brother. Mike had retreated into a dark grimness untouched by his family's love and his children's laughter. Tom's grip tightened on the rim of the cooler. Its plastic bit into the flesh of his palms. "With all the miracles of modern medicine, having someone die like that, a bitter, lingering death with their own body eating away at them from the inside out? It's really hard to watch."

Moira's arms slid around his waist. She rested her head on his back. When she spoke, her voice was soft and muffled, as if she'd buried her face in his shirt. "Yer family had time to say its goodbyes. Some never have the chance."

He smoothed his hands over hers, warming her, grateful for the comfort of her touch. "That doesn't make death easier."

"Nothing does." Her arms tightened briefly around him, then she stepped away. "I won't take too much of yer space, kind Thomas."

He peered at her over his shoulder. "You're the only person who calls me that."

Her gaze dropped to the floor. "I'll stop, if ye wish."

"No," he said, and turned back to the cooler. "I kinda like it."

He checked the date on a bag of carrots and tucked it under the ones already in his fridge. Her silence dragged on, so unusual, he glanced back. The space where she'd stood was empty. She'd moved away so silently, he hadn't heard her leave. He pulled out a plastic container of Bibb lettuce and stored it on top of the carrots. One step forward and twelve back, that was life around Moira. One day, maybe he'd earn enough of her trust that she wasn't so leery of him.

That day needed to come soon. He had a feeling he no longer stood at the crossroads between Naomi and Moira, that he'd already stepped onto the path leading to the uncouth Irishwoman with her wide, kissable mouth and a spark of wildness in her eyes. He closed the fridge and stared at the door, certainty bolstering the strength of his will. He'd have to tell Naomi, and soon. He owed her that much, out of friendship if not common courtesy.

The minute he severed those ties, Moira would no longer have the luxury of backing away from him. She'd set them on this path the day she'd walked into the Archives, her fine strawberry blonde hair a halo around the delicate features of her face, so beautiful he'd nearly fallen prostrate at her narrow feet. In the meantime, he'd court her the way he'd always longed to court the woman of his dreams, with slow kisses and the steadfast promises of the heart.

He narrowed his eyes on the bedroom where she moved quietly to and fro, rearranging a space he'd never shared with another woman, and a cunning grin blossomed on his face. Until that moment, Moira had led him around by the short hairs, calling the shots in every aspect of their relationship. Not anymore. By golly, if she wanted him, then she'd have him, and he her, and that would be that. He rubbed his hands down his thighs as a plan formed in his mind. Dinner, a movie, and a night spent holding her, slowly seducing her down the path *he* wanted *her* to take. Oh, yeah, this should be interesting.

He left the cooler airing out on the counter and strode into the bedroom, determination etched into every line of his body, his mind bent on taming a wild Irish doe to his touch.

68

LUNCH WENT more smoothly than Moira would've imagined, given the long, speculative looks Tom directed her way. He was planning something, the cogs and gears in his mind whirring near loud enough to hear. No telling what the man was up to, nor whether it would bode ill or well for either of them.

After lunch, he directed his new assistant to what he called an easier task and cloistered himself in his office with Moira, sitting thigh to thigh with her on a cushy sofa upholstered in a rough earth tone plaid, a legal pad on his lap, pen in hand, reading glasses perched on his slim nose.

She'd been inside his office less than a handful of times. It was neat as a pin, much like his apartment. A massive scarred wooden desk sat strategically in front of an entire wall of books, its surface holding a white-shaded, brass lamp, a pen, a legal pad, and his laptop centered precisely on a desk calendar. He'd pushed one end of the desk against an adjacent wall, leaving just enough room for two battered four-drawer filing cabinets on the opposite wall. The sofa and the coffee table placed in front of it, both situated parallel to the desk along the wall next to the entrance, were the only other pieces of furniture in the room. The top half of the visible walls were painted a bright white, the bottom half covered in bead board wainscoting stained walnut. The office was cozy and warm in spite of its location in the middle of a mountain.

Tom's thigh nudged hers. "I was thinking about something you said, that I might already have clues to Sanctuary buried in my head. To jog my memory, I started making a list of keywords. Sanctuary, Seven Sisters, oasis..."

"Why oasis?"

"James showed me a picture of a cylinder seal found at Sandby borg with what he thinks is a depiction of Sanctuary. Looked like an oasis to me."

"Hunh." She eyed the list of keywords he'd written down and ignored the warm friction of his thigh brushing along hers. "What else?"

"Well, I went through the Legend of Beginnings and the Prophecy of Light, using those as guidelines, so I have Mother, Father, murder, savages, bones, burials, graves. Things like that." He dropped a casual hand over hers and rubbed his thumb across her knuckles. "I was hoping you could help. Once we're finished, I thought I'd make a list of any documents that come to mind and maybe retrieve them, have you look them over."

"So the keywords will help ye pinpoint what ye might've already come across." Not a bad idea. She tugged at her hand. His grip tightened, and she huffed out an impatient breath. "Need me hand, Tom."

He kept his gaze on the legal pad on his lap and the notes he was making. "I like holding it."

"We're working."

"Not so hard I can't hold your hand." He peered at her over the rims of his glasses. "It seems a bit much to protest holding hands when you're sharing my bed."

She furrowed her eyebrows over a glare. "Spillfeite..."

"*Naomi* isn't sleeping naked in my bed, nor will she be. In fact, I don't intend to share a bed with her at all, naked or otherwise." He glanced down at the legal pad and jotted another note. "When I started updating the Archives' organization and cataloging system, I added keywords to the Preliminary Descriptive Inventories. I was trying to standardize them, make them easier to search as we switched over to a digital catalog, and that could be useful here."

She slumped into the couch. Did he really think she believed he wouldn't sleep with Naomi, and hadn't already, as he'd claimed that morning? She tensed her hand under his. A Daughter never allowed a man to lead her by the nose with half-truths and deflections. She had no intention of giving Tom that leeway.

"Don't test me, sweetheart," he said mildly. "Tonight when we get home, you can rail at me, throw me over your shoulder, spank my ass if you want to, but right now, I need your devious

70

little mind focused on this."

She pressed her lips together over a laugh. "Spank your arse, eh?"

"Believe me, that's the mildest fantasy I've had about you." He flicked a glance down her body, so quickly she nearly missed its heat. "Keywords?"

Her mind caught on that fantasy. Tom naked, sprawled across his bed, his face buried in the sheets as he begged her to touch him. Heat curled through her nethers and her skin tingled. Aye, she had a few fantasies of her own. Now that he'd mentioned his, it'd be that much harder for her to hold back, that much harder not to dwell on the fantasies she'd been brewing since the first time he'd asked her to dance.

She locked her need for him carefully away and turned her mind to his work, adding texts she thought might be helpful to his growing list, and spent the afternoon digging through the outdated catalog in the main research room while he searched the nascent digital one from his laptop at a nearby table.

As had happened since the beginning of their search, they were hampered by both catalogs' incompleteness, by the random nature of the Archives' holdings, and by the haphazard and inconsistent inventories that had been created by previous archivists, if they'd been created in the first place. The room Moira had started in was just one of several housing documents and artifacts that had never been inventoried or cataloged at all. Then there were the number of languages represented. Most of the documents were written in a language neither Tom nor Moira could easily read, as were some of the inventories. James had helped somewhat, but they'd need more than his gift with languages to sift through the Archives' vast holdings.

By five thirty, Tom's normally patient demeanor had disintegrated into obvious frustration. He yanked his glasses off and scrubbed a hand over his eyes. "I vote we head to my place and see if the steaks have thawed out enough to grill."

Moira marked her place with a slip of pink paper and closed

the catalog drawer she'd been working in. Her own eyes were gritty with fatigue and dust, and in sore need of respite. "I second yer vote. Salad or baked sweet potatoes?"

"Both. I'm starving." He stood and stretched, ruffled his hair with wide-spread fingers. "Let me drop these notes off in my office and we can go."

He checked on Diana on the way out and draped a casual arm around Moira's shoulders as they walked between the Archives and his apartment. She kept a wary eye on their surroundings and checked his rooms before letting him wander inside, then helped him prepare their meal. Over supper taken with a glass of a truly fine red wine, she updated him on Bobby's situation, what she knew of it, and teased him into sharing stories of his family. He spoke easily of growing up, his expression animated, his laughter never far away. His casual manner soaked into her, easing some of the loneliness she'd lived with for nigh on a century, since war had rent the two most important parts of her family into shreds.

After clearing the supper dishes, they changed into pajamas and watched a movie with the lights off. He insisted on wrapping an arm around her and brushed his cheek over the top of her head from time to time. She could scarce pay attention to the on-screen action, so roused was she by the weight of his arm and the press of his thigh against hers.

At the end, he switched the TV off with the remote and put the DVD away, then pulled her into a stand. "If this were a real date, I'd walk you to your door and steal a goodnight kiss."

"This wasn't a date a'tall, Tom."

"More's the pity," he muttered. "You want the bathroom first?"

"Why not?"

She wandered into the bathroom, keenly aware of him hot on her heels, and performed her nightly ablutions with thoughts of the night ahead strong in her mind. When she came out, he was sitting on the bed dressed only in his pajama bottoms, reading from his Kindle, his nude torso partially lit by the light thrown from the bedside lamp. He had a fine body, tall and lean. Not heavily muscled, no, but well-built all the same.

Her gaze lingered on his flat stomach and the faint bump of his sex, hidden beneath the thin flannel of his pajama bottoms. Would he cuddle up to her again, press his firm erection to her arse as they slept? And why would she want him to, when his words regarding another woman and his actions concerning the same were at opposite ends of the spectrum? Best she discourage him until he sorted the matter out, bluntly if needs be, and rein in her own need to feel his skin on hers.

"You keep looking at me like that and I'm liable to do something about it." He closed the Kindle and set it on the nightstand. "All done?"

She nodded and sidled out of his way, her resolve drooping in the face of this new Tom. *This* Tom had tucked much of his natural reserve away and appeared unafraid of speaking his mind. *This* Tom had held her hand and told her plainly that he had no interest in bedding the fair Naomi. *This* Tom had kissed her skin that morning and claimed a need to mark her, a need she shared, both to carry his mark and to place hers upon his skin in return.

Moira checked the apartment's locks and retrieved her phone, setting it on the nightstand next to her side of the bed with the ringer turned low. Margaret had promised to text with news, and had agreed that the Order wouldn't dillydally in arranging an exchange point. Within the next twenty-four hours, they'd know where Bobby was. Moira intended to be out there hunting for her brother when they did and punishing the ones who'd dared spirit him away from the love of his family.

She stripped her pajamas off and slid into the bed, curling into a ball as her mind whirled and her heart thundered and her breaths hitched, anticipation of Tom's touch warring with worry over Bobby's welfare.

Tom came out of the bathroom moments later and flipped off the bedside lamp. The covers rustled and the bed dipped under his weight. He scooted close to her, spooning her as he had the night before, his hand on her stomach, his legs supporting hers. "Mmm. This is nice."

She lay still beside him, her eyes wide open, staring into the darkened room. He nuzzled her neck and his breath feathered over her skin, sparking ripples of heat wherever it touched. She shivered and buried her face in the pillow. How much longer did she have to hold out against him? How much longer could she?

He nipped the skin of her throat with sharp teeth. "How mad would you be if I left a mark here?"

Her moan mingled with laughter. "We're not children, Thomas."

"I know. You're right. I'm getting a little carried away." He sighed and pressed a gentle kiss to the place he'd nipped. "I've never wanted to be rough with a woman before. Should've known better than to try it with you."

"I didn't say ye couldn't be rough. If ye wish to leave a mark, ye may." She shrugged, aiming for casual unconcern, hoping he missed the breathy need in her voice. "'Twill heal soon enough."

"Seriously?"

"Have I not said so?"

His breath hitched and shuddered softly. "Mind if I cut the light back on for a minute?"

She bit her lower lip, containing a moan. Sweet blessed Mother, he wanted to see his handiwork. "As ye wish."

The mattress shifted, the light flicked on. His hands came to her shoulders, tugging her onto her back. He tucked the covers over her breasts and braced his upper body above hers, his lower body pressed into the bed beside her. "This isn't how I imagined kissing you the first time."

"Ye wish to kiss me?"

"Since the moment I saw you." He smoothed her hair back and touched his lips to her nose, her eyelids, her chin, leaving spots of heat along her skin. "I thought I'd finally talk you into a real date, and after, I'd walk you to your door and press you into

74

it and take my time exploring you."

She twisted the sheet between her fingers and lowered her gaze. He made it sound so sweet, as if he wished to court her. Was that how he'd treated Naomi, with tender words and proper kisses?

He sighed and dropped his forehead to hers. "Guess you're not ready for that yet, huh."

"Need I be?"

His brows shot down into an angry vee over his eyes. "What kind of question is that?"

"A fair one. Ye've been flirting with Spillfeite as long as I've known ye. It makes me wonder if it's really me ye desire or if ye're using me to slake yer need for her."

The emotion bled slowly out of his expression as he stared down at her, leaving his face cold and hard. "If that's the kind of man you think I am, maybe you should leave now."

"I've a duty to protect ye."

"And that's all I am, huh, a duty?" He glanced away, his mouth a thin slash across his face. When he spoke again, his voice was soft and flat. "I apologize for bothering your rest."

He pushed himself carefully away from her, flipped off the light, and settled quietly onto the other half of the bed with a good foot of empty mattress between them. She threw a forearm across her eyes, cursing the heat simmering in her blood. Why had she opened her mouth? A minute more and his would've been on her, touching her the way she'd yearned for him to for donkey's years. But no, she'd had to yip and yammer and ruin the moment, and wasn't that a fine how-de-do?

She rolled onto her side and fell into a fitful sleep filled with dreams of Tom's beautiful eyes turning cold and bitter as wind blowing off the Atlantic across the rugged hills of her homeland.

EIGHT

SHARP BEEPS woke Moira. She groaned and rubbed her face along Tom's back. Sometime in the night, they'd met in the middle of the bed, seeking warmth or comfort or the promise of a lover's touch. It annoyed her no end that she'd been the one to give in and cuddle up to him instead of the other way around. She checked the time on the digital clock on his nightstand and cursed roundly. Five oh eight. Feckin' sun wasn't even up yet.

She rolled away from him and fumbled for her phone, glaring at the screen through bleary eyes. Margaret had sent a text. Moira opened it, staring blankly at it for a good long while as her mind shifted and rearranged, and finally woke enough to understand the letters forming words across her phone.

Have an address. BDH asap.

Tom turned over and curled himself around her, cupping her stomach with one gentle hand. "Izzit?"

"They've found Bobby," she whispered. "Go back to sleep."

He *mmphed* and wiggled closer, and his breaths evened out, deepening into soft snores. She grinned and eased away from him. He was a snorer. How darling and sweet and...

She caught herself in the middle of bending over to kiss his stubbled cheek. The man had driven her barmy, that's what he'd done. She slid out of bed, foraged for clothes in the dark, and

76

crept into the bathroom. Aye, he'd pushed her right over the edge with his sweet little snores and hand-holding and promises of kisses. The very devil, he was, sent to tempt her from the crooked path she walked onto the straight and narrow.

She snickered over it through a quick shower, using his soap so she'd have his smell around her all the day long. Tom as the devil. That was rich, and she'd be certain to tell him, soon as she sorted out her brother.

Assuming Thomas would speak to her again.

She dried off, shrugging the worry away. He'd speak to her, a'right. A man who couldn't keep his hands to himself during the night would forget his grudge, and he'd right damn well explain when he intended to cut off Naomi so there'd be no further misunderstandings.

Moira texted Ruanna, an immortal Daughter who'd leveraged an informal claim on Tom's young friend, Phil, sharing the handsome historian with another Daughter. Ruanna had promised to watch over Tom should Moira be needed in the search for Bobby, at least until the Order had been rooted out. Though Moira knew very little about Ruanna, she knew enough to understand that the other Daughter would never jeopardize Phil and would therefore never knowingly betray Tom. If nothing else, Ruanna's actions would be checked by the certainty of Moira's wrath raining down, not a pleasant prospect in the best of times.

Having a reputation as a mercurial brawler came in handy on occasion.

With the strength of the entire family gathered behind the search for Bobby, it was the best Moira could do. She ignored the pinch of worry gathering in her chest. Tom would be fine as long as he stayed on campus, and there was no reason for him to stray outside its walls.

She finished dressing and scrawled a note for him, tucking it under his alarm clock where he'd be sure to find it first thing. While she'd been in the shower, he'd rolled onto his back and thrown an arm over his head, baring the silky hair underneath and the long line of his ribs. It was so tempting to explore him there, to trail her fingers over the smooth expanse of muscle and bone, to discover if her touch tickled or aroused him. She sat on the edge of the bed and rested her ear over his heartbeat, measuring the slow thump against her own. It soothed her, rounding off the edges of grumpy temper stirred by the early morning wakeup call.

His arms came around her, holding her tight. "Moira," he said, his voice soft and hoarse. "Thought you'd left."

"Not yet."

He yawned, exhaling his breath on a low *mmm*. "Come back to bed."

She wanted to, so much, wanted to strip off her clothes and slip under the covers and tangle herself up with him, and would if it were anything other than family calling her away. "Can't. Have to help get Bobby back."

"Mmkay. Be careful."

"And ye as well, Thomas." She eased out of his embrace and sat up. His eyes were closed, his face turned toward her, and his hand burrowed under the hem of her shirt, resting on the bare skin of her waist. He loved to touch her there, did Tom. "I'll be back as soon as I can."

"Hold you to that."

A soft tap came at the front door. Moira pressed fleeting kisses to Tom's mouth and forehead, expecting him to protest or respond, but he'd already dozed back off. She smoothed his hair back, kissed his forehead a final time, and went to open the door.

Ruanna stood on the other side, her rich blonde hair falling in a braid down the center of her back, wearing a thin t-shirt and pajama bottoms under a knee-length white wool coat with a backpack slung over one shoulder and a pillow in one hand. Moira went over Tom's schedule, promised to check in as often as she could, and left before temptation got the better of her.

The streets were nigh on empty between Tellowee and

BDH Security, the morning air too chill for casual outings. The sun hid behind the mountains, its rays barely peeking over the tops when Moira pulled into the parking lot next to the building housing her brother's company. She raced inside, passing easily through building security, and found her mother in Bobby's office, sitting on the sofa between Jerusha and Charlotte, who scooted closer to Rebecca and patted the cushion next to her lap.

Moira flopped into the small space and rested her head on Charlotte's shoulder. "Another hour in bed would've been dandy."

Charlotte harrumphed. "Like there's anything good waiting in that cold bed of yours."

"Fat lot you know," Moira muttered. She closed her eyes as a small smile touched her mouth. Her bed was feckin' cozy with Tom in it. "Where's Maggie May?"

"Coordinating rescue efforts with Hiro and Drew. Dani's at home with Dave, Robert, and Charlotte's family, and Indigo's on her way in. What I'm curious about is you." Rebecca's calm voice turned sly. "Margaret said you'd taken Tom to your bed. I thought she was pulling my leg, but judging by the satisfied smile on your face, I'd guess not."

Moira slapped a hand over her eyes. Why had she let her big sister goad her into giving up that secret? "He's accepted no woman's claim. It leaves him vulnerable. Since he's under your protection and I'm yer daughter, the least I could do is watch over him."

"Been kissing the Blarney Stone again, sister?" Jerusha asked.

Charlotte snickered. "I bet that's not all she's kissing."

"Oh, har." Moira crossed her arms over her chest and snuggled into the couch, amused in spite of herself. "I'll have ye know I've only touched his lips once and that was this morning on the way out with him sleeping sound as a babe."

"All these years, I thought I'd reared daughters who knew what to do with themselves," Rebecca said, "but if you haven't figured out where else to kiss a man yet, perhaps I missed the mark."

The office's door opened, interrupting Moira's retort. She opened one gritty eye and peered at Margaret as her sister dropped into a chair in front of Bobby's desk, across the coffee table from them.

"We're a go soon," Margaret said. "What did I miss?"

"Nothing," Moira said.

"Oh, right, nothing," Jerusha jeered. "Moira's got a new lover."

"Demme." Margaret leaned forward, bracing her forearms on her knees. "I gave him three nights to seduce her and he did it in one. Seems I overestimated his reserve."

"Jaysus." Moira glared at the varying expressions of amusement her family wore. "He didn't seduce me, though, give him credit, he's edging his way 'round to it, and that's not the point. The point is it's nobody's business aside from mine and Tom's, and I'll thank ye all to butt out of it."

Charlotte nudged Moira's arm with her elbow. "Don't get your panties in a twist. We're happy you've found somebody, especially after..."

Rebecca tapped a gentle hand on Charlotte's thigh. "Not now, darling. Let Moira wake up. Her humor will return once the sleep's faded from her mind. You can needle her all you want after that."

"Ye're all heart," Moira muttered.

Margaret took the lead, outlining the plan she and Bobby's partners had come up with, smoothly drawing the attention away from Moira's near non-existent love life.

Moira's mind lingered on Tom and the previous night's near miss, on the soft concern in his voice that morning when he'd been vulnerable and relaxed and likely unaware of what he was doing. In his sleep, he'd turned to her, calling *her* name. It had been *her* he'd reached for, *her* he'd asked to return to his embrace. Perhaps he was forgetting the fair Naomi after all.

It warmed Moira through and through. She gripped that comfort, holding it tightly within her heart, and concentrated on Margaret's plan to rescue their brother from the clutches of his woman's sister.

TOM WOKE SLOWLY, groggy after a restless night. He stretched a hand out, expecting Moira, and encountered a smooth expanse of cool flannel. His gut twisted into a knot. She'd left. God, she'd really left him. He huffed a bitter laugh into her pillow, breathing in the scent of her pine shampoo lingering in the cloth. What had he expected? She'd flat out accused him of using her and he'd told her to leave, so she had, though he'd never thought her the kind of woman who'd sneak off in the middle of the night without even saying goodbye.

He rolled onto his back and blinked at the ceiling, an awful emptiness echoing through him. Unless she'd left town all together, he'd see her again. Surely she wouldn't abandon her work at the Archives. It was too important to the People, too important to her mother, and Moira was nothing if not dedicated. Sassy, temperamental, and flat out bawdy, but never one to shirk her duty. She couldn't avoid him forever, not when they were working so closely together on such an important project.

His alarm clock buzzed, the digital drone annoying on top of the ache lodged in his chest. He slapped a hand over it and fumbled the switches, shutting it off. Paper crinkled, catching his attention. He pulled a single sheet of notebook paper from under the clock, flipped on the lamp, and patted his bare chest. Glasses, glasses. They were probably on the coffee table where he usually left them at night. He shook his head and threw the covers off, padding into the living room with the note in one hand, feeling his way through the darkened rooms by memory.

A soft, feminine breath sighed from the area around the couch. *Moira.* He loped toward it, stumbling over its edge with a muttered curse, and nearly missed the rustle of cloth and the metal snick of a gun cocking.

He froze where he stood, half leaning over the end of the sofa, and his heart leapt into double time, pounding against his sternum.

"Identify yourself," a hard, not quite familiar voice said, "and I might aim far enough to the left to miss your heart."

"Tom Fairfax. This is my apartment. Who are you?"

Metal hit wood and the sofa's springs creaked. "Sorry, Tom. It's Ruanna. One of Phil's women? Cut the light on so we can meet."

He sucked in a breath around the hammering of his heart. "Are you going to shoot me?"

"Hardly. Moira would kill me, if Phil didn't first."

He edged his way to the light switch, flipped it on, and exhaled a shaky breath. The woman sitting on the couch was smiling at him, her honey blonde hair twisted into a long braid. "Ruanna. Nice to put a name with the face."

"The pleasure's mine. Phil talks about you all the time, though he's a little shy about introducing us." She shrugged and her smile edged over from friendly into knowing. "What with him courting two women at the same time and all."

"If I were him, I'd have a hard time choosing, too." And wasn't Tom in the same boat, though he was under no delusions as to whether or not Naomi and Moira would share him. He couldn't handle two women at once anyway. Phil, on the other hand, appeared more than up to the challenge. "No offense, but what are you doing in my apartment?"

"Moira asked me to watch over you while she worked with her family to retrieve Bobby." Ruanna glanced toward Tom's hand. "She left a note."

A vague memory surfaced, of Moira sitting beside him on the bed telling him they'd found Bobby. Tom sagged against the wall and clutched the note. She hadn't left him, not for the reasons he'd believed anyway. Thank God for favors small and large. "I was coming in to get my glasses."

82

Ruanna rose gracefully from the sofa. "Mind if I use your bathroom?"

"Help yourself. It's through the bedroom."

She slipped through the apartment while he scrounged for his reading glasses, carrying them and the note into the kitchen. He started the coffee, then perched his glasses on his nose and read Moira's note.

Dearest Thomas,

A small bubble of humor worked it's way out of his throat. Thomas, huh? He shook his head and continued reading.

Margaret, et al., have found Bobby. I'm needed there, likely will be through the day. Hope to be home by supper, though, so plan accordingly. Ruanna will watch over you until then. Mind her well and keep your head down, there's a dear. Will text when I can. Ever, Moira.

He read the note twice more, searching for anything indicating a softening in her. Home. She'd called his apartment home. It was where she was resting her head at night, so he didn't put much store in it or the way she'd started and signed the note. He sighed and tugged his glasses off. Why had he bothered getting his hopes up? Hadn't he already known what kind of woman she was, that it was unlikely she'd ever truly care for him? Hadn't that been why he'd pursued Naomi in the first place, in spite of the sparks flying between him and Moira?

As soon as Ruanna came out of the bathroom, he took a quick shower and dressed for the day. A workout would be heavenly, but he wouldn't drag her through that. Chances were good she'd escort him to the Archives and leave him there while she went about her day. Maybe once she had, he could clear his head and work the disappointment out of his system. If not, he'd slip out later and go to the gym on his own, Moira's cautions be damned. The IECS had more security than the White House, for pete's sake. If he wasn't safe there, he wasn't safe anywhere.

NINE

MUCH TO TOM'S CHAGRIN, Ruanna didn't drop him off at the Archives and go about her day. She dogged every step he made, going so far as to stand outside the bathroom when he had to relieve himself. If he left his office, she walked beside him, halting him well back from corners so she could peer around them and check for God only knew what.

As if ninja assassins were waiting just out of reach to conk her on the head and spirit him away.

Tom scowled at her over his laptop's screen. For crying out loud, she'd tasted his lunch for poison right in front of the cafeteria's staff before letting him eat. He'd ended up apologizing to them, earning knowing grins and a wink from one rotund woman, who'd added, "Happens all the time. This lot's got paranoia down cold."

Well, it wouldn't be happening anymore, not because of him. Soon as Moira returned from helping find Bobby, he intended to sit her down and explain, calmly and rationally, that her overprotectiveness had to stop. He was a grown man and fully capable of caring for himself.

And if she didn't listen to reason, he'd do what a man should do to his woman in those situations. He'd kiss her senseless.

Though it was annoying to have Ruanna treat him as if his life was in danger every second, she turned out to be useful. After lunch, he'd settled into his office with stacks of documents Moira had asked him to catalog, organizing them into collections for storage and creating inventories for them. Ruanna had declared herself bored and begun scanning the ones she could read, seemingly anything written in English, Latin, Greek, Arabic, and, of all things, Aramaic and archaic Hebrew. She sat on his sofa, studiously searching the texts for the keywords he'd given her, summarizing and classifying those he couldn't read on his own.

Halfway through the afternoon, Ruanna's phone beeped. She checked it, then casually tossed it onto the sofa beside her. "They found Bobby."

"Thank God," Tom said. "Is he ok?"

Ruanna's fingers tapped quickly across her tablet's free-standing keyboard. "Beat up pretty bad. Otherwise fine. Doc Phillips is gonna keep him for a coupla days."

Tom straightened the folders stacked beside his laptop, lining the edges up precisely. "And Moira?"

She flipped a document over and ran a finger down the page. "Took a knife to the thigh. Been sleeping it off."

"What?" Tom's heart leapt into his throat. He stood, pushing his chair back. It spun around and banged against the bookshelves behind him. "Why the hell didn't she text earlier?"

"If it were something to worry over, she would've."

"If it were…" He shoved his fingers into his hair. Trust a Daughter to take what had probably been a serious wound as if it were nothing. "What hospital is she in?"

"County, about twenty minutes from here." Ruanna eyed him, her expression wary. "Why?"

"We're going right now. Mule-headed woman." He strode around the desk and snatched up his coat, shrugging it on, then riffled through his pants pockets for his car keys. "She's probably near death and too stubborn to admit it."

Metal snicked against metal. Tom swung around and stared

aghast at the gun Ruanna held on him.

"Moira told me to keep you here until she came for you," she said. "That's exactly what I aim to do."

"You won't shoot me."

Her expression hardened. "Try me. There are lots and lots of places I can put a bullet that'll slow you down without killing you, and I don't mind doctoring you right here on the carpet."

"Jesus Christ," he breathed. "Fine. Shoot me, then, but I'm going after her."

Ruanna held the gun steadily, aiming it straight at his heart. After a while, she sighed and dropped her hand. "Fuck. I hate it when people call my bluff."

A fine tremor ran through Tom's limbs. He leaned against the edge of the desk, propping himself upright, and in a hoarse voice said, "I didn't think you were bluffing."

"Hunh. So you were gonna make me shoot you."

"If that's what it took."

She stood and gathered her things together, stuffing them into her backpack. "You must love her a lot."

"Getting there," he muttered. "Can we go already?"

She grinned and stuffed her gun behind her back. "Anybody ever tell you you're not as mild-mannered as you look?"

"You're the first."

Though she probably wouldn't be the last, especially once he got ahold of Moira. He fully intended to be anything but mild-mannered the next time he saw his Irish Daughter.

Ruanna escorted him out of the Archives, then drove him to the hospital. She took a firm hold on his elbow and led him through the corridors, stopping outside a room with people lined up and down the hallways, their voices so quiet, he could barely hear them.

One of the waiting women raised an eyebrow. "He's a bit scrawny for you, isn't he, Rue?"

Ruanna pulled a sour face. "Jerusha, this is Tom Fairfax. He's here after Moira."

Jerusha eyed him, open interest gracing her tanned features. "Well, well, well. Big sis caught a handsome one."

"Where is she?" Tom asked.

Jerusha jerked a thumb over her shoulder at the open door. "Resting. Some idiot tried to saw her leg in two with a dull blade. It ain't pretty."

He paled and sucked in a breath, willing the nausea churning in his gut to stay put. "I knew it had to be bad. Can I see her?"

"Please, take him off my hands," Ruanna said. "He was willing to let me shoot him to get here. Short of knocking him out cold, there's no way I can keep him from doing whatever he wants."

Jerusha wrapped a firm hand around his upper arm. "I'll make sure Moira doesn't come after you."

Ruanna blew out a sigh. "Thanks. Let me know if you need an extra sword."

"Will do." Jerusha's mouth turned up at one corner as Ruanna slipped away. "Come along, brother. Try not to rile Moira too much. Bobby's still out and he needs his rest."

She muscled Tom through the doorway and shut the door behind them, leaning her back against it as she released him. His gaze zeroed in on Moira, resting on the hospital bed on the far side of the room.

"Tom, thank you for coming."

His gaze jerked around. Rebecca Upton stood in front of an empty chair wearing faded jeans and a ragged flannel shirt two sizes too big for her. A blonde with the director's pale blue eyes sat in the chair next to her, her shrewd gaze narrowed on Tom. A beautiful young woman with her black hair pulled into a long ponytail sat by the bed, holding the hand of a man with bandages over his eyes and an IV attached to his other hand. Dark bruises bloomed across the man's body, clearly visible on the bare skin not covered by a thin hospital gown, in spite of the lack of overhead lighting and the curtains drawn over the room's windows.

"Jesus Christ," Tom breathed. "Is he ok?"

"He will be." Rebecca stepped forward and cupped Tom's shoulder. "But you're not here to visit Bobby, are you?"

Her voice held a faint hint of humor. He cleared his throat and glanced at Moira. "Not exactly."

"She told us she was protecting you, since no woman had claimed you."

The black-haired woman exchanged a small smile with the blonde. "Two more nights."

"Maybe one, judging by his expression." The blonde stood and raked a cold gaze over him. "Though she could've found a man with a little more meat on his bones."

Jerusha coughed softly. "Twenty says he gets her out of here without a fuss."

"I'll take that one," Rebecca said mildly.

Heat crept up Tom's cheeks. "I can't believe y'all are betting when two people have been seriously hurt."

Rebecca squeezed his shoulder. "They'll be fine or we wouldn't be so cavalier. Margaret will help you get Moira home, if you can overcome her pigheaded nature and persuade her to leave."

"If the doctor says she can leave, she will by golly leave," he gritted out.

"This should be interesting." The blonde stuck out her hand and nodded toward the black-haired woman. "Margaret, Rebecca's eldest living. That's Indigo, Bobby's woman."

Tom took Margaret's hand. "How many more of you are there?"

Rebecca smiled and sank gracefully into her chair. "Charlotte, who's married and mortal, and Dani, the youngest."

"I've met Dani."

"Who hasn't?" Jerusha muttered

Rebecca slid a chiding look at her daughter. "Moira's starting to stir, Tom. Best head off her temper before she wakes fully."

He inhaled a fortifying breath and wound through the narrow space between the end of Bobby's bed and the people gathered around the injured man. Moira grimaced and touched pale fingers to her forehead, groaning softly. He sat gingerly on the side of the bed, careful not to jostle her, and examined her from head to toe.

A vivid bruise colored her left cheekbone, which was swollen around a small cut. Her black turtleneck was slit open across the right arm. A white bandage peeped through the fabric, thankfully also small. The real damage seemed to be her leg. Her olive cargo pants had a jagged tear across the right thigh, and underneath, gauze wrapped around her thigh, bright dots of blood running down its center.

He hissed in a breath and took her hand, holding it gently. "Moira, sweetheart. You awake?"

She rolled back and forth on the bed, her grimace deepening. "Tom. What in blazes are ye doing here?"

Her words slurred together and held none of the sharp retort he was used to hearing from her. His breath caught on worry and stuttered out. "Ruanna told me you were hurt. I've come to take you home."

She cursed under her breath. "I told her to keep ye safe."

"We're surrounded by your family. That's safe enough." He brushed her hair back with trembling fingers. "Stop trying to open your eyes. I'll get a wheelchair and you can sleep this off at home where I can keep an eye on you."

She scoffed, though her eyes stayed shut. "Ye daft? I can walk fine."

"It's either a wheelchair or I'm carrying you out," he said evenly, "but you are absolutely not going to walk out of here."

Her fingers tightened on his hand, and for a moment, he thought she'd argue with him. Instead, she sighed and pulled his hand to her chest, wrapping her arms around it. One corner of her mouth turned up in a sleepy smile. "Lovely Tom. Will ye kiss me now?"

Jerusha snorted. "Should've bet more."

Rebecca tutted. "I never thought I'd see the day she'd give in to a man. It only took four and a half centuries."

"Says the woman who took nearly a millennium." Margaret appeared at Tom's shoulder, her footsteps so quiet along the tiled floor, he hadn't heard them. "I'll carry her out. You go fetch a wheelchair."

He heaved a relieved sigh and eased off the bed, out of her way. "Thanks."

Rebecca stood as he passed by and placed a gentle hand on his forearm. "Be patient with her, Tom. She's got a good heart, if you care enough to find it."

He nodded and gripped her hand. "I'll remember that. Let me know if I can help with your son."

Jerusha followed him out of the room and trailed behind while he rounded up a wheelchair. They met Margaret, holding a woozy Moira, at the entrance to Bobby's room. Margaret placed her sister in the chair and walked with them to the parking lot, leaving Jerusha behind with the pack of others waiting for news on Bobby.

Tom went slowly, easing his way over bumps in the floor, his hands white-knuckled on the wheelchair's handles. Everybody had made light of her injuries, but the very fact that she'd let him talk her into leaving with him said it all. She was badly wounded, so badly she slumped in the wheelchair, her head propped on her hand. His mind delineated her injuries and the nausea came roaring back. Another inch inside her thigh and the tip of that blade would've nicked her femoral artery. She could've bled out and died, immortal curse or not, and he would've lost the brightest star in his life before he'd had a real chance to know her.

Margaret lifted Moira into his Prius and buckled her in, shutting the car's door quietly. "She'll be able to walk on it by the end of the day. You'll be lucky to keep her down after that. Try, though. We still need her to help hunt down the people who took Bobby."

"Find somebody else," he said through clenched teeth.

Margaret's cold gaze warmed fractionally. "She'll be fine, Tom. Feed her up and encourage her to rest. Sex is optional."

He pinched the bridge of his nose, refusing to acknowledge the heat blushing across his skin. "Thank you for helping me with her."

"Any time." She patted his shoulder, sending him swaying under the force of her hand. "Don't let her Irish tongue rip you to shreds."

"Too late," he muttered, and went around the car. By the time he slid into the driver's seat, Margaret had disappeared inside the hospital. He stared at the entrance for a moment, then checked on Moira, touching the back of his hand to her forehead and cheeks. She had the most bizarre family he'd ever met. Treating her and Bobby's injuries so casually, betting on the outcome of him asking her to leave. He checked the parking lot behind him and to the sides, and backed out, heading toward his apartment, his thoughts caught on the assumptions her family had made about her relationship with him.

THE THROB in Moira's cheek eventually woke her. She prodded it gently and winced. Feckin' elbow had caught her unawares as she came through the back door of the house where Bobby had been held. She'd lashed out at her attacker with a quick strike to the gut and earned a slice across her arm and a jab in her thigh for the trouble. Blast it. Shoulda been a quick in and out, not an ambush. She'd not even caught her attacker's face. Margaret would've though, and as soon as Moira caught up with her sister, she'd hunt down the unknown knife wielder and deliver a timely lesson of her own.

The faint scent of roast beef caught her nose. She sniffed and sighed appreciatively, and rubbed a hand over the hunger gnawing at her innards. Hospitals sure had come along since the last time she'd been in one. No, wait. She'd visited Dani the month before after her baby sis had tangled with the irritatingly hardy Lilith. Rebecca had snuck meals in, the food there had been so bad. Moira prodded her memory, teasing out images of previous visits to the hospital. Come to think on it, the county hospital had never had good food.

She frowned. How had she made it out of the hospital and landed in an unfamiliar place dressed in her knickers and not a stitch more?

She slit a single eye open and peered cautiously around. The room was dark, lit by a slice of light shining under a door on the opposite side of the room. She sniffed again and detected an unmistakable hint of Tom's cologne. A shadow crossed the light and a moment later, he opened the door and walked in carrying something in his hand. He set it on the nightstand and sat beside her, his hands checking over her in swift, tender strokes.

"What am I doing in your apartment?" she asked.

"Resting. If you know what's good for you, you'll stay in bed and let me take care of you."

His voice held a thread of steel he seldom used on her, even as his fingers gently prodded the cut on her arm.

"I need to move or me leg muscles'll seize up."

"Later." He tucked the covers around her shoulders and smoothed her hair back. "Hungry?"

"Starved."

"Want to clean up first?"

"Love to, if ye can help me. Doc said I'm not to wet the stitches, not 'til tomorrow."

"Sponge bath then, or a shallow one. I brought you some water."

She groaned and shoved herself into a sit, not minding his steadying hands one whit. "Ye're a saint."

He laughed softly. "That's not what you told me when I carried you in and undressed you. Here."

She sipped from the straw he held to her mouth. The cool water soothed her parched throat, easing its ache. She pushed his hand away and sighed. "I'll apologize then, since ye meant it kindly."

"You were a little out of your head," he said easily. "Margaret brought pain pills if you need them."

She wiggled her foot and measured the sharp ache the movement shot along her thigh muscles, then glanced at the clock. "Jaysus. What day is it?"

"Same day you left." He set the water down and picked up her hand, cradling it between his. "You've been sleeping most of the day. Your family told me it was normal, that you'd heal quickly and be on your way before I knew it."

"I will, Tom." She rested her head against the headboard and considered him. His skin was pale and thin, and his mouth formed a tense line. "Ye shouldn't worry."

"You could've died. Another inch, just one more, and we would've lost you." His voice had gone hoarse and hollow. He brought her fingers to his mouth and kissed each one, then pressed her hand to his cheek. "Don't do that to me again."

She stared at him, baffled by the concern. "It's a flesh wound, little more than a pinprick. I've had far worse in me life and bounced back admirably."

He flinched and what little color his skin held leached out. "Don't make light of this, Moira. I changed your bandage earlier. I know exactly how deep that pinprick is and I know exactly how many stitches are holding your leg together. Another inch. Sweet Jesus."

His head bowed, not before she caught the tremble in his lower lip and the bright glint of tears in his eyes. She scooted forward, easing her way down the bed, and touched her forehead to his, cupping the back of his head with her free hand. "Thomas, darling, ye should know I'm too stubborn to die and too contrary to make that many others happy with me passing."

He huffed out a gentle laugh. "Can't have that."

"No, we can't."

She pressed her mouth to his, lingering in spite of the twinge of healing muscles pulled too far too soon. He was still under her touch, his hands a stiff vise around her one hand, his mouth soft and unmoving. She sighed and drew away. For all his concern, he held himself back. Still pining for Naomi, no doubt.

"I'll get a bath ready," he said. "I think you'll be ok in three or four inches of hot water, as long as we keep your leg elevated."

He slipped out of her grasp and stood, turning toward the bathroom.

"Tom." His name spilled out in a rush, a desperate effort to hold him a while longer. "Thank ye for caring for me."

He nodded and stalked into the bathroom, shutting the door firmly behind himself. The whir of the small heater he kept in there sounded, followed by the splash of water. Moira sank into the pillows, her heart falling right through the floor into the earth below. Why had he bothered to come after her? Was he merely repaying a debt by taking care of her after she'd given him her protection or was his heart too kind to turn away an injured woman, no matter the lack of feeling on his behalf?

Her throat tightened and her sinuses clogged, and an ache pinged through her, filling her to the brim with sorrow. She rolled onto her side and covered her face with her hands, hiding the tears pricking at her eyes. Fuck him, then. If he didn't want her, she'd find another, and good riddance. One man was as good as any, wasn't he? That philosophy had served Sigrid well for better than twelve hundred years, hadn't it?

Moira suspected the sentiment had worn thin in her own heart, rubbed away by a lanky archivist with a slow drawl and the most tempting mouth she'd ever kissed.

Gentle hands tugged back the covers and lifted her high, snug against a familiar chest. "Shh. Don't cry, sweetheart. We'll get you fed and some more meds in you, and that'll take care of the pain."

She clung to him, curling her fingers into his cotton shirt, and sniffed back the tears. Let him think what he wanted. It was better than him knowing the truth, that the wound he'd dealt to her heart hurt far worse than the ones marring her body.

TEN

MOIRA SAT QUIETLY in the shallow bath Tom had drawn, her eyes closed, willing her heart to calm and her breaths to even. He'd already washed her face using a warm, soapy cloth, and now ran that same cloth gently over her arms.

Maybe it would be easier to endure his impersonal touch if he hadn't stripped down to his skin and gotten in the tub with her, kneeling between her legs with her injured thigh draped over one of his. She was open to him, completely open, and he'd looked right through her.

The cloth moved to her ribs, touching a sensitive spot. She flinched and her breath hissed out.

"Sorry," he murmured. "You've got a dandy bruise there."

"It'll heal."

"Your arm's almost there."

She peeked at him through one narrowed eye. "Ye sound surprised."

His gaze was fixed on her stomach. He soaped the cloth and ran it over her skin, up her abdomen, over her breasts, around her collarbone. "Margaret said you'd be able to walk by tonight. I didn't think you could heal quickly enough. Now I have to wonder if she was right."

"I heal quick, even for a Daughter."

His ministrations moved to her left arm. She lifted it for him and watched him. He was careful, scrubbing only hard enough to clean. Her skin tingled under his touch, from the scratch of the cloth, and because it was him.

He dipped the cloth in the water and rinsed it out. "If this makes you uncomfortable, I can leave, come back when you're done."

"It's nice, having ye care for me." She sighed and closed her eyes, relaxing against the tub's ceramic side. "Ye're not obligated, if it's a bother."

"Oh, it's not a bother," he said, a hint of amusement sparking in his drawl. "How often do I get to bathe a beautiful woman when she's too weak to resist me?"

She smiled and met his gaze, surprised at the warmth in his eyes. "I'm not so weak I can't handle meself."

"You're weak enough to worry me."

He shifted, opening his thighs, leaving one under her injured leg. He lifted her other leg and ran the cloth over it in slow strokes, beginning with the top of her thigh. Her gaze fell down the sleek lines of his torso, past his flat stomach to his proud erection, jutting up from between his thighs. It wasn't overly long, perhaps the length of her hand or a little more, but it was thick, the head broad, and would make a good mouthful, if she wished it.

Heat spiraled through her, coiling in her nethers, warming her skin. She dug her nails into her palms. Oh, how she wished to touch him there, to taste him. Would he let her, later, when she could kneel in front of him? Would he tangle his fingers in her hair and guide her, showing her what he enjoyed? Would he moan her name as she pleasured him and come in her mouth, or would he pull back and release on her skin as ecstasy tightened his features?

"Don't say it," he warned. "I can't help how I respond to you."

She swallowed the need, tasting its thickness in her throat. "Ye have to know how pleasing I find ye."

He turned his face away, concentrating on bathing her foot, her ankle, her calf and shin, his hands strong and competent and tender. "Is that why you kissed me?"

"Ye seemed to need it, but aye. Ye said ye wished it. Have ye changed yer mind, then?"

"I don't think that's possible." His voice was as soft as the swish of water over her skin. He eased her leg down and soaped the washcloth again, then turned to her injured leg. "But you're hurt and not quite in your right mind, and I'm not going to take advantage of it."

"I'm fine, Tom, truly," she said, humor coloring her words, lightening them. "This time tomorrow, I'll be running again."

He slid a disbelieving glance at her and washed carefully around the bandage on her thigh. She let him be, content to receive his care, and more than willing to ogle him when he thought her too weak to act on the heat gathering in her blood.

He rinsed her with his hands, cupping water in them, sluicing it over her limbs and across her torso. A hint of pink colored the skin over his sharp cheekbones. "Would you rather wash your privates?"

"Don't go shy on me now, Thomas."

"It's not..." He rubbed a knuckle along the bridge of his nose, leaving a faint trail of water behind. "I was imagining what it would be like to watch you do that."

"And I was wondering what it would feel like to have your hands there."

"Moira," he groaned, and his stomach muscles tightened, pushing his breath out. "Once I start, I don't think I can stop."

"Try." She tugged the cloth from his hand, guiding him to the soap. "Touch me, Tom, just for a moment. Give me something to cling to."

His eyes met hers, their brown-green depths holding the same heat coursing through her. He soaped his hands and touched her, his fingers scratching gently through the curls protecting her sex. "Too rough?"

98

His hoarse voice washed over her, and she shivered. "Never."

He slid his fingers down her labia, inside and out, circling around her clitoris, flicking across the sensitive nub, drawing a sweet cry from her. His thumb outlined the opening of her pussy beneath the water. "I want to be here."

"I want ye there, Tom." Her voice softened to a whisper and her hands found his, clutching them tightly against her skin. "Wanted ye there for so long. Will ye not take me, let me pleasure ye?"

His gaze dropped, resting on her hands covering his, and the need there pushed her own high. "You won't date me, but you'll have sex with me. You're sleeping in my bed. You think I'm with another woman." He shook his head and tugged his hands out from under hers, the tenderness in his expression shuttering. "Let me wash your back, then I'll tackle your hair. I think I have a blow dryer around here somewhere, if you can wait that long on food."

She let her own hands slide away, masking her disappointment. "I've one in me bag somewhere."

"Good. Here, lean forward."

He did as he'd said, finishing her bath, helping her out of the tub with the same courtesy as a man assisting his date out of a vehicle. He wrapped a soft towel around her, dried her off. Sat her on the toilet while he rubbed lotion into every inch of her skin and blow dried her hair, his naked abdomen inches from her mouth. She breathed him in, the soft mist of his cologne, the clean fragrance of his soap, the faint hint of his softening arousal.

He dressed her in clean pajamas, one of his long-sleeved shirts and plaid flannel bottoms, and coaxed her into wearing a pair of his wool socks. She leaned on him as they walked slowly from the bathroom into the living area, placing her weight carefully on her injured leg, unsurprised when it twinged and balked.

He helped her into a seat at the dining room table and

dropped a fleeting kiss to the top of her head. "Let me get dressed and I'll dish you up a plate."

Moments later, he was back, fully dressed in the ratty UGA sweatshirt he preferred and a pair of pajama bottoms similar to the ones he'd given her. He fiddled in the kitchen, the microwave dinged, and out he came, bearing a solitary plate laden with enough pot roast, potatoes, and carrots for two people.

Her eyes widened. "How hungry do ye think me?"

"Margaret said you'd need a lot while your body's healing. Something about the curse speeding your metabolism." He shrugged and dropped into the chair across from her, pulling over a stack of hand-written notes attached to photocopies. "If you need more, there's plenty."

"This is more than fine, thank ye. Are ye not hungry?"

He slid his glasses on and peered at the pages in front of him. "Ate earlier, while you were out. Didn't know when you'd wake up."

His words trailed off, his attention caught by whatever he was reading. She tucked into the meal he'd fixed her, savoring the fork tender beef and the vegetables baked in rich broth. How offended would he be to hear she intended to keep him for his skills in the kitchen, without having tried him in the bedroom first?

She hid her smile behind a sip of the water he'd given her, certain he'd be perplexed if she voiced the sentiment, and equally certain he'd blush to the tips of his finely made ears when she coaxed him into sleeping beside her as he'd been born.

His finger swept over one of the pages and his eyebrows furrowed. "I don't know why Ruanna gave me this one. She promised to pick out the most important ones. This is just a letter written by somebody called Begni."

Moira set her fork down and swallowed hastily. "Give it over."

"It's in archaic Hebrew." He passed it to her and snagged her empty glass, rising and moving into the kitchen.

She scanned the detailed summary Ruanna had made, her nerves zinging. "Begni was rumored to be a granddaughter of the youngest Sister, Abragni, and was supposedly the keeper of the People's history."

Tom set her glass down, now full of water, and stood behind her, his hand loose on her shoulder. "That would explain it then."

"Here, look." Moira stabbed her finger at the pertinent line, excitement jangling through her. " 'And there the Bones of the Just shall forever lie in sacred slumber.' It's how the older Daughters referenced the Seven Sisters."

"The Just," he murmured. "I wish you'd told me. I vaguely remember running across this term before, though I think it was in a much later text."

"Sorry, love." She covered his hand with hers, caressing his fingers. "Ye blend so well, I sometimes forget ye're not of the People and wouldn't know all our history."

"I'm learning." He squeezed her shoulder and took the pages from her. "If you clean your plate, I'll let you stay up late and watch a movie."

She snorted out a laugh. "Ye're fair generous there, Da."

His mouth turned down. "I'm not that old."

"Aye, ye're a doddering old man, all of what, thirty-five?"

"Forty," he grumbled. "That's old in mortal years, smarty pants."

"Not so very old yet." She pushed her plate away and stood, stretching her bum leg out in slow increments. "All yer parts appear to be in working order."

His lips pressed together, though humor lit his eyes. "You had to look, didn't you."

"Oh, aye, look and yearn I did, memorized every blessed inch, and plan to do more as soon as ye're willing." She winked at him, keeping it saucy and flirty and light. "Be a love and undress for me, real slow like."

"Tomorrow," he said firmly, "when you can move around

on your own and there's no danger of reopening that wound."

"I'm all yers then, Thomas."

His gaze sharpened on her, then fell away. He gathered her plate and went into the kitchen, his shoulders tense.

Moira shook her head and hobbled to the sofa, bracing her hands on the back. What had she said this time to drive him away? If it wasn't one thing, 'twas another, and she was getting feckin' tired of trying to figure out where she'd gone wrong. One more day, that's all he had, and another woman or not, Tom would yield to her or satisfy her curiosity as to why not.

THEY SPENT THE NIGHT wrapped around each other. Tom hadn't given in to Moira's sly plea for him to come to bed naked. He hadn't been able to resist sleeping beside her, though, even knowing he should take the couch.

He'd always thought himself strong enough to resist any temptation. Apparently not.

After she woke, he threw together a sausage, egg, and cheese casserole, listening with a small smile and a light heart to the rain pattering down outside the kitchen window and the low curses she muttered from the living room.

When had her uncouth language become so charming?

"Do you need help?" he called.

"Only if ye can heal me feckin' leg." A moment later, she limped into the kitchen, the delicate lines of her face marred by a ferocious scowl, and leaned against the counter next to the sink. "Soon as I know the Daughter that did this, she's a dead woman."

"No killing," he said firmly.

Her features lightened into humor. "Ye think one bath and a few good meals give ye the right to stay me hand?"

"As long as you're living under my roof."

She laughed, and he let his words trail off.

"Now ye sound like Rebecca," she said.

He pulled a honeydew melon out of the fridge and set it on the counter. "She's a wise woman."

"Figures ye'd say that." She winced and her hand fell to her thigh, kneading the muscle around the wound through the thin pajama bottoms she wore. His once, now forever hers. "Are ye certain I can't go head hunting?"

He washed his hands and dried them off, dug a sharp carving knife out of the drawer beside her. "Positive. Though a little closer to the inside of your thigh and I might've gone after her myself."

She arched one perfect eyebrow. "Ye'd resort to violence, Thomas? Surely not."

"Surely so." He centered the melon on the carving board and sliced it in two. "You forget I'm a Southern man. We don't take kindly to people hurting our..." *Women*, he wanted to say. He bit the word back. Moira wasn't his. Soon, maybe, but not now. He settled for the innocuous. "Friends."

"So we're friends now."

"I don't watch movies with just anybody."

He finished preparing the melon in silence, oddly comforted by her presence in the tiny kitchen. She watched him, one hand gently massaging her thigh. The timer dinged for the casserole. He snagged two potholders and pulled it out, checking its doneness with a fork.

"Where did ye learn to cook so well?"

He cut the oven off and rummaged for plates in the cabinet above her head, nudging her out of the way. "Here and there. I like to eat and I've never had anybody else around to feed me."

Her eyes narrowed into pale slits. "Ye've never married?"

"Never married, never lived with anybody." Until her. "You?"

"I've never taken a man as me own. Lovers, aye, but never for long. Men are all fuss and bother, and not much use elsewise."

He grinned, couldn't help it. "Yet here we are."

"Oh, ye're a right handy gent, Thomas."

"You just like having ready meals." He tapped the top of the casserole, testing its firmness. "Speaking of, go sit down and I'll bring you a plate."

She tilted her head to the side, a soft smile stretching her wide mouth. "Ye needn't wait on me."

"I'm taking care of you. There's a difference." He turned her toward the door and patted her firm bottom, tempted to linger in spite of her injury. "Go."

She muttered under her breath, but she went, limping slowly from the room. He dished up two plates of casserole, added chunks of melon, and joined her at the table, going back for silverware and glasses of chilled orange juice.

"What's on the schedule for today?" he asked as he slid into his chair.

She speared a piece of melon and eyed it dubiously. "Rest. Stretch. Wait for Margaret's call."

He sliced off a bite of casserole and forked it up. "She could just come by."

"She's on the hunt, searching for India Furia. The woman who kidnapped Bobby?"

"She wasn't captured?"

"None of them were." Moira slid the melon off her fork with one finger. "Until the Order's rounded up, I'll be staying, unless ye'd rather another guard ye."

Not just no, but hell no. He liked having her around, and he still had some hope of persuading her to have a real relationship with him, something deeper than whatever it was they were falling into. "I'm just getting used to you," he said mildly. "Eat that."

She sneered at the melon. "It's green."

"You eat lettuce."

"Lettuce is supposed to be green. Melons aren't."

"That melon has nutrients in it you need so you'll heal properly." He set his fork down and eyed her sternly. "If I have to hold you down and feed it to you, you're eating it."

A slow smile spread across her face. "Promise?"

Of course she'd say that. "Eat the melon, Moira."

She grimaced and took a bite of the hefty slice of casserole he'd portioned onto her plate.

He ate a bite of his own, chewing slowly, and washed it down with a sip of orange juice. "Can I ask you something?"

"Anything ye wish," she said softly.

"Who are Siobhan and Hannah?"

Her fork clattered onto her plate and her face paled. "Where did ye hear those names?"

"Last night, when you were sleeping. You called for them."

She slumped against the back of her chair and covered her face with her hands. "I'm sorry, Tom. So sorry. Did I hurt ye?"

"You weren't violent." Not at all. Her voice had been soft, tender, and her hand had gripped his, holding it to her heart. "Who are they?"

"Me daughters." Her hands dropped and her beautiful eyes, so pale and clear, stared right through him. "They died a long time ago."

"I'm sorry. God, Moira." He clutched his napkin. His heart hurt just seeing the pain etched into her expression. "What happened?"

"A war. A bloody war with no winners and many losers." Her breath shuddered out of her, so hard her shoulders shimmied, and her gaze found his, so stark and lost, his own breath failed him. "Can we talk about something else?"

"Sure." He reached across the table, holding his hand out to her, and she took it, gripping it tightly, her fingers icy and stiff. "Sure, we can. It's raining. How about a movie after I clean up? We can cuddle on the couch and I can feed you that melon you're determined not to eat."

Her lashes fluttered and a hoarse laugh huffed out of her. "Is there a woman alive ye haven't charmed into doing as ye wish?"

"She's sitting across from me right now."

Her laughter rang out again, lighter and looser than it had been before, and his worry bled away. Moira had daughters. She'd never mentioned them, holding that part of herself back as she did so many other things. He held her hand and ate, drawing her humor out with light-hearted banter, but somewhere during that meal, a hard determination formed in his gut.

One day, Moira would share all her secrets with him, every single one, even if he had to pull them from her one hidden moment at a time.

AFTER BRUNCH and a movie, Tom declared a need to run into Clayton and restock, since Evangeline's, the grocery store in Tellowee, had closed for the day. Moira grumbled, but she dressed and endured the light drizzle, bundling into the passenger seat of his Prius for the trip there and back. He matched his pace to hers as they strolled up and down the aisles, didn't bat an eye at the food she threw into the cart, and only shook his head when she whipped out her debit card and paid for the lot.

They watched another movie, ate the simple supper Tom prepared, and sprawled on the couch together with a third movie playing on the tele, one of the romantic comedies he claimed to despise. He spooned her, his hand resting on her bare stomach under her shirt, his gentle breaths feathering across her hair. She stretched her bum leg over his, grateful for the support, thankful his kindness extended to tending injured Daughters who'd forced their way into his life.

He'd not pressed to learn more of her children. In a way, she was grateful. Their deaths were a festering canker on her heart, a wound that had never healed in spite of the growing distance from that cursed day 'til the present. In another way, his refusal to demand answers sank another nail into the coffin of the hope she clung to that he'd accept her suit.

She couldn't think on it while his fingers toyed with her skin, stroking her stomach lightly, delving under the waistband of the pajamas he'd lent her as if he had every right to explore the area between her bellybutton and her sex. Desire stirred beneath his touch, a desperate yearning for more. She buried her face in the pillow he'd brought in for her and stifled a moan, rocking into the erection growing steadily behind her arse.

His lips brushed over her neck, found her ear. He nipped gently, drawing the lobe into his mouth, flicking it with his tongue. She shivered and sighed as lightning raced from there through her body, landing in a shimmering pool of heat in her nethers.

His fingers slid into the curls above her sex, pressing into her flesh with a firm tenderness. "Want me to stop?"

"Not ever," she said, and her voice was wispy and needy, a bare whisper above the music and laughter spilling from the movie.

"You don't mind?"

She huffed out a breathy laugh. "Why in blazes would I?"

"You're still hurt."

"I'm well enough for sex."

His voice took on the mildness she'd come to associate with genuine humor. "Who said anything about sex? This is seduction, teasing, learning what pleases you."

She scooted onto her back and cupped his jaw. "Ye please me, Tom."

"Do I." His gaze dropped to her mouth, held there for long moments as his fingers circled lightly into her mons. "I think you should tell me no before I take a notion to kiss you."

"I'll not tell ye no and I'll never settle for a kiss."

Something wild and greedy flashed through his eyes, followed by a steady, burning heat. "So be it."

He lowered his mouth slowly, fitted his lips to hers as if he'd kissed her a million times before and knew exactly how she wanted him there. She opened for him, accepting the gentle pressure, aching for him to do more, to take and give and build her up so high she knew only him.

His finger slid into the slick folds of her pussy and a low, broken groan sounded deep in his throat. He tore away from her, his breaths panting sharply across her mouth, his eyes green and hungry and knowing. "You're so wet. God, Moira. You're so hot and wet, it's all I can do to be gentle."

"Don't be." She arched into his touch, undulating her hips under the steady strum of his finger across her clit, welcoming the pleasure searing through her. "I want ye in me."

"Not yet," he murmured, and his mouth claimed hers again, hard and demanding. A second finger joined the first and his tongue dipped into her mouth, tasting her in light flicks. His fingers moved faster, lighter, barely stroking her, pushing her closer and closer to the edge of something great and wondrous and terrifyingly high. She dug her fingernails into his triceps. His muscles rippled under her grip and he pleased her, sweet Lady, he pleased her so much. She squirmed and writhed and gasped her pleasure into his mouth, and he broke the kiss burying his face in her throat, biting into her skin, the sharp nips devastatingly blissful.

"Please, Tom. Please."

Her voice was a near sob. His fingers shifted over her, urgent and quick, and he sucked the skin of her throat into his mouth, suckling hard, and it was enough. The release spiraled out of her in a dizzying rush of beauty and light, and she arched and clamped her thighs around his hand as her pussy clenched and throbbed.

His hand slipped from between her thighs and clutched her hip, and his mouth released her skin. He cradled her close to him, peppering kisses across her face, her name a soft whisper on his lips. "Better?"

"Jaysus, Tom. How could it not be?" She shifted onto her side facing him, ignoring the twinge in her healing thigh and her heart clamoring against her sternum, and settled against him, her quick breaths melding into a happy sigh. "Ye'll allow me to pleasure ye now in the same way, won't ye? I have a powerful urge to taste yer manhood."

A strangled laugh erupted from him. "And here I was, all set to wait until you'd healed."

"I haven't yer endless patience." Her cell beeped, signaling an incoming text. Moira rolled her eyes and bit back a curse, for Tom's benefit more than her own. He'd relaxed somewhat where her vocabulary was concerned, though he still flinched every once in a while when her temper riled and her tongue ran free. "That best be important or I'll be strangling someone's neck."

"How is anybody still alive after being around you?" He squeezed her hard and dropped a smacking kiss to her mouth. "It's probably Margaret."

"Aye, likely so." She glared at the satisfied smile on his face and scratched his chest through that infernal, ratty UGA sweatshirt he insisted on wearing. "Ye're not supposed to be the Cheshire until after ye get yer way, Tom."

"That was my way, sweetheart, and later, after you answer that text, I'll get my way again." He rubbed the tip of his nose across hers. "Maybe I'll even part those beautiful thighs of yours and taste you, the way I wanted to earlier when you were open for me in the bathtub."

A second text beeped. Moira rolled away from Tom and grabbed her phone. Feckin' timing. Another minute and she'd've talked him into stripping down for her. She pushed herself into a sit in front of him as his hand slid under her shirt, caressing her bare stomach. She rested one hand over his and flicked through her messages with the other, reading the texts in the order they'd arrived.

Her ardor cooled abruptly. "They've found India."

His hand stilled on her hip. He propped his head on his hand and drew his legs up until they near touched her thigh. "Where?"

"County hospital." Moira's fingers flew over her phone,

109

sending a response to her mother, then framed a politely worded request for Ruanna's presence in Tom's apartment and sent it. "I need to dress and arm."

He stiffened. "No."

Ruanna texted back immediately and Moira grunted, satisfied with the arrangement. "No, what?"

"No, you're not going." His arm came around her middle and he buried his face in her side. "Your leg isn't well enough. Jesus, Moira, the stitches aren't even out yet, and you're talking about going after a woman who took down a man twice your size? Forget it, sweetheart. You're staying here."

An odd feeling rose in her as they sat, poised in a tableau with the movie playing in the background, his warm breath filtering through her clothing, her heart torn between duty to her family and the unmitigated fear in Tom's voice. Humor that he'd dare set limits on her actions, eagerness for the battle ahead, and a quiet need to soothe his worry the only way she knew how, with a lover's kiss and a woman's need.

"Sweet Thomas." She twisted around on the couch, pulling free of his arm as gently as she could, and stared down at him, bemused by the determination in his expression and the sudden urge she had to give in to his pleading, to remain here with him for as long as he'd have her. "Ye've not been around enough Daughters if ye believe we'll yield to the commands of a man, even one we hold dear. I'm not a weakling mortal."

He flinched and paled, and his eyes slid closed. "You're going after her."

"I must."

"No matter what I say."

She tamped down her impatience, fighting back the need to force his understanding. "She harmed a Son. That can't go unanswered."

He threw an arm over his eyes and turned his head away, his mouth an uncompromising slash across his face. Three hard raps hit the front door. Moira sighed and dropped her phone onto the coffee table, then made her way slowly to the door, unlocking it and throwing it wide. Ruanna stood on the other side, pillow in hand, backpack slung over her shoulder, and behind her was Phil, a grungy sweatshirt stretched tight over his broad shoulders, his handsome face set in a sheepish expression.

Moira stepped back, waved them in, and excused herself. She went into the bedroom, ignoring Tom's softly called greeting and Phil's response, ignoring the acid souring her stomach and the twist of regret in her heart. She'd been *that close* to having him and maybe binding him to her. It was better this way, better that he find out who and what she was now at the beginning rather than later on. Better he learn quickly that a man had no hope of staying a Daughter's vengeance.

She bandaged her leg and yanked on a black crewneck and loose, black cargo pants, calming the unsteady beat of her heart with the familiar routine as her mind ran through what she knew of India. Hot temper, far hotter than Moira's and far more unpredictable. Favored her fists and close combat over a sword, though she was rumored to be proficient in any weapon she chose. She never gave up, even when she was down. A warrior through and through, was India.

The thought sparked a reluctant admiration in Moira. In another time, she might've welcomed the other Daughter as an equal, banding with her as needed to cut down their enemies. To India Furia, though, everybody was an enemy, including, apparently, her own sister. For that, for breaking the tender Indigo's heart and laying harm to the man they both loved, Moira would see that India paid her pound of flesh.

Moira stretched slowly, pleased when her leg held firm. She twisted her hair into a French braid and selected her weapons carefully, tucking them around her body in quick, efficient motions. She chose a black fleecy zip-up as outerwear and matched it with fitted black leather gloves and a black toboggan Dani had knit.

Tom slipped into the room and shut the door quietly

behind himself. "I wish you wouldn't go."

"I have to, Tom. Ye should understand the whys by now."

"Doesn't mean I agree with them." He crossed his arms over his chest, grasping his triceps with one hand and his ribs with the other. The stance tugged his shoulders down, erasing the pride inherent in his normally erect spine, curving it under the weight of the uneasiness settling between them. "Be careful."

"I always am." She pulled the toboggan on, jamming stray strands of hair under its edge. "Will ye welcome me back or should I arrange for another protector?"

His short laugh was bitter. He glanced away, fixing his gaze on a point beyond her left shoulder. "I honestly didn't think you'd give me a say in it."

His words speared through her, opening a wound deeper than any wielded by his hand could have. "If ye wish me gone, ye need only say so. I'll not impose on ye a minute longer than ye desire to have me."

She brushed past him, her heart throbbing a painful patter in her chest. He caught her arm and pulled her around, tugging her into his embrace. His own heart pounded under her ear. She clutched him to her, breathing him in, absorbing his goodness.

"Come back to me, Moira, safe and whole. No more knife wounds, no more bruises."

He bent and captured her mouth, kissing her with a muted desperation that called to her own need to claim him, protect him, cherish him for what he was, a good man with a good heart. He released her slowly, and she slipped past him, leaving before he tempted her into forgetting the lessons drummed into her over a lifetime of service to the People's cause.

ELEVEN

REBECCA UPTON stepped out of the elevator into the corridor leading to the Oracle's room. A small hospital in rural Georgia had seemed like the perfect hiding place for one of the People's most highly guarded treasures. How the Order had found the woman's location was beyond Rebecca, but she would find out, and quickly. Bobby's kidnapping had interrupted his company's work tracking down the People's enemies, but as soon as he was healthy and whole again, she'd see to it that his hunt continued.

She followed the sounds of a muted conversation around a corner and halted in her tracks. Bobby and India held Indigo between them, bracing the swaying Daughter.

Bobby glanced at Rebecca and his mouth thinned. "Get out now, India."

India's gaze met Rebecca's. Margaret appeared behind the trio at the other end of the hallway, her boots quiet on the plain floor. India slid Indigo's arm off her shoulder and turned to Bobby. "Get her out of here. If I don't make it, tell her I love her. Tell her..."

"You can tell her yourself," he said. "They won't kill you."

India laughed, the hollow sound echoing through the sterile hallway. "For what I've done, I deserve to die."

She turned on her heel, racing toward Margaret, and Bobby

dragged Indigo toward Rebecca, murmuring to his woman as he urged her steadily forward. He stopped beside Rebecca, his gaze flinty. "Make sure Margaret doesn't kill her."

Rebecca's smile was as cold and furious as her heart. For kidnapping a beloved Son, for beating him when he was helpless to defend himself, India deserved a harsh sentence, even death. Her knowledge of the Order's workings saved her from such a fate, an irony not lost on Rebecca. "We don't want her dead, darling. She's far too valuable to lose."

"You're not talking about her being Indigo's sister, are you?" he said flatly.

"No, but I'll keep that in mind."

"You do that."

Rebecca strode past him, closer to the combatants. Moira had edged her way silently into the fray. She and Margaret were attempting to flank India. Indigo's sister countered their moves with an impressively fluid grace, her hands a blur as she fought off Rebecca's daughters.

A slight bruise on Moira's neck, barely visible above the line of her shirt, drew Rebecca's gaze. A hickey. Blessed Mother, her daughter had a hickey on her throat, likely given by the reserved archivist she'd taken under her protective wing.

Tom Fairfax had put a love mark on Moira.

And Moira was checking her blows, deliberately tempering her strength, placing her punches to bring India down and not inflict the maximum damage, the first time Rebecca had ever seen her do so.

She pressed her lips together, containing a delighted laugh. Well, well, well. The mighty Moira was well on her way to falling and couldn't have found a nicer man to catch her. Rebecca made a mental note to personally call Tom and invite him to Thanksgiving dinner, if for no other reason than to thank him for having the patience to deal with her temperamental daughter.

One of Margaret's concrete-like right hooks landed on India's jaw, knocking her to the floor. Indigo's twin defended herself as long as she could, deflecting well-aimed kicks and punches, then curled into a ball, protecting her head and vital organs.

"That's enough," Rebecca said, keeping her voice sharp and soft, just loud enough for her daughters to hear.

They drew back immediately. India slumped onto the cool, tile floor, her breaths so shallow, her chest barely rose. Rebecca knelt and pressed her fingers to the pulse under India's jaw. It beat steadily, strong and regular as a Daughter's should. "Get a gurney and call Dr. Phillips. She'll need care before we can question her."

Margaret jogged off, her long strides even, her footsteps quiet. Moira braced herself against a wall and called Ethan, asking him to come to the hospital as quickly as he could, then slid her phone into her back pocket.

"How's the leg?" Rebecca asked.

Moira grimaced. "Feckin' hurts. Be better if the stitches were out."

"I'm sure someone can take care of that while you're here."

Rebecca brushed the back of her fingers along India's forehead and frowned. The skin was warm to the touch, far warmer than it should've been. India inhaled a ragged breath and her eyelids fluttered. Broken rib, likely more than one. Margaret had probably seen to that, a fitting retaliation for the ribs India had broken when she'd beaten Bobby.

Margaret entered the hallway pushing a rolling gurney, two nurses trailing after her. The five of them lifted India onto it far more gently than she deserved. Rebecca jerked her chin at Margaret, silently requesting her guard on the errant Daughter, and followed more slowly, matching her pace to Moira's mincing gate.

Rebecca cleared her throat. "I'm surprised Tom didn't object to your coming out tonight."

"He tried."

"And you ignored him."

115

Moira ducked her head, fixing her gaze on the floor in front of them. "He was worried. That's to be expected, but I still have me duties."

"You'll bring him for Thanksgiving," Rebecca said, keeping her tone light.

"If his family obligations permit." Moira paused in the hallway and inhaled deeply, her hands opening and closing into fists. "I'm thinking of..."

Rebecca eyed her daughter. Uncertainty. Yet another first. "Go on, darling."

"Claiming him. I'm of a mind to keep him."

"He's under my protection."

"Aye." Moira yanked her knit cap off and twisted it between her hands. "If ye have the time, I'd appreciate it if ye'd draw up a fair contract."

"Has he accepted your offer?"

Moira's gaze sharpened, hardening her clear blue eyes into brittle chips in her pale face. "Haven't asked."

A tendril of unease curled through Rebecca's gut. "You plan to, though, surely."

Moira's lips thinned. She jerked her gaze away and tugged her cap back on, stuffing her hair beneath it.

Rebecca placed a firm hand on her daughter's arm. "Tread carefully, Moira."

"I intend to."

Moira strode away, a slight limp slowing her, and the unease blossomed into worry. Rebecca's middle daughter had always been headstrong, always had a blind spot where men were concerned, starting with her father. The arrogant Irish rebel had embroiled his daughter in enough plots and wars to last any mortal a lifetime.

Rebecca shook her worry off and made her way to Bobby's room. She'd keep a close eye on what developed between those two and would step in if Moira didn't treat Tom as he deserved. In the meantime, she had a family to hold together and a prophecy to fulfill, somehow.

She checked in on Bobby and Indigo, relieved to find them cuddled together on Bobby's hospital bed sleeping soundly, and left instructions at the nurse's station regarding India's care and handling. Margaret would oversee India, of that Rebecca had no doubt, but an extra word of caution never hurt.

She made it home half an hour later, parked at the curb, and eased her way into the house. Robert had probably gone to bed early. She closed the door and locked it, listening for the quiet chatter of Charlotte's voice, the deep reply of her husband's, and heard only the click of the heater coming on and the tick of the grandfather clock sitting in the living room.

Charlotte must've gone home, though it was unlike any of Rebecca's daughters to leave without saying anything. Even in these relatively quiet times, the People were cautious.

Rebecca checked in the kitchen, her unease growing, separate and distinct from her worries over Moira. No note. Rebecca veered off toward the garage, intending to check it in case Charlotte had pulled her car into it.

A muffled hiss of pain came from the library.

The hairs on the back of Rebecca's neck stood on end and a chill shivered down her spine. She pulled her Glock 26 from its holster and crept silently down the hallway. The door to the library was open, the room a black void between there and the windows on the far side of the room, lit only by the faint hint of moonlight shining through the remnants of the evening's rain.

Another gasp, bitten off, sounded from behind the far couch. A chilly breeze blew through the room, billowing the gauzy curtain draped over the middle window.

"Shadow." The voice was hoarse, the word flat and muffled. "Blade."

Rebecca searched for the voice, narrowing its speaker's location to the left-hand side of the couch, near the empty fireplace. "Who's there?"

"Shadow approaches." A scraping sound, as if the person

117

was trying to drag herself across the floor. "Blade must..."

Rebecca flipped on the overhead light and tucked her Baby Glock away. The Woman with No Face was propped against the end of the couch, mask firmly in place, her legs sprawled in front of her. One gloved hand held a bloodied sword and the other clutched her side. Blood seeped through her fingers, spilling over the Woman's hand, soaking into the black tank top she wore under a sturdy, knee-length canvas coat.

"You're wounded." Rebecca took one step forward, then another, approaching the other woman slowly. "Let me help you."

"The Shadow approaches."

"I know," Rebecca said, sliding her right foot forward in another tentative step. "We know they're coming. We found a warehouse full of their weapons."

The Woman shook her head, the movement brisk and edged with desperation. "The *Shadow* approaches, and the Blade...the Blade..."

"That's me. Tell me what I need to do." Another step, one more. *Almost there.* "Tell me what you see."

"The Blade...yields. The Blade..."

The Woman slumped. Her head drooped and her hand fell away, leaving a trail of blood on the hardwood floor along the edge of the carpet protecting the area under the couch. Rebecca dropped to the floor beside her and pressed gentle fingers to the wound. She peeled back the Woman's shirt, revealing a precise hole. Gunshot wound. Rebecca eyed the bloodied sword. Older Daughters were forever bringing a sword to a gunfight. It almost never ended well for either party.

Rebecca reached under the Woman, grappling for a hold so she could turn the injured woman over and check for an exit wound. Her hands slid along bare skin and a jolt of light seized her, freezing her where she knelt.

Shadows drifted into her mind, dark and foamy, rolling like mist over the water toward a solitary sword suspended point-

118

down in mid-air, it's outline achingly familiar. Silverthorn, her first sword, the weapon she'd earned during her first battle centuries before. The shadow surrounded the sword completely, thin and tenuous, failing to hide the metal's gleaming sharpness.

The Woman stepped through the darkness and her voice floated between them. *The Shadow approaches and the Blade must yield.* She pointed toward the sword, focusing Rebecca's attention there. The sword fell, clanging onto an unseen floor. It's glow flickered and dimmed, snuffed out by the encroaching blackness.

Rebecca gasped and came to, her heart pounding furiously in her chest, fear clogging her throat. The Woman was gone, vanished through the still open window, her path evident as an uneven trail of blood smeared across the floor. Rebecca pushed herself into a stand, willing her limbs to steady.

The Shadow approaches and the Blade must yield.

The Woman had come at great risk to warn Rebecca of her impending death.

A tremor ran through her and her knees gave out. She braced herself against the edge of the couch, her mind whirling with the vision implanted in her mind. She'd lived nearly a millennium, and of that time, she'd had more than thirty years with a man who loved her so deeply, he'd married her in spite of her long and bloody past.

Rebecca swiped a trembling hand over her forehead. Robert would miss her. He would mourn, and she didn't want him to. They'd had a good life together, so good, and far longer than she'd ever hoped.

She laughed, tried to. It came out weak and breathy, more sorrow than joy. The Shadow Enemy would kill her. After all this time fighting them, they'd finally win this one small battle.

Her gaze fell to the blood congealing on the hardwood floor and her mind sharpened. Blood carried many secrets. It could identify a suspect in a crime. It could pinpoint genetic defects in a child.

And it could tie a Daughter to her kin.

Her death might be imminent, but Rebecca still had a job to do. She would carry out her duties until the bitter end, content with the knowledge that she'd given everything she could to her People and her family.

She slipped her phone out of her pocket, her hands steady as a rock, and dialed Sigrid Glyvynsdatter. The other Daughter answered on the first ring, her greeting sharp and alert.

"Sigrid," Rebecca said. "I have a blood sample for you at my house. Get here as quickly as you can and bring something to collect it with."

She hung up and pushed herself into a stand, resolved to fight on for as long as life allowed.

THE APARTMENT was dark and quiet by the time Moira made it back. She slipped inside, bone tired, her thigh muscles aching, and sent Ruanna and Phil home where they could rest comfortably through the remainder of the night.

Tom was in bed, sprawled across the mattress on his stomach. Moira padded into the bathroom, stripped, and turned the shower on. While the water warmed, she brushed her teeth, her mind too numb to focus. Feckin' nurse had taken a might too much pleasure in ripping out the stitches along the cut in her leg. Moira had burned through the last of her patience trying not to strangle the woman, certain Tom would chide her rash behavior.

She rinsed her mouth and replaced her toothbrush in the nifty holder Tom had set out. It warmed her, thinking on the way he cared for his home. He'd make a good one wherever he roamed, his knack for detail aiding him here as it did in work.

Her eye caught on her reflection in the mirror set above the sink. A tiny bruise marred the line of her throat. She ran a finger along it, remembering the manner in which the mark had been given, under the insistent pressure of Tom's mouth on her skin.

Heat shot through her, unexpected and bold. His time was

up. Tonight, she'd claim him, and he'd come under her official protection willingly, mingling his life with hers. He was a practical man, after all, and reasonable, and she was the elder by far, her experience outmatching his by centuries. She pressed a shaky hand to the nerves jumping in her stomach and exhaled slowly. Aye, he'd see the logic of her words and not fuss over her intentions. That was Tom, quiet and steady and rational.

She stepped into the shower and bathed quickly, scrubbing away the sweat raised during the brief fight with India and the goo the nurse had spread over the cut on Moira's thigh.

Already, Tom had influenced her more than any other man ever had, save her father, long dead. Had she not muzzled her temper for him, guarding her tongue so as not to offend him? Had she not reined in her blows, sparing India the harm Moira usually meted out to her enemies? Her heart softened and a small smile curved her lips. She was changing, because of him, because he wished her to, and because she couldn't stand to disappoint him any more than she already had. Maybe someday, she'd trust him enough to submit her will and become mortal, living beside him until death carried them into the Lady Ki's eternal mercy.

Moira turned off the water, toweled herself dry. Slapped lotion on her skin and blow dried her hair, humming a happy tune softly under her breath. She padded into the bedroom, her heart filled with buoyant hope.

He hadn't moved an inch, as far as she could tell. She slipped between the covers and scooted over to him, draping herself across his long length.

He stirred and sighed. "Moira, mmm. When did you get home?"

"Not long ago."

He turned onto his back and held out an arm for her, wrapping it around her shoulders as she laid her head on his chest. She rubbed her fingertips through the hair scattered across his skin, inhaling the clean fragrance of his skin.

"Are ye very tired?" she asked.

He yawned and placed his hand over hers, his fingers stroking her lightly. "Not been asleep long."

"Oh."

"Why?"

A nervous flutter shivered through her. "I was wondering if ye'd mind continuing our explorations from earlier, before I was called away."

He huffed out a gentle laugh and his heartbeat tripped and stuttered under her touch. "I would absolutely love to, as long as your leg's up to it."

"Stitches are out." She eased her hand out from under his and skimmed it down his lean abdomen, resting it on his hardening manhood, covered by the thin cotton of his pajamas. "Would ye mind terribly if I loved ye?"

His breath hissed in. He stretched under her, and a moment later, the bedside lamp clicked on. She blinked in the sudden light, tilting her face up to his.

"I want to watch you," he said, his brown-green eyes hot as he held her gaze. "I want to see everything you do, and when you've had your fill, I want to slide into you and make love to you all night long."

"Tom." Her voice broke on the need ripping through her. "Kiss me now."

He did, pressing his lips to hers with a surprising urgency, claiming her in a fierce kiss. His mouth moved under hers, demanding a response, and she opened for him, welcoming the hot slide of his tongue against her own and the scrape of his teeth over her lips.

She moaned and pressed into him, inching her hand beneath the waistband of his pajamas. He was hard and thick under her hand, his skin smooth as silk. She encircled him, measuring his breadth, and ran a testing stroke along his length.

His hips arched into her touch, pushing his erection through her circled fingers. He broke the kiss on a gasp. "That feels so

122

good."

"It gets better," she said, and he laughed.

She kissed her way down his body, savoring the taste of his skin on her tongue. He was cool water and spicy heat, and warm beneath her lips. She dipped into his bellybutton, flicking in and out, and he groaned, his stomach muscles clenching tight.

"Moira," he whispered, and the need was as thick in his voice as it was within her.

She tugged his pajama bottoms off, dropping them on the floor beside the bed, and straddled his legs. "Ye're never to wear pajamas to bed again, not as long as ye're with me."

He arched an eyebrow at her. "What if I get cold?"

"Ye won't," she promised.

His mouth curled into a grin, all manly and knowing. She took his erection in a firm grip and bent, sucking its tip into her mouth.

His hands tangled in her hair, a light weight pressing her down. "Moira. God, that's...*mmm.*"

Mmm, indeed. She ran her tongue over him, around the broad head, along the sensitive slit at the tip of his penis, sucking lightly as she learned him. His hands tightened in her hair and his breath panted out of him in irregular gasps and his hips moved in counterpoint to her mouth.

Her Tom, so reserved and conservative with others, so responsive and open with her.

She would've thought him prudish in bed. A spark of pleasure flitted through her, joining the heat writhing within her. How could another woman have passed him over so easily and missed this passion?

She shook the thought off. He was hers now, only hers, and that's what mattered. *She* would care for him as those other women hadn't. *She* would tap his hidden depths, allowing him to find his full potential, and he would love her as he'd never loved another.

"Moira, please. I'm... I'm close."

His hands pushed at her shoulders, and she relented, loosening her hold on him only because she wished him to release within her this first time. She crawled her way up his body and guided herself to his erection, seating the tip against her pussy.

The backs of his fingers brushed over the tips of her breasts, teasing her gently, and his gaze met hers, his eyes near a deep green, the brown washed completely away under the flood of desire tightening his features. "That's it, sweetheart."

She held his gaze as she rocked herself gently down over his hard length, allowing her body to acclimate to his breadth. "Ye fill me, Tom, so lovely firm. It seems ye're not so old ye can't pleasure me."

He laughed softly, happiness radiating in his smile and from the glint in his beautiful eyes. "The way I feel now, I'll never be too old for that."

"Love me now," she said, and his hands dug into her hips, urging her to take him. She eased him out of her, then tilted her hips, seating herself fully against him. "Love me as long as ye can."

She braced her hands against his chest and rotated her hips, matching her rhythm to his gentle thrusts and the tightening of his fingers in her skin. Wild pleasure speared through her with every brush of her clitoris along his skin, with each rub of his erection inside her. It consumed her fully, lifting her high, carrying her along a tight wave of heat, and she gasped his name again and again as her hips whipped around and his pushed desperately into her. They flew together, their breaths rasping through the room's quiet, lost in each other and the passion holding them in its grip, and she teetered on a precipice, awaiting the fall into bliss. His fingers found her clitoris, tugging and pinching, and she came, her pussy throbbing hard around his erection. She threw her head back and met his hard thrust, and he released into her, spilling his seed inside her welcoming body, his lean form shuddering beneath her.

She collapsed on top of him. Their breaths panted out of their bodies in near unison and her heart matched the unfettered beat of his, so near her own.

He smoothed his hand over her hair and gathered her close, pressing tender kisses to the top of her head. "Not bad for a couple of geezers, huh?"

Laughter stuttered out of her. He moaned as her pussy tightened around his erection one final time.

She slid off him and rolled away, hopping off the bed. "I'll be just a moment."

She cleaned herself quickly, wet a washcloth for him, and found him waiting for her, his hands behind his head, a satisfied smile stretching his mouth.

"There's yer Cheshire grin again." She knelt over him, washing the sex from his softening body. "Well-earned this time."

"Is that so?"

He caught her gaze with his own. She studied the soft light in the brown-green depths and her heart flipped and muttered in her chest. Was that the first trace of love or merely the glow of good sex?

She tossed the washcloth into the bathroom. "I've something to ask ye."

"Shoot."

"I want ye to take me mark." She blurted it out in a nervous rush. Her fingers trembled along his stomach where she'd placed them. "I've never asked a man before, but I want ye to."

His eyebrows shot up. "I thought that was the equivalent of getting married for y'all."

"'Tis precisely that."

He huffed out a laugh. "After one bout of sex, you want to marry me." He shoved a hand through his hair and glanced away. "That's a little sudden, even for you."

Temper stirred, and with it, the first rumblings of fear. "What's that supposed to mean?"

"You're not exactly known for your steadfastness, Moira."

He rolled a shoulder against the bed and the happy glow faded from his face. "What happens when I grow old and you don't and you find somebody younger to fill your life?"

Her eyebrows shot down over her eyes. "Ye think I'll tire of ye and discard ye, like stink and rubbish instead of the fine man ye are."

"Yes, that's exactly what I think will happen."

"Ye don't know me very well if ye think that."

"That's my point," he said, and his own brow furrowed. "You won't even go on a real date with me. Hell, Moira, I bet you think I'm still pining after Naomi and you want to marry me?"

Moira's hand shot out, gripping his jaw firmly. She turned his gaze to hers and dropped her voice into a deadly growl. "Never mention another woman in me bed, Tom."

He jerked his chin out of her hand. "This is my bed and I will goddamn well say what I want to here."

"Ye think so?" She braced her hands on either side of his head and lowered her face to his, leaving a foot of space between them. "Ye'll accept me claim tonight, Tom. Ye'll take me mark and live in the house I provide for ye. Ye'll shop in the stores I tell ye to and dress in the clothes I buy for ye, and ye will never, ever again truck with the fair Naomi. Is that clear?"

The last flame died in his eyes, leaving them grim and dark. "I guess you want me to quit my job, too, stay home and be a dutiful husband while you gallivant all over the world, fighting anybody stupid enough to irritate you."

"Ye'll not quit unless ye wish it. The People need the keen strength of yer mind. Would be a shame to lose it to husbandly duties."

"What if I say no?"

Her heart wavered and a sick acidic nausea clawed at her. "Ye'll accept me."

He scrubbed a hand over his eyes, and when he spoke, his voice held all the weariness emanating from his gaze. "You make it sound like I have no choice."

She pinched her lips together and uttered the first lie she'd ever told a man. "None whatsoever. A Daughter wishes to claim ye, Thomas. Bow down graciously and be thankful I don't chain ye to me bed as I did me last lover."

He stared at her for long moments, his expression empty and flat, so unlike the animation flashing across it earlier. "Do I need your permission to take a piss and go to sleep?"

His words hit hard, the mild rancor eliciting an exponentially larger amount of damage than they should've. "Not for that."

He nodded and rolled away from her off the bed, and padded into the bathroom. The door clicked shut behind him. She sagged into the mattress, swallowing the hurt down over the lump in her throat. Why hadn't he accepted her? Why had he forced her hand on such a simple matter? Did he not understand the privilege she extended or the life she could give him? He never need work again, should he wish. He'd never worry over money, nor would she ever allow danger to befall him.

She stared at the bathroom door. He'd grow to love her, in time, he had to. He'd love her and give her children, and she would cherish him until the day he died.

127

TWELVE

EARLY MONDAY MORNING, Tom sat at his desk in his office deep within the Archives, staring blankly at the full translation Ruanna had made of Begni's letter. Moira had left him there with strict instructions to lock the door after her and not leave without calling her first, not for any reason.

Apparently, she'd lied when she'd told him he didn't need her permission to go to the bathroom.

As soon as he'd judged her safely away, he'd unlocked the door and sat down, and had promptly lost himself in thoughts of her.

He yanked off his reading glasses and dropped them onto the desk. God. How could a man deal with a woman like her? He'd been furious with her on Saturday, for knowingly putting herself in harm's way when she clearly hadn't been up to it, and for the asinine ultimatum she'd laid down, brushing off his say as if it didn't matter one bit what he wanted out of life, only what *she* wanted him to do.

The funny thing was, he was pretty sure it didn't. Spending so much time with her, beginning to learn her inside and out, had pushed him beyond infatuation and precariously close to the edge of love. He rubbed a hand over the ache in his heart. For as long as he'd known Moira, one certainty had guided his actions. She'd never fall in love with him, never submit her will, never become mortal. He'd thought the situation hopeless, well beyond his control, and had chosen to pursue a less passionate romance with Naomi rather than risk losing his heart to an uncaring Moira.

That had been before she'd elbowed her way into his life and given him a chance to get to know her. How charming she could be when they were together, her laughter over the silliest things. Her refusal to eat anything green other than lettuce no matter how much he coaxed. The warmth in her lilting voice, in odd moments when other women would've loosed their tempers. The way she fell asleep instantly at night and woke the same way in the morning, clinging to him every moment in between, her nude body tangled in his.

He was beginning to depend on her being there with him. She'd wiggled her way under his skin, and he liked it, so much he was willing to consider the insane and bend to her will.

What if accepting her claim and allowing her to dictate nearly every aspect of his life was the only way he could have her?

A light hand rapped on the door. Naomi poked her head in, a shy smile on her face. "Hello, Tom. Are you busy?"

He smiled and stood, waving her in. "Never too busy for you. How's Kara?"

"Wonderful. Her husband came home Saturday night." Naomi shut the door behind herself and sank gracefully into a chair in front of his desk. "I see you survived all the drama and fuss."

"You could say that."

Her dark gaze turned speculative. "Moira treated you well?"

Oh, God, had she, until that blasted ultimatum. "Well enough."

"You slept with her."

Heat flooded his cheeks. He pinched the bridge of his nose and inhaled sharply.

"You have that look," she said softly. "I'm not judging.

129

Moira's a beautiful woman and quite tenacious."

She could say that again. "I'm sorry, Naomi, really I am."

"I won't hold it against you."

He glanced sharply at her. "That's good."

She crossed her legs and eyed him coolly. "As long as you don't see her again, there's no reason why you and I can't continue our relationship."

"Wait." He shook his head, certain he hadn't heard her right. "What?"

"I have no intention of losing a man of your caliber to another woman, Tom. I'm prepared to forgive your indiscretion, as long as your relationship with Moira ends now."

"Jesus. Are all Daughters as insane as the two of you?"

Naomi arched an eyebrow and a small smile curved her beautiful mouth. "We're practical. Moira is a distant cousin. If you're sexually compatible with her, chances are good you and I will be compatible as well. We've already proven we're compatible in other areas."

"I can't believe we're having this conversation," he muttered. "Look, it's not like that. I mean, it is. She and I, er, hit it off, but the truth is, that's happened since the first time I saw her. The very first time." He caught Naomi's gaze, his desperate for understanding, hers losing its soft glow, and scrubbed his palms down his jean-clad thighs. "I wanted it to be you, Naomi, so badly. I wanted to love you and settle down with you and have children with you, but it's just not going to happen. You're not the one for me. I knew that as soon as I saw Moira."

"Yet you tried for me anyway."

"I kept hoping," he admitted. "Like a dummy, I ignored reality, hoping your quiet grace and beauty would win me over. It never did, and now..."

His voice trailed off and he glanced away, scowling at the door. Somewhere behind it, Moira was working, likely content in the knowledge that he'd accepted her claim. He hadn't forgiven her for forcing it on him, not by a long shot, and he wasn't willing to go down quietly, either.

"What has she done?" Naomi asked.

He met her cold gaze with a calm one. "She claimed me."

She hissed and leaned forward, her even features marred by the feral gleam in her eyes. "Not formally, not this quickly."

"Afraid so. She informed me..."

"You have a say."

"Apparently not." He shook his head again and slumped into his chair, suddenly so tired he couldn't think straight. "It doesn't matter."

"It does, Tom. This isn't the nineteenth century. She can't force your hand."

"Maybe I want her to," he said softly.

Naomi sat back, her expression impassive. "I see."

"I didn't mean to hurt you."

"You wouldn't. You're too kind, your heart too tender, and she's trampling right over it in her usual roughshod manner."

"It's her way." And likely always would be. "I wish things had turned out differently."

"Me, too." She stood, came around the desk, and leaned against its edge next to him. "Promise me you'll be careful."

Too late for that, far too late. "Promise me I didn't break your heart."

"Not quite."

He sighed and grasped her hand, squeezing it gently. "You'll find somebody."

"One always hopes, though I was quite set on you." She cupped his face and pressed a soft kiss to his forehead. "Why couldn't you have fallen for me instead of that Irish hellion?"

He laughed and placed his hand over hers, grateful for her understanding, thankful she hadn't kicked his ass from there to Atlanta and back for treating her so poorly. "I ask myself that question every single day."

The door popped open and Moira strode in. "Tom, you won't believe... What the fuck?"

131

Tom yanked away from Naomi. He stood and held out a hand, warding Moira off. She dropped a dusty box onto his couch, her expression furious, her hands forming tense fists at her sides.

"It's not what you think," he said. "I was just explaining to Naomi that I can't see her anymore."

"Is that what ye were doing, explaining to yer former lover about yer new one." A murderous glint flitted through Moira's pale blue eyes. "I warned ye, Tom, warned ye plain as I could."

"Naomi is a friend of mine," he gritted out.

Naomi held her hand out to him. "No, Tom. Let her get it out. It's well past time she and I settled this."

Tom shook his head. "If settling involves fists or weapons, you'll do no such thing. She's just jealous, that's all, and I can deal with that."

Naomi's expression turned pitying. "She's not jealous, Tom, she's possessive. Jealousy requires some depth of feeling. Everyone knows Moira's heart is too jaded for emotion."

"In the hallway," Moira said, her voice low. "I'll kick the shite out of ye for that and then I'll kill ye for touching me man."

"That's enough," Tom snapped. "I will not allow the two of you to fight over me as if I were a toy. Moira, Naomi is a friend of mine. She will always be a friend of mine, so get over it already." He inhaled deeply, willing his heart's thudding beat to calm. *God.* Moira pissed him off so easily, he who'd never had much of a temper to speak of. "Naomi, I'll come by your office later and catch you up on what's been happening here."

"E-mail me," she said, her sharp gaze focused on Moira. "I'm turning in my resignation to the director and will be gone by lunchtime."

He deflated, the anger leaving him in a rush, leaving only weariness. "That's not necessary."

"It's for the best all around." She patted his arm and smiled. "Don't worry. There are plenty of Daughters more qualified than I to assist with your work, though I'd appreciate your keeping me

132

informed. This work is important to all of us."

She circled past Moira, facing the other Daughter as she left, her hands held loosely at her sides. Moira circled with her, closing the door in Naomi's face as soon as the other woman crossed the threshold. She whirled and faced him, her whole body braced for battle. "I turn me back for an hour and ye fall in with another woman."

He leaned a hip against the side of his desk and crossed his arms over his chest. "Forget it, Moira. That's not what was going on here and you know it."

"I..." She stared at him, her eyes wide, her mouth not quite firm. When she spoke, her voice was much softer and held none of the rancor she'd thrown at him since entering his office. "I asked ye not to truck with her. Have ye no respect for me wishes?"

He laughed, bitter and hard. "Oh, that's rich, asking me to respect you when you have none for me."

"That's not true, Tom, not true at all." She edged toward him, her steps tentative, and placed a gentle hand on his arm. "I have the deepest respect for ye. How could I claim ye elsewise?"

He shook her off and sidestepped her, making his way to the couch and the box she'd thrown there. Damned if he'd argue with her when her actions said plainly exactly what she thought about him.

The box was about three feet long and nearly that wide, the cardboard a creamy color darkened in irregular blotches to a non-descript beige. A layer of dust covered the lid and strands of cobwebs clung to the sides. He lifted a corner of the lid and did a double take. "Why do you have a human skeleton in my office?"

"Found it, just now. It's one of the last items left in that room I'm cleaning." She appeared at his elbow and lifted the lid away. "Thought ye might be interested."

"I'm interested in what a skeleton is doing in the Archives. I bet George and Sigrid would be very interested in whether or not they can get DNA out of the bones." He pulled the box closer by one of its edges and peered in, counting them. A skull, a jawbone, several longer bones that could've once been arms and legs, two ribs attached to vertebrae, and an assortment of other bones. Not a complete skeleton, but hopefully enough for the Dynamic Duo. "Any idea where it came from?"

"Not a one. The box was unlabeled. There were no papers inside." She lifted one shoulder in a careless shrug. "It was tucked into a back corner under a box of fire-damaged scrolls."

He groaned and rubbed the nape of his neck. "Ugh. Not more of those. We've barely begun restoring the first ones you found."

A grin flashed across her face. "Buck up, Thomas. This is only the first room. There's bound to be more in the other unexplored ones."

"You had to remind me," he muttered. "Let me call George and have him come fetch these. I can make a rough inventory while we're waiting for him so we don't lose track of the whens, wheres, and whats."

"I'll help, if ye don't mind."

"You mean I have a choice?"

She stiffened and the humor fled her expression.

He sighed. Why hadn't he left well-enough alone? As ticked as he was at her, she didn't deserve his flippancy. "Moira..."

"No, ye've a right to define yer limits, Tom, as I've a right to define mine. Text me when ye're ready for lunch and I'll escort ye to the cafeteria."

She pivoted and walked out, leaving him to the solitude of the cage she'd built so hastily around him.

DINNER WAS QUIET. Moira sat across from Tom, shifting the meal he'd made back and forth on her plate with the tines of her fork. He'd thrown a whole chicken into the crock pot before they'd left for the gym that morning and turned it into chicken and dumplings when they'd come home from work. It was fragrant and probably as delicious as anything else he'd fed her.

She couldn't bring herself to eat. Since Saturday night, her appetite had steadily diminished, no doubt fleeing in the face of the distance that had sprung up between her and Tom.

How could it all have gone so wrong?

She studied him from beneath lowered lashes. He ate slowly, thoughtfully, as was his way, though his shoulders held a tension new to him. His expression was grim and somehow hopeless, and had been since lunch. No, he'd been that way since Saturday night, and she hadn't yet found the means to jolt him into his normal self again.

"Thanksgiving's coming up quickly," she said.

Her words fell into the silence between them, breaking it into jagged pieces.

"Mmm." He swallowed and patted his mouth with his napkin. "Your mother called earlier and invited me over on Thursday, said your family will eat around seven."

She stabbed a dumpling and edged it into the whipped potatoes. "And yer own family?"

"We'll eat around one or so, if I'm allowed to go."

She stifled a wince, though the ache in her chest grew too large to hide. "Of course, ye are, Tom. I'd never keep ye from yer family, not without good reason."

"Hunh." His eyes dropped to his plate. He picked up his fork, stirred it through his potatoes, set it down again. "I guess you'll want to go with me."

Her breath left her in a rush so fierce, her head spun. He didn't want her there, didn't want her to meet his family and partake of a meal with them, when she'd counted on him wanting to be with her. Her heart throbbed and cracked, and that was it for her, a broken heart delivered by the man she'd hoped could love her.

She stood abruptly and dropped her napkin next to her plate. "Thank ye kindly for dinner, Tom. Ye're an excellent cook and I appreciate yer efforts."

135

She left quietly, walking into the bedroom when her heart prodded her to *run, run*. The ache of it gathered there, so large and hard she could scarcely breathe around it. She stopped in the middle of the room, unsure why she was there, not certain where else she should be.

He didn't want her.

She moved to the closet and stripped off the clothes she'd worn to work, throwing them in the hamper with Tom's dirty clothes. She should wash them. He'd been taking care of the apartment and the cooking while she'd been gallivanting, as he called it. He wasn't her maid, wasn't her caretaker. A Daughter on her own had no need for either, and she wouldn't force that on him anyway. That wasn't why she wanted him in her life, not by any means.

She tugged on pajamas and gathered the towels, bundling them into the hamper. When she came out of the closet, Tom was leaning against the doorframe of the bedroom entrance, his expression closed.

"What are you doing?" he asked.

"Laundry." She hefted the hamper out and set it on the floor beside the closet. "Have ye washing powders and such?"

"Under the kitchen sink. Not that I mind, but why are you doing laundry?"

"It needs doing. 'Sides, ye do enough."

"It's not like you add a lot of work, Moira. Jesus. I've never seen a woman so determined not to leave her mark."

The bitterness in his voice slapped at her and she flinched. She turned her back to him and stared down at the dirty clothes, his overlapping hers, mingling in exactly the way she'd wanted to join his life with hers. "I was willing enough to leave me mark with ye, Tom."

"You say that like you've changed your mind."

"Never." The word broke, echoing the crack in her heart. Naomi could believe what she wanted, but the truth was, Moira felt all too keenly the hardships life had thrown at her. That she tried not to wallow in them should've been a credit to her, not a criticism. "I'll not willingly lose ye, not ever."

"So I gathered," he said flatly. "I'll get the laundry detergent."

She turned and stared after him, watching him disappear around the corner into the kitchen. Where had she gone so wrong? How could she have miscalculated his interest so badly?

Perhaps it would be better if she let him go. Her knees wobbled and her stomach roiled. She braced a hand on the hamper, breathing through the ache. No, she couldn't let him go. She'd simply have to work harder to bring him 'round, that's all, and hope she could before the happy glow in his beautiful eyes dulled forever.

Tom re-entered the room and dropped the laundry detergent into the hamper.

"Thank ye," she said softly.

"Anything to get out of laundry duty." His voice was light and held a hint of laughter, and his arms slid around her waist, pulling her back against him. "If you're gonna do them, though, you should be thorough, right?"

She melted into him, so thankful for his warm touch, she could've cried. "A good Daughter is always thorough."

"What about a Daughter's, ah. What will I be when I get the *aenkanien*?"

"My mate."

"Right. What about a Daughter's mate? Are they thorough?"

She twisted around and eyed him, surprised at the mischief dancing in his eyes. "I suppose that would depend on the situation."

His mouth curled in that Cheshire grin of his. "I'd say this situation calls for a very, very thorough hand."

She knew that grin, knew it very well. Heat skipped and skidded under her skin. She jerked her gaze away from his even as a small smile tugged at her own mouth. "Laundry duty?"

"Oh, no, sweetheart." He lifted the hem of her shirt and pulled it off, leaving her bare from the waist up. "Hmm. Look what I found."

His hands skimmed up her stomach and cupped her breasts, kneading gently, thumbs brushing over her nipples, teasing them into tight nubs. Each caress shot an arc of pleasure through her, layering upon the last, building, building.

"Tom," she whispered. "What are ye about?"

"My mom has a saying. *Begin as you mean to go.* This is our beginning. This is how I intend for things to go from now on."

His mouth found the side of her neck, sucking lightly, dissolving every coherent thought she had. She dropped her head back, rolling it to the side, silently begging for more. His hands slid down her torso and into the waistband of her pajamas, pushing them down past her hips.

His mouth left her skin. "Bed. Face down," he said, his voice low and thick, the need in it nearly tangible.

She stepped out of the pajama bottoms and collapsed onto the bed face down, burying her face in her pillow. The soft rustle of clothing came from behind her, the light thump of it into the hamper. She clutched the covers between greedy fingers, eager for his touch, eager to learn what he planned. The mattress dipped as he stretched out on top of her fully nude, his skin warming hers.

He brushed her hair aside and trailed his mouth over her nape. "I've wanted to do this for a while."

"Do what?" she asked, and he laughed, soft and husky.

His mouth went lower, tracing every knob of her spine, his kisses feather light. She shivered and moaned, and her breath came in ever faster pants, matching the dazzling pleasure racing through her.

His breath feathered across the faint traces of moisture he'd left behind on her skin. "Cold?"

"No," she managed at last. No, she wasn't cold, not a'tall. Could he not feel the heat arcing between them? Could he not see his effect on her? His slightest touch sparked a flame within her. He had to know. He *had* to. "Tom, I..."

"Shh, sweetheart. I've got you."

His hand came down on her arse, a hard grasp of possession, and his tongue traced over her lower back in random circles, near burning his touch into her skin. She groaned, low and breathy, and arched into him. "Tom, please."

"Yes." He raised up, grabbed one of his pillows, and stuffed it under her hips. "Now, you just lay there and let me do my almost-husbandly duties, ok?"

She snickered. "Almost husbandly?"

"Hush it, woman," he said, but his voice was light and his touch so beautiful, her laughter morphed into a low, greedy moan.

He covered her, bracing most of his weight on one forearm near her head. His erection prodded at her pussy and his fingers found her clitoris, circling lightly, and she nearly came from the twin pleasures.

"Not yet," he murmured. He slid into her, filling her so completely, so tightly. She tilted her hips back, accepting his gentle thrusts and his fingertips barely grazing her sex. His breath feathered across her hair, stirring her as much as his body. Tom, sweet Tom. Her man, the one carrying all her hopes. He built her passion in tender increments, and she let him pleasure her, let desire roam free within her. Up and up she went, ever higher, carried by his soft rocking thrusts and his fingers teasing her clit. He pushed her closer to the edge of passion, held her there for long moments, poised on the brink of wonder and awe, his own heart pounding against her spine, his breaths panting faster. He thrust into her a final time and grunted softly, his release throbbing through her, and his fingers circled and tugged. He shifted and bit gently into her shoulder, and the pleasure-pain was too much. She shattered into a million pieces, fragmented until he breathed her name and made her whole again.

She came down slowly, drifting safely within the confines of his embrace, her lungs empty, her body full. He slid off of her, winding himself around her, and a keen sense of loss pressed into her. It was so right, being one with him, so sweet. She inhaled a shuddering breath, sighing her pleasure out in a long gust.

Tom nuzzled her neck, peppering her skin with soft kisses. "That sounded like the sigh of a woman well-satisfied."

"Ye have the right of it, Thomas." His hand slid to her stomach, and she covered it with her own, tracing the long lines with her fingers. "Though I have to wonder what brought on yer sudden bout of lust."

"Laundry," he said with a small laugh. "All the way into the kitchen and back, I kept thinking about your clothes and how you should really get out of them and what I'd do when you did."

She clucked her tongue. "Ye've a strange mind."

"You have no idea," he muttered. "I've wanted to get my mouth on those tattoos since the first time I saw them. I didn't even know immortal Daughters could have tattoos."

"'Tis difficult. Our skin heals so quickly, the ink must be reapplied frequently."

"Why do you do it, then?"

She shifted around, facing him. "They're for me daughters, the only memorial I could give them."

Sorrow flitted through his gaze. He cupped her face and kissed her tenderly. "I'm sorry. If I'd known that, I'd've done something else."

"What ye did was perfectly fine. In fact, I insist ye do it again, and soon."

His eyes narrowed. "You've done enough insisting, Moira."

She pressed her lips together, stifling a smart retort. Aye, he was bang on. She'd insisted, and though he hadn't balked, he wasn't happy with her decision.

"Though maybe if you ask nicely," he added, his mouth curving into a small smile, "I'll take your request into consideration, but only after I go through the long, long list of things I want to do with you."

She slid her thigh over his and rubbed her fingers through the hair scattered across his chest. "Such as?"

"Thanksgiving. Mom wants to meet you."

Her heart leapt into a ragged, nervous beat. "Oh?"

"I told her you were my fiancée. After all this time trying to marry me off, she's so thankful I've found a woman who'll take me." He rolled his eyes, and she snickered. "She's willing to do whatever it takes to meet you."

"I'd like to meet her, too," she said softly. All of his family, really, his brother and his brother's children and any relatives he'd see fit to introduce her to. They must be wonderful people to have produced such a kind man as her Tom.

"Then you should've said so when I asked you."

She huffed. "That wasn't precisely asking ye did."

"Yeah, you're right, and I'm sorry. I didn't mean it the way it came out." He stroked his hand up and down her arm, soothing her. "I guess I'm still a little pissed about the whole claiming thing. I'm not really happy about you trying to dictate my life, either."

"It's our way."

"No, Moira. It's *your* way. Naomi said I don't have to yield to you."

Moira stilled and lowered her gaze to his chest. Feckin' Naomi and her big fat mouth. What right had she to interfere? "And ye believed her?"

"She's never lied to me, unlike some people I know," he said mildly. "Don't do it again."

"Do ye intend to reject me now?" she asked softly.

"No, sweetheart. No." He sighed and draped his arm over her, pulling her close. "We'll do things your way, for a while. Don't think I'm such a pushover that you can get away with the high-handed-ancient-Daughter crap all the time, though."

She sputtered out a laugh. "High-handed, am I?"

"High-handed might be an understatement." His hand

drifted to her arse and squeezed. "I'm a man, Moira, not a slave, and I have my own way of doing things, my own notions of how our relationship should go."

"And yet ye're willing to accept me claim. Why would ye, Tom?"

"I have my reasons."

And that, she thought, was all she'd get out of him. He had that look on his face, one she'd only seen a handful of times, usually when she'd told him to do one thing and he thought to do another. Stubborn man. He wasn't the only one who could play along, though, and if he accepted her claim willingly, why shouldn't she? Particularly if it meant keeping him, as she'd intended.

"So, now the question remains, what are we gonna do with our holiday. I vote going out on a date, a real one, and making love for three days straight."

She eyed the wide grin growing on his lovely face, her own humor growing apace. "I think ye're a feckin' genius, Tom."

He laughed and claimed her mouth in a fierce kiss, and they practiced for the long weekend ahead through the rest of the evening, so hard Moira forgot all about her resolve to do the laundry.

THIRTEEN

BEGNI'S LETTER drew Tom's attention again and again over the next few days. There was something there, something he couldn't pinpoint. *The Bones of the Just.* The phrase leapt out at him every time he read the letter. He studied every document he could find related to bones and the Sisters, and still, it nagged at him like water hitting his brain one meager drop at a time. He e-mailed Naomi and sent her a transcription, pleading for any assistance she could give, and asked the director's permission to bring Ruanna in, anything to help him break through the wall he was banging against.

Moira continued to dig through the forgotten rooms in the Archives, rooms Naomi hadn't discovered or had time for in her own explorations. She'd moved to another room since finding the bones now in the eager company of young George. He'd come out the same day Tom had called him and picked up the remains, promising to keep Tom and Moira both in the loop on any findings.

Maybe it was too much to ask, but Tom sincerely hoped George could identify those remains and possibly fill a hole in the People's history.

Thanksgiving morning dawned clear and cold. Moira chased Tom out of the bedroom an hour before they were supposed to leave for his family's get together. The evening before, while he'd cooked the pumpkin pies his mother had asked him to bring, she'd slipped out of the apartment, leaving the ever-faithful Ruanna behind to watch him. Two hours later, Moira had come back carrying a hanging garment bag and another one of her duffel bags. She'd hidden them in the closet and refused to discuss their contents or the reason she'd left, but now he had to wander what she was up to.

He filled his time sitting on the couch, going over his notes on Begni's letter. Ruanna had translated the section containing the reference to the Seven Sisters as, "Five shall there be, together (unintelligible phrase; name?), and there the Bones of the Just shall forever lie in sacred slumber."

The Bones of the Just. A metaphor? A literal reference? Bones, bones. He turned the phrase over in his mind, contemplating the possibilities. Interpreted literally, the phrase likely referred to the remains of the Seven Sisters, but if it wasn't a literal reference, it could refer to anything, like the laws and customs of the People or even the People themselves.

He rubbed his fingers over his forehead and stared at his laptop's screen. Literally interpreting the phrase was an idea he kept returning to. The Prophecy of Light was, well, a prophecy, full of portents both mysteriously vague and absolutely clear, but this was a letter, a communication from one party to another, written by a woman who could very well have known one of the Sisters personally. If bones literally referred to the Sisters' remains, then there existed a slim possibility that somehow, somewhere, their locations had been recorded and the remains could be found. If they could, perhaps they would, in turn, somehow point to Sanctuary.

He rested his head against the back of the sofa and closed his eyes. Moira had found bones. No chance those were a Sister's, though, surely not. Who would cram the remains of such an important person into an unmarked box in a near-forgotten room? But the bones of a Sister had been found not long back, when Dani had fought her mother. Or had those been the bones of a Daughter?

The bedroom door opened and soft footsteps swished along the carpet.

"Hey, Moira, those bones found when y'all went to that nightclub..."

He twisted around and his thoughts trailed into nothingness. Moira stood just outside the bedroom's entrance wearing a slinky black long-sleeved sweater held up by thin straps, leaving her creamy shoulders bare. It fell in loose, elegant folds over her hips, encased in a tight black skirt that fell to mid-thigh, hiding the healing scar on her upper leg. Her legs were covered by sheer hose and she wore black heels so delicately fashioned, they looked like they'd fall apart with the next step she took. He jerked his gaze upward. She'd curled her soft strawberry blonde hair and piled it on top of her head, baring the elegant line of her neck, and she'd somehow made her eyes bigger and bluer and her whole face more exotic.

Tom Junior stirred to life and poked at the fly of Tom's slacks.

Moira's eyebrows veed into a furrow. "Well. Say something, ye big lug."

He stood slowly and stuffed his hands in his pants pockets where they'd do no harm to her outfit. "You are by far the most beautiful woman I've ever known."

She twisted her hands together and dropped her gaze. "Oh."

"Yes, oh." But she always was, even in her chunky sweaters and baggy cargo pants, the exact outfit she'd been wearing the day he'd first seen her and nearly swallowed his tongue. "Mom will never believe a woman like you is willing to marry me."

"Ye must know ye're an appealing man."

"Not that appealing." He slid a glance down her long, toned legs and imagined them wrapped around his waist, minus the hose, heels on and digging into his back with every thrust of his body into hers. "You sure you want to go out? I don't mind staying in."

She laughed and strolled toward him, her normally quick walk now a slow, seductive glide. She rested her hands on his chest and leaned into him, eyeing him from beneath lowered lashes. "If we stay in, how can I flirt with ye in front of our families and seduce ye with me womanly charms?"

"Oh, you do that every day." He kept his hands in his pockets, certain they'd get ideas, though he leaned close enough to catch a whiff of her perfume, something smoky and dark. "God, you smell good. Let me call Mom and tell her we'll be late."

Moira whirled away from him, sashaying toward the bedroom with all the grace of a runway model. "Not a chance, Thomas. It's too much of a bother getting this way to have ye ruin it with yer grabby man hands."

He smiled and eyed her luscious curves, outlined very clearly by her mini-skirt. "I do not have grabby man hands."

"Aye, ye do, and ye can use them to help me with me coat, like a gentleman of your breeding should do."

He caught up with her in three strides and snagged her around her hips, drawing her back against him. "Tonight when we get home, I'm gonna kiss your pretty shoulders, sink my teeth into your neck, and bend you over the bed while you're wearing this outfit, and then I'm gonna make love to you for a very long time."

She shuddered and relaxed against him, and her hands covered his, soft and gentle. "I'll think of nothing else the whole day through."

Neither would he and that suited him just fine.

TOM'S MOTHER'S HOME was a gray, one-story, board and batten house sitting flat dab in the middle of a huge tract of rolling pasture outside of Gainesville. Moira accepted Tom's help out of his Prius. Feckin' heels made walking nigh on impossible. Wearing them had been worth the trouble, though, if only for the dazed look on his face when he'd first seen her and the lingering gleam in his brown-green eyes.

She should've tried wearing a skirt sooner.

He carried the pies in, leading her up the rock-lined walkway through the neatly trimmed front yard, its grass yellowing under winter's coming cold. Her stomach roiled and jittered, each step irritating her nerves something fierce. Why had she agreed to this? To all outward appearances, there was a huge age gap between her and Tom, though his family would hardly countenance the truth, that there was, indeed, an age gap much greater than it seemed, only her the elder by centuries.

And they had so little in common. A love of the written word and of history, a love of good food, and enough chemistry to set the world on fire, but what did they truly know of one another?

Worry pinched at her. She inhaled around the dizziness rising within her. What was she doing, about to meet Tom's family? She should've kept him at home, should've sent him on his own, should've done anything other than face the critical stare of a mother over her eldest son's choice in a mate.

"Moira, sweetheart, what is it?"

Tom's voice pierced through the fog enveloping her head. She glanced up and met his concerned gaze. He stood on the top step of the house's porch. She'd stopped halfway between his Prius and the house, standing as still as a doe trapped by a car's headlights, frozen by fear and insecurity.

Foolishness. Daughters faced their fears head on and wrestled them into submission.

She pressed a calming hand to her stomach and forced herself to close the distance between them. Tom had met her halfway, allowing her to claim him though he felt another path more prudent. The least she could do was return the favor.

She followed him through the main entrance into a warmly lit living room, shedding her coat as she went. The space was cozy. A merry fire burned in the fireplace on the far side of the room, caught within a glass-fronted insert. A long sofa upholstered in sturdy earth-tone plaids was placed at a right angle beside the fire and a matching recliner sat across from the fire next to the sofa, arranged around a coffee table. Bookcases lined the wall behind the sofa, filled to the brim with books and family photos and mementos. Two doors bracketed the fireplace, one leading into what appeared to be a dining room and the other into a hallway.

A man with Tom's dark hair and slightly hooked nose sat on the sofa between two teenagers, a tow headed boy with a spatter of freckles across his upturned nose and a solemn-eyed girl with braces. They were watching the Thanksgiving Day parade on the tele across from them. The man rose and nodded, his tanned face holding the weary lines of someone who'd handled more than his share of sorrow.

"Moira, this is my brother Mike and his kids, Jilly and Josh. Everybody, this is Moira, my fiancée."

Moira murmured polite greetings to the somber crowd. Tom disappeared into the dining room, and she perched carefully on the edge of the recliner, her gaze pinned politely on the giant, blown-up turkey floating above the parade on the tele.

"Tom said you work with him."

Moira glanced at Mike. He regarded her with such a neutral expression, she thought he must be reserving a poor judgment. The acid in her gut leapt high, gnawing on her innards. She willed it down, willed her heart to calm, and met his stare evenly. "I do."

"Just out of college?"

"Hardly." She smiled, aiming for friendly, or at least polite. "Me youth is donkey's years behind me, Mr. Fairfax, with many hard miles between here and there."

Jilly fixed a round-eyed stare on Moira. "Where are you from?"

"Ireland, all over." And that was the truth. She'd spent enough time in each county to know them all like the veins in her skin. "Where are ye from, young Jilly?"

"Here." The girl's voice was a scant whisper, barely loud enough to hear over the announcers on the tele and the pop and crackle of the fire. "We live next door."

"I run the farm," Mike said.

Moira waited politely for him to elaborate, though it was clear he'd said all he intended to. His face had that pinched look to it, closed and hard, not from anger or disinterest, but from simple habit.

After a short silence, she took pity on him. "The cows must be yers then."

"Lowline Angus. Dad started the farm years ago. Tom had his books, but I..." Mike's mouth snapped shut and his lips thinned.

He wasn't used to talking, Moira guessed, not about himself leastwise.

Tom walked back in followed by a raw-boned woman, her graying hair twisted into braids on either side of her head. She wore a beaming smile on her thin face and a flour-specked red-and-white checkered apron over a flannel shirt and jeans.

"Mom, this is Moira, my fiancée. Moira, this is my mother, Dolores."

Moira rose and threaded her icy fingers together in front of her.

"Call me Do," Dolores said, her voice husky and firm. "Everybody does."

"Pleasure to meet you," Moira said, and wasn't at all surprised by the quaver in her own voice.

Dolores parked herself in front of Moira and placed bony hands on her shoulders. "Well, now. Let's look at you. Right pretty, you are, and younger than Tom let on."

"Not nearly so young as I look, I promise," Moira murmured.

"Good breeding. It's in the genes." Dolores nodded, sharp and decisive, her Carolina blue eyes dancing. "And the hair.

149

Tom always was a sucker for the red-heads."

Tom coughed into his hand, though Moira saw the smile he hid behind his fist plain enough. "She's not a heifer at auction, Mom."

"Didn't say a thing about her breeding hips, now, did I."

Josh snickered, turning it into a hum when his father speared him with a stern glare.

"We haven't talked about kids yet," Tom said. "In fact, that subject is completely off limits for the foreseeable future."

Moira's stomach dipped and rolled. Would Tom want children with her? She glanced at his niece and nephew. Their gazes avidly followed the adults' conversation. Tom had spoken of them in the days leading up to this one, always with a proud fondness. Men always wanted their own seed to prosper, sons especially, and he'd want a son.

Her heart sank down to her knees. Tom would want a son, and she could never give him one. Daughters, though, that was a different story. She met his gaze across the room. A soft smile played along his mouth and he'd tucked his hands into the loose pockets of his slacks. He'd be a good father, would Tom, never abandoning his children, never leaving them to a Daughter's hard fate.

The tattoos in her back burned and itched. If Siobhan and Hannah had had fathers such as him, ones who'd protected them and talked sense into their hard, stubborn heads, they might still be alive today, and Moira wouldn't be living with the agony of watching them die.

Dolores slung an arm around Moira's shoulders and squeezed, taking Moira's breath. "Don't suppose you know how to baste a turkey."

"I've a fair hand in the kitchen, though nothing near as good as Tom's," Moira admitted.

"That'll do, then. Jilly-girl, it's your turn in the kitchen. We'll leave the boys to the TV."

Jilly rolled her eyes, though she rose quickly enough, a

familiar smile tugging at her mouth.

Moira tagged along behind Dolores and Jilly. Tom stopped her with a hand on her shoulder. "Don't let Mom pester you," he said softly.

"We'll be fine." She cupped his jaw and pressed a gentle kiss to his lovely mouth. "I'm safe with her, and she and Jilly with me. The turkey might squawk a protest, though."

He grinned and stole another kiss, then let her go. She glided past him, moving slowly more to humor her shoes than to entice her lover, and was well aware of accomplishing both.

Would he want children, her Tom? Would he mate with her during the needing and see her through the pregnancy that would surely follow? Would he stand beside her as she gave birth and welcome the life she pushed from her body?

Once in the kitchen, a cramped, cheerily decorated space full of light and the delicious scent of turkey roasting, Dolores handed out aprons. Moira pulled one carefully over her hair and secured it, then helped Jilly do the same, the small routine achingly familiar and nowhere near forgotten.

Daughters had long, long memories, crisp, clear memories sharpened by the enduring centuries and the curse levied by an unjust hand. The pain of her daughters' deaths would never heal, not entirely, and though she'd sworn to think carefully on having another, her mind couldn't quite push aside the tiny need buried deep in her heart, to carry Tom's child under it and gift him with a love like no other.

FOURTEEN

TOM SANK into the recliner in his mother's living room, his gaze on the television, his ears tuned to the quiet conversation emanating from the kitchen. Moira would be fine. She hadn't threatened to skin anybody in days, and his mom would be on her best behavior for fear of alienating the first woman he'd brought home in a decade and a half.

Moira had gotten the funniest look on her face when he'd mentioned children. Had she been remembering her daughters or had she been thinking, as he had, of what they'd have to do for her to become pregnant?

His mind drifted to the possibilities and heat throbbed in his groin. He shifted in the chair and crossed an ankle over his knee, hiding Tom Junior's insistent poke for attention.

"She's pretty," Mike said.

The daydreams running through Tom's head ground to a screeching halt. "She is."

On the TV, the camera focused on a university marching band playing a pop medley. A short burst of laughter came from the kitchen, and Tom smiled. Mom must've started in on tales of his youthful foibles. Maybe she'd have pity on him and throw in a few good ones, too.

Mike cleared his throat and crossed his arms over his chest, his gaze never leaving the TV. "Awful young, though."

Tom's pleasure in hearing Moira's laughter soured. "Not nearly as young as she looks, trust me."

"Looks like a damn kid."

"Well, she's not," Tom snapped. He inhaled sharply through his nose, tamping down on his impatience. He'd expected his brother's objections, expected more from his mom, though he'd been happy enough to have her easy acceptance. "She's a full-grown woman with her own money and her own life."

"Never said she wasn't."

He'd implied it, though, and that was close enough. "Give her time, Mike. Get to know her. She's a good woman. Got a temper on her a mile wide, but her heart more than makes up for it."

Mike grunted. "Hair like that, I guess so."

"Comes out in other ways, too."

"Yeah?"

The question held enough speculation to return the smile to Tom's face.

"What's that mean?" Josh asked. "What other ways?"

Mike ran a hand over his son's unruly hair and said, his voice gruff, "You'll find out when you're older."

Tom turned his gaze back to the TV and chose his next words carefully. "She has sisters and a whole slew of extended family, a lot of them unmarried."

"So?" Mike said.

Tom cleared his throat. "So, if you're interested in dating again..."

"Not ready for that, Tom."

"It's been five years," Tom said, as gently as he could. "I know you miss Carolyn, Mike. We all do."

Mike scrubbed a hand over his face and slumped in his seat, drawing Tom's gaze. Josh leaned into Mike's shoulder, his blond head nearly touching his father's dark one. Tom let it go. Today wasn't the day to push, but maybe he'd at least planted the seed in Mike's mind.

The meal was a roaring success. They piled their plates high with turkey and dressing, mashed potatoes, sweet potato soufflé, green beans, creamed corn, and rolls fresh from the oven, and squeezed together in his mother's tiny dining room. Moira charmed them all with stories from Ireland. Even Mike unbent enough to chuckle a time or two.

Moira picked at her food, eating sparingly. After the main meal, Tom cornered her over the spread of desserts his mother had laid out. "You're not eating much."

"Not very hungry." She pressed a hand flat against her stomach. "I'm a bit unsettled today, truth be told."

Tom set his plate down and cupped her shoulders, rubbing gently. "Not coming down with something, are you?"

"Hardly, Tom. Daughters never sicken." She glanced around and lowered her voice. "It's not in our nature."

"Then what?" He lowered his own voice and leaned down. "Are you pregnant?"

She drew back and goggled at him. "Think I'd know if I was, Thomas Fairfax, and ye'd be the first to hear tale of it."

That wasn't disappointment tugging at his gut, couldn't be. He was still trying to talk her into something resembling a normal relationship. They weren't even close to a place where they could talk about having kids, and wouldn't be until he convinced her she needed to treat him like an equal. "I'd better be," he said, smiling to ease the words' sting.

IN MID-AFTERNOON, after helping his mom clean up, he and Moira headed back to Tellowee. She was unusually quiet, subdued even, and the first stirrings of worry pricked at him.

"You sure you're ok?" he asked.

Her wide mouth curved into a small smile. "No worries, Tom."

She curled up in the seat, resting her head on her arm

where it was propped against the car door. The next time he glanced over, she was sound asleep. He turned the radio down and slowed his speed slightly, driving as smoothly as he could. Moira had a knack for falling asleep quickly, but he'd never seen her do it outside of a bed. In spite of what she'd said to the contrary, he wondered if she wasn't coming down with something, a cold maybe. Or maybe she simply needed more rest. The past few weeks had been busy for both of them, the last two especially.

More sleep then. She'd get it, even if he had to tie her to the bed at night and sleep on the couch.

She woke as they crossed into Tellowee, yawning and stretching like a kitten. "Oy, Tom. Why'd ye let me sleep so long?"

"You needed it."

She snorted. "Daughters can go days without sleep, needs must."

"There's no *needs must* here, Moira." He parked along the curb in front of Director Upton's house, edging into a tiny space between an aging truck and a spiffy Beemer. "If you're not getting enough sleep at night, maybe we need to change our routine."

She placed a hand on his thigh and her expression softened. "Ye've such a good heart, Tom."

"And you have a stubborn one," he retorted.

"There is that," she said mildly. "Come along, now. I want to present ye formally to me mother."

"Is this one of those People things?"

"'Tis indeed." She threaded her fingers through his and pressed a gentle kiss to his lips. "I'm eager to have ye become a part of me family."

He squeezed her fingers, rubbing a thumb over her knuckles. "There's no rush. You've already got me."

Her eyes narrowed. "Perhaps, and perhaps ye'll run off with the fair Naomi as soon as me back's turned."

He dropped his head against the seat. "Not that again."

155

"Aye, that again, until I'm certain ye're mine."

He was, very nearly all of him. All that remained was the sane part of his heart that hadn't quite fallen for her yet. It wouldn't be long, though. He could already feel it caving, but it didn't matter. He was already in too deep, had been since the first night she'd curled up beside him and fallen asleep in his arms, before their first kiss, before they'd had sex, before he'd come to know the depths of her sorrow or the lengths she'd go to in order to protect him or the mercurial nature of her temper, equally matched by her humor.

He'd been such a fool to cling to Naomi and the cockeyed dream he'd had of the perfect woman as long as he had.

They walked hand in hand up the concrete sidewalk toward the director's home, a two-storied, dark green monstrosity with tan trim and an irregularly shaped outline, as if rooms had been added on as they were needed rather than having been planned from the start. The wide front porch jutted out into the yard, its foundation hidden by ancient rhododendron and azaleas, their leaves drooping under the dimming sunlight.

The main entrance opened into a foyer with a gleaming wooden floor and a chandelier hanging overhead. Moira took his jacket and hung it in the closet behind the front door, then led him into the living room where a portion of her family had gathered around a football game playing on the TV.

No one batted an eye at his presence or at her hand holding his.

Moira gestured toward an older gentleman sitting on one end of the couch next to a little girl with golden hair and huge blue eyes. "Tom, ye know me step-father, Robert, and the rug rat is Becka, me sister Charlotte's only daughter. Ye've met me brother, Bobby, and this is Charlotte's husband, Howard."

Tom nodded politely at Bobby. The other man's face appeared remarkably normal for somebody who'd been badly beaten less than a week before. Tom shook hands with Howard, a balding man with an easy-going smile and a stocky build. "I

156

think your wife is the only one of Moira's sisters I haven't met yet."

Howard grinned. "She's the quiet one."

"That's what they all claim," Robert said, chuckling. "And they're all correct, right up to the moment one of them says something another one disagrees with."

"Not a lot of quiet after that," Bobby said wryly.

"Says the one doing most of the instigating." Moira tugged at Tom's hand. "Don't listen to him, Tom, else he'll sway ye to the dark side. I'm going to the kitchen where the sane portion of me family is likely to be."

"Mind if I watch the game?"

Her voice dropped to a soft murmur. "If ye wish it, aye, Tom. Ye needn't ask permission."

"I wasn't," he said mildly. "It's football. I'm a man."

A smile creased her face and her blue eyes danced. "Now ye decide to be typical, when there's work to be done."

"I'm a man," he repeated, and she laughed.

"So ye are, Thomas, and glad I am of it." She smacked a loud kiss to his mouth. "Don't let Bobby lead ye into trouble."

"Hey, now," Bobby said.

Moira dropped a kiss to his forehead on her way past. "Don't deny it, brother."

"A man can't get away with anything around this crowd." Bobby twisted around and watched Moira walk out, then turned and speared Tom with a curious look. "What did you have to do to get Moira into a dress?"

Tom dropped into an upholstered armchair across from Howard. "Took her to meet my mom."

"That'd do it," Howard said. "First time I've seen her in heels since me and Charlotte got married, and even then, she wore a pants suit."

"And she had on lipstick, too." Bobby's eyes narrowed. "So I guess it's true. She really is claiming you. Has she submitted?"

Tom's stomach twisted into knots low in his gut. He fixed

unseeing eyes on the game. "No."

A heavy silence fell in the room, broken by the announcer's voices and the muted sound of women's laughter drifting from the back of the house. Tom didn't need to hear what the other men were thinking. He was thinking it himself. Moira didn't trust him. Chances were good she never would. He'd continue to age while she remained forever young and his heart would crumble into dust when she moved on. It was inevitable, but he hadn't lost all hope yet. She'd claimed him, hadn't she? And she was softening toward him. Maybe someday she'd fall in love with him, the way he was falling for her.

Though the Uptons' Thanksgiving dinner was much noisier than his own family's had been, the gratitude was the same. At the beginning, before the platters of turkey and fixings were passed around, everyone joined hands and listened respectfully as Rebecca thanked the Lady Ki for her mercy and goodness. Moira's hand held his in a tight grip, her fingers stiff and her expression troubled. As soon as Rebecca finished speaking, Moira leaned close, her voice low, and said, "The Lady Ki blessed me when she brought ye into me life, Tom. Never think I don't appreciate the gift of yer presence."

The worry slid from him. He cupped her face and kissed her, a real kiss, not the pecks they'd given each other all day, drawing away only when Dani whistled.

Moira would love him. He clung to that hope as fiercely as a man lost at sea, his only refuge a woman whose heart had never yielded, not in nearly five centuries of living.

MOIRA WAITED until the meal was finished before pulling her mother aside and quietly requesting a formal audience. The pleasure in Rebecca's smile couldn't quite override the touch of concern in her expression. Moira shrugged it off and sent Tom ahead, slipping into the guest bathroom for a moment of quiet.

Her stomach was a tense knot lying low and heavy in her

abdomen. She touched light fingers to it and breathed deeply, inhaling and exhaling in slow beats, calming herself as much as was possible. When that didn't work, she ran cool water over the insides of her wrists.

Nerves, that's all it was. She'd never claimed a man before, not formally leastwise, and the few men she'd had relations with had spent such a brief time in her life, she would've forgotten them if not for her curse-enhanced memory.

Her reflection caught her attention and she winced. Even through the make-up she'd plastered on, dark circles marred the skin under her eyes and her face seemed too pale, bleached of any natural color. Jaysus. No wonder Rebecca had looked askance at her. She was a feckin' zombie.

Moira lifted the hem of her skirt and prodded the jagged, virulently red scar through her stockings. Tender still, but that was to be expected. No sign of infection, and that was to be expected as well. It was healing nicely. Other than her lack of appetite and a sudden, nagging fatigue she couldn't quite shake, she was fine. Healthy as a horse. Happy as a lamb.

About to join her life to another for the foreseeable future.

She sagged against the sink and pressed icy fingers to her eyes. Who was she kidding? Tom could still back out, probably would when the contract was read, and she'd lose him.

Tears clogged her throat and her chest filled with a fierce agony. Aye, she'd lose him, and then where would she be, forsaken by the first man she'd found who could love her, whom she could love in return.

She wrestled down the fear and stiffened her spine. If he rejected her, she'd simply have to find another way to talk him 'round, that was all, and if that didn't work, she could always chain him down until he agreed to give her a chance.

She slipped into the library a few minutes later, interrupting Tom's explanation of their recent findings. This room was as much the heart of the house as the kitchen was, with its walls of books, inset fireplace, and two leather sofas, facing one another over a coffee table. Here, Rebecca dispensed justice and advice to her family in equal measure. It was here that she regrouped and pondered her duties to the People, and here that her husband and children sought her when their own duties grew too heavy to endure.

Tom stood slowly and smiled, and Moira's worries slithered away. "Hey, sweetheart. I was just catching your mother up on my thoughts about Begni's letter."

Moira shut the door behind herself and walked to him, perching on the edge of the sofa facing her mother, who sat primly on the opposite sofa. "We've come a ways, though there remains much to be done."

"I didn't expect your work to be completed overnight," Rebecca said. "In fact, I'm pleased with the progress you've made. Uncovering a reference to the Seven Sisters is more than a step toward finding Sanctuary. You've recovered a piece of our history, for which we are all grateful."

Tom nodded and draped an arm around Moira's shoulders, his skin warm along hers through the slits in her sweater. "I'm hoping to go full-tilt after the holiday break, maybe get James on board more often. The biggest barrier after organization is language. We could really use his help."

"Plus a few more hands to sift through the rubble," Moira said. "It's still a mess, though we're making steady progress."

"James' schedule is his own, but I'll see what I can do on the extra hands." Rebecca smoothed her hands down her tailored slacks. "Well. Now that business is out of the way, I suppose we should deal with family matters."

Tom's fingers squeezed her shoulder. She placed a hand over them, drawing strength from his touch.

Rebecca smiled. "Moira, daughter of my heart, you may begin."

"Maetyrm, I come before you with a gift to your line, a man from a reputable family with a good heart and mind who will do much credit to our family, and to the People who have accepted him as their own."

Rebecca's eyebrows lifted slightly, the only outward expression of the surprise Moira was certain her mother felt at the wording she'd used. It had been more for Tom, she admitted to herself as Rebecca questioned them both, more to remind him of his place among the People and in her heart than to praise his worth to her mother. Rebecca would never deny Moira a man such as him, but Tom might well deny his value, should the question arise.

It didn't, and Moira was grateful. Her breath shuddered out of her at the end of the interview and her mother's casual acceptance of this man into their family. The contract was next. Rebecca handed it to Tom rather than reading it aloud. He promptly handed it to Moira.

"No glasses," he explained. "You never said anything about a contract."

"It outlines me duties to ye and yers to me. It's traditional among the People, similar to a pre-nuptial agreement among mortals, though more binding."

"Read it to me."

She gripped the pages between stiff fingers and stared down at it, the words a blur. He nudged her with his elbow and said softly, "Go on."

She cleared her throat and began reading, enunciating carefully, going through each clause one by one. He sat beside her with his forearms braced on his widely spread knees, nodding in response to some parts, grunting at others, shaking his head at odd moments. She finished and set the contract aside, folding her hands together in her lap, stilling the slight tremble spreading through her.

He sat back and rubbed a thumb along the bridge of his nose. "You realize how crazy some of that is, don't you?"

Moira glanced at Rebecca, whose knowing smile never budged. "Like what?"

"You setting me up with property, me keeping it no matter

what happens. I have my own investments, you know."

Temper spiked in a heady rush. "I'll not touch yer money, Tom. A Daughter cares for her man, not the other way around."

He rolled his eyes and sent a pleading look to Rebecca. "You see what I'm up against?"

Rebecca lifted one elegant shoulder. "Any Daughter would say the same."

"Crazy." He shook his head and sighed. "Are you really ready to have children now? I mean, two children in five years or you pay a penalty? That sounds kinda harsh. We haven't even talked about kids yet, anyway."

The temper drained out of her, leaving her so weary she swayed. "Ye don't want children?"

"Yeah, I do, but I..." He covered her hands with his, rubbing gently, warming her numb skin. "We could always wait a year, get to know one another better, and then decide if this is really what we want to do."

"Ye're rejecting me." The words came out so low and harsh, they were barely recognizable. Moira swallowed past the lump in her throat and blinked back tears.

He pulled her close, kissing her temple softly. "Hey, now. I'm not rejecting you. Where did you get an idea like that? I just think we should wait a little longer, not jump into anything."

She sniffed and turned her face into his chest, rubbing her cheek over his shirt. It was soft and warm and comforting, like him, and she was so very grateful for his kindness, the tears threatened to spill over.

"How long as she been like this?" Rebecca asked softly.

"All week at least." Tom circled his hand over her shoulder, soothing her. "And she hasn't eaten enough today to keep an ant alive, though she swears she's ok."

"Hmm." Rebecca rose from the couch and moved around the coffee table. She pressed her fingers to Moira's forehead, testing the skin in gentle touches and sweeps. "I'm sure she'll be fine, if not in the next few days, then soon afterward. I won't expect the two of you in to work until next weekend."

Tom stilled. "But we're so close. A delay now..."

"No buts, Tom. Trust me. You'll need the time."

Moira peered at her mother. "What aren't ye saying, Mother?"

"What aren't you?" Rebecca shot back. "Take your man home and let him tend you, Moira. We'll deal with the contract as soon as you're back to normal."

Moira pushed away from Tom and sat up, glaring at Rebecca's implacable expression. "I'm normal now."

Rebecca cut off an exasperated sigh. "If that's what you think, you're not paying attention. Go home. Let Tom take care of you. I'll talk to you next week."

Moira grumbled, but she went along as Tom bundled her up and they said their goodbyes. She slumped into the seat of his Prius and fell asleep. The engine switching off woke her. She gazed around, surprised to find them parked next to Tom's apartment building on the IECS campus.

"Why'd ye let me sleep?" she asked.

He slid a side-eyed glance at her. "No matter how many times you ask that question, I'm gonna give you the same answer."

She leaned on him as they made their way inside, held still while he pulled off her coat and shoes and clothes and tucked her into bed. "Just for a little while," she told him. "And then, I'll expect ye to make good on yer promise to make love to me all weekend."

"That's a promise I intend to keep." He smoothed back her hair and kissed her forehead. "I'll be in in a while."

"There's a dear," she murmured, and promptly fell asleep.

She woke on a gasp, sitting straight up in bed, her blood burning with a need so strong, her body ached and twinged. She shoved the covers off with shaky hands. Her breath came in pants and liquid fire pooled in her nethers.

Oh, aye, there was nothing wrong with her, nothing a'tall

163

except for the blasted needing sneaking up on her, taking her unawares, and the man she desired above all others unknowing of the consequences.

FIFTEEN

TOM GLANCED at his wristwatch and slumped against the back of his chair, scowling at the catalog pulled up on his laptop. He'd been searching through it for hours while Moira slept restlessly in the bedroom and the wind howled outside, blowing in a thunderstorm. Rain lashed across the windows and thunder rolled in the distance, matching his mood.

How many more times would he go through the catalog trying to find references to Sanctuary or the Seven Sisters?

He closed the laptop gently and rubbed his eyes, holding his fingers against his eyelids for a long moment. The longer he spent looking for answers, the more frustrated he got, and the more certain he became that he was missing something important.

The bedroom door creaked open, followed by a quiet shuffle of feet across the carpeted floor. Tom lowered his hands and glanced up. Moira stood in the doorway fully dressed in a black turtleneck and cargo pants, her cheeks flushed, a gentle tremor shuddering through her in irregular intervals.

He rose and strode toward her. "What are you doing up?"

Her eyes went round. She held a hand up and backed away from him, bumping into the doorframe. "Don't, Tom. Not a step closer if ye value yer precious distance."

He halted halfway to her. "What are you talking about?"

165

"I'm... I can't..." She inhaled sharply and eased toward the door, keeping her back pressed flat against the wall. When she spoke again, her voice was reed thin and held enough panic to worry him. "I can still smell yer scent, Tom. I love the way ye smell, like the ocean at sunrise."

"I'll be sure to e-mail the company that makes my aftershave," he said drily. "Let me get you back to bed."

"Ye smell so nice, Tom, so masculine and clean," she said, as if he hadn't spoken. "I want to bury me face in your throat and take ye in, make ye forever a part of me, and I can't. I... Ye want another."

His breath huffed out of him as impatience rose. "How many times do I have to tell you...?"

"And no children. Not a one for me Tom. Such a fine thing he is, strong of mind and heart." She sagged against the wall, her pale eyes unfocused. Her hand dropped to her side with a thump. "I would've liked another daughter. Siobhan and Hannah, too. They wanted a sister, a brother more, but a sister would've done, and I couldn't. Couldn't bring meself to have another when they died. And now ye're here, Tom, and I want ye so fierce, and ye don't."

He gentled his voice and edged toward her. "You're not making any sense, Moira. Come on, sweetheart. Let me help you."

"Can't. No help for me, none a'tall." Her eyes swung to his and in them he saw such pain, such longing, it staggered him. "Have to protect him. Have to protect me heart."

"I know, baby." He closed the distance and swung her up in his arms. Her forehead cradled in his throat, hot and dry. His gut clenched as he carried her into the bedroom and laid her gently on the bed. "You're running a fever, sweetheart. I'm calling Rebecca. Don't get up again, ok?"

She gasped and clutched his wrist. Her fingers dug into his skin, bruising him. "Don't leave me, Tom, not like this. Please."

"I'm getting the phone, that's all."

166

"Won't help." A laugh shuddered out of her and a tear streaked out of the corner of her eye. "Too late. I need ye so, need ye in me."

"Moira..."

"Ye'll hate me when it's done, aye, ye will, Tom." She released his wrist and sat up, shucking her turtleneck quickly. She was nude underneath, her skin flushed a light pink. "Come to me now, Tom."

He backed away even as a perverse heat shot through him. Damn it all, she was sick and half out of her head, and already, Tom Junior stirred behind the loose pajama bottoms he wore.

She yanked off her boots and wiggled out of her cargo pants, dropping her clothing into a messy heap on the floor. "Undress now, lover."

"Come on, Moira. You're not in any shape for sex."

She rose from the bed, her eyes fixed on him, and her wide mouth turned up into a smile full of seduction and determination. "A Daughter wishes to fuck and ye back away. What does reason tell ye will happen if ye don't comply?"

She stepped forward, stalking him, and he eased away, circling around, his body hardening and a wicked need lighting within him. She was beautiful, her eyes lit with a dangerous glint, her steps graceful and sure. He lifted a hand, intending to hold her off, and she pounced, rushing at him so quickly, her limbs were a blur. She shoved her shoulder into his stomach and circled her arms around his waist, using her momentum and native strength to lift him high and flip him onto the bed. He landed on his back with a solid thud, bouncing as the breath whooshed out of him. She was on him before he could move, straddling his hips, her hands anchoring his wrists to the bed on either side of his head.

"Now, we shall discuss compliance." Her voice was a low, silky purr. She rotated her hips over his growing erection and threw her head back on a gasp. "Ye feel so good, Tom, so feckin' good. I want to fuck ye all night."

He bit back a moan and fought to keep his hips from rising to meet her. Even through his clothing, her heat beckoned, warming him, tempting him. And she was still sick, still in need of care. "Moira, sweetheart..."

Her mouth came down on his, claiming him, demanding his surrender. Reason deserted him, its place filled by a clawing need. He strained upward, meeting her demands with his own, giving in to the wild brush of her lips against his, the sharp nip of her teeth, the bold sweeps of her tongue. His world narrowed to her, to their breaths panting into the stillness of his bedroom, to the rain beating down outside.

She released his wrists and shimmied down his body, shoving his clothes out of the way as she went. He lifted his hips, held them off the bed while she pulled his pants down, freeing his erection. Her fingernails raked down his stomach, leaving four stinging trails behind.

He hissed in a breath. "Careful there."

She laughed and crawled her way back up, snagging his wrists, pinning them to the mattress again. "I've marked ye good, Tom. Tell me ye don't wish it."

He did, so much. He wanted her to dig her fingernails into his back while he made love to her, wanted to feel her breaths panting across his skin, wanted to hear her gasps of pleasure as she found her release. He pushed against her hands and arched his hips, and the tip of his erection slid into her welcoming heat. He shuddered and gasped and said, "Oh God, yes," and she tilted her hips back, taking all of him, burying him deep within her slick heat.

Her hips set a hard rhythm, grinding against him in quick, sure strokes. He matched her pace, flexing his body under hers, the ache building in him pushing him to move faster, harder. She was wild above him, her red-gold hair streaming in fine tendrils around her delicate features, her blue eyes fierce as they met his and held, enrapturing him with the sheer wanton need glowing from her.

"Ye need to come, Tom," she panted, her hips pounding against his, whipping the heat building between them high. "Need to..." Her eyes fluttered shut and she gasped and her hips tilted back one final time, hard and sure. Her pussy clenched around him and he gritted his teeth, struggling to ride out her release, struggling not to come, but it was too late. He shoved into her and came, spurting his seed into her in long waves of hot pleasure. It rippled through him, on and on, stealing his breath and his reason, leaving him with nothing but the certainty that he'd do anything she asked, anything at all if it meant being with her like this, with nothing between them save the heat racing through them.

"Tom," she whispered, and collapsed onto his chest, releasing his wrists. Her heart hammered against his skin, bold and fierce. He huffed out a laugh. Just like her, his wild Irish Daughter. He caught her hand and brought it to his mouth, kissing the tips of each of her slender fingers.

When his breath settled, he said, "What was that? Not that I'm complaining, but you're not usually that wild."

"It's the needing." She rubbed her cheek along his chest and exhaled a shuddering sigh. "I'm sorry, Tom, so very sorry. If I'd known it was close, I would've left, would've spared ye."

"God, Moira. Don't ever spare me from sex like that."

"'Tisn't funny, ye daft man." Her voice snapped out of her, still husky from the need spooling between them. "The needing is the rare time when a Daughter is fertile and her womb best able to receive a man's seed."

His heart sputtered to a halt, then rebounded, racing under hers. "You're fertile? Now? Right this minute?"

"Oh, aye, Tom, so fertile it's likely I'll conceive as soon as yer little Toms swim their way upstream."

He brushed her hair back, relieved to find her skin much cooler than it had been before, in spite of the hot monkey sex they'd just had. "You say that like it's a bad thing."

She buried her face in his throat, and when she spoke, her

words were tight and thin. "I know ye don't want children with me."

"Whoa, now. I never said that." He rolled her onto her back, slipping out of her, missing her heat as soon as he did. She turned her face away, hiding her beautiful gaze from his, and the flush returned to her delicate skin. He brushed his fingers along her cheek. Not fever, he thought, eyeing the hard set of her mouth. "I said I thought we should wait and maybe make sure we wanted to be together before we made a commitment. Not once did I say I didn't want kids."

"Ye said ye didn't wish to discuss it and ye said it often, to yer mum and mine both."

"Because you and I haven't talked about it yet." He bit back exasperation and cupped her face, stroking his thumb over her skin. "In a normal relationship, these things go in stages. We date, we discuss what we want out of life and each other. We fall in love and get married, and *then* we have kids."

A small smile softened her mouth and her eyes peeked at him through lowered lashes. "Is that the way mortals do it, then."

"When they do it right, yes, but not you." He returned her smile and rubbed his nose across hers. "Rebecca should've named you *impatient.*"

"It's me middle name," she murmured. "Ye're taking this awful well."

"I'm not getting any younger. Besides, I kinda have a hankering for an impetuous daughter with red hair and bright blue eyes."

"Not a son, then."

Humor drained out of him. A son was impossible. Moira would never submit to him, never love him enough to even try, and that was the only way she could give him a son. He'd always wanted one of each like his brother had, a son to carry on his name and a little girl who'd twine his heart around her finger, holding him there forever. He tucked the dream away without a single regret. If Moira could only give him daughters, it wasn't settling, not at all, not when they were hers. And he wanted hers so much.

"A daughter," he said firmly, "and she'll not step a foot out of the house until she's at least thirty."

"Tom." She turned her head into his hand and kissed his palm gently. "Ye'll be a good father, I know ye will."

"I'll do my very best," he vowed. "Now, about this needing. It's a rare and hushed secret among the People."

"Not so very much. Ye must've never run across another Daughter in need of a child or ye'd already be wed and bed." She grinned, the corners of her eyes crinkling with laughter. "We think it's a way to ensure the survival of the People, this need Daughters have every year or so to find a man and mate with him. It's a powerful thirst, Tom, and I'm thankful ye're so accepting as it's a trying time for a woman and her mate."

A shadow crossed his heart, dimming his pleasure in her humor. That's exactly what was happening here, he feared. *This* was the reason Moira had pursued him so fiercely, this odd compulsion she'd had to conceive a child. She just hadn't figured it out yet. Damned if he'd be the one to tell her, though. A small kernel of hope still resided within him that she might find it in herself to love him someday.

She pulled his head down, capturing his mouth in a gentle kiss, and a powerful need of his own rose, pushing aside the worry that she might never trust him, no matter how much he wanted her to.

THE FIRE HAD burned low by the time Rebecca finished reading through a photocopy of her will. After the Thanksgiving meal's leftovers had been stored away and all the dishes cleaned, and after her children and their families had left, she'd retreated to the comfort of the library, intent on ensuring that her personal affairs were as up to date as possible.

The Woman's words rang clearly in her mind. *The Shadow*

approaches and the Blade must yield.

Death might find Rebecca ten years from then or in the next ten minutes, but she'd be ready. She'd be prepared, and she'd face it head on as she'd always faced the challenges life threw in front of her.

Rebecca shuffled the pages she was working on back into order and set them on the coffee table, satisfied with the changes she'd made. So much had happened since the last time she'd updated her will. Charlotte had given her two more grandchildren, Dani had found love, Bobby's heart had healed, and now Moira was in her needing and likely to become pregnant. Life would go on, carried forward by the younger generations as it always was.

The door creaked open. Robert pushed through, his gate slow and steady. He dropped onto the couch beside her and placed a warm hand on her thigh. "You're spending more and more time here lately. What's bothering you?"

She leaned her head on his shoulder. He'd been her rock for decades now, her strength and will, in spite of the terrible disease ravaging his body. "It's nothing, Robert. Nothing for you to worry over, anyway."

"You're my wife," he said gently. "If something's bothering you, I should know. Tell me what's going on. Let me help."

"There's nothing you can do, not this time."

Her throat tightened around the last few words, nearly cutting them off. His arm came around her shoulders, heavy and comforting, and she curled her fingers into the fabric of his shirt. He'd follow her into battle if he could, would follow her anywhere if she let him. Not this time, though. This time, he'd remain firmly in the land of the living, and she would greet fate with her sword raised high and her heart full of his love.

"You're going through your will again," he said.

"The family's grown so much, I thought it best."

"No hopes for Margaret and Jerusha, then."

The mild humor in his voice stirred her own. "Can you

172

honestly see Margaret settling down with a modern man? The last time she took a long-term lover, it nearly started a war."

Robert's low chuckle vibrated through her. "Maybe she should've picked someone other than a minor prince to kidnap and chain to her bed."

"Margaret never did anything the easy way."

"Much like her mother. Tell me what's wrong."

Rebecca sighed and brushed her face over his shirt, the fabric worn thin and soft over time. "Change is coming, Robert. I'm simply doing my best to accommodate it."

"By updating your will? I know what that means, Becca." His breath rushed out of him in an audible sigh. "Give me a little credit for understanding you."

"I do. It's just..." She pressed her lips together around the need to blurt everything out, to detail the Woman's vision and its implications for their family and the People. The need for honesty, the need to give him everything, battered at her, but she held it back. No good would come of Robert knowing. "You'll worry and I don't want you to."

"I'm worried now." He squeezed her shoulder and drew her closer. "How much worse could it get just by you telling me what's on your mind?"

Much, much worse, she feared. He wouldn't simply worry, he would mourn, and the last part of their life together, however long they might have, would be overshadowed by her certain death. Not knowing the method of that death would've been far kinder. The Woman had had her reasons for sharing it, though, and whatever those were, Rebecca trusted that they were sound and whole, just as she'd trusted the Woman the day she'd brought Dani into Rebecca's life.

"Robert, darling, I love you beyond measure."

"But you aren't going to tell me what's troubling you."

She smoothed a gentle hand over his stomach. "Someday, when the time is right. For now, I want to enjoy every minute we have together."

They settled down side by side and watched the fire's flickering flames slowly fade to coals.

THE ARCHIVES was quiet in spite of the small crowd gathered in the public area. Moira sat at one of the wooden tables arranged in rows in front of the old card catalog, sorting through a loose stack of documents she'd found in an abandoned room. Tom stood with James one table away, rooting through a box together, their quiet conversation drifting easily to Moira's ear. Ruanna and Phil occupied another table in the second row, her with documents Tom had asked her to translate, him compiling his research on Tellowee's history into an outline. A few others had drifted in, eager to lend a hand tracking down the location of Sanctuary, and Tom had given them simple, necessary tasks.

Moira sighed and studied the scroll in front of her. Like so many other documents she'd found in the past few months, this one had gradually been forgotten. Worse, its originating data had been lost as well, stripping its contents of any context or clues as to the writer.

Perhaps those could be discovered with time, though Moira found the task beyond her patience at that moment.

Her needing had begun nearly a week before and run its course so quickly, she was certain Tom's seed had taken root in her womb.

She glanced at him beneath lowered lashes and worried at her lower lip. For nigh on a day and a half, he'd serviced her gladly, never once complaining over the task, though the needing had afforded him little rest and few opportunities to gather sustenance, and left them both so weak, they'd had to prop each other up in the shower. After, though, when she'd assured him the needing was over, he'd taken such good care of her, cooking a decent meal, holding her close, and his expression had softened into one of a man well on his way to loving the woman he was with.

By the Lady Ki, let it be so.

She pressed her fingertips to her heart, hoping against hope that he'd one day live there. To have his child, to live with him, those things would never be enough for her. Would that she could submit simply by willing it and thereafter live with him as mortal couples did. Squabbles and disagreements she would gladly accept, if it meant having him in her life for the rest of her days.

She didn't love him, not quite yet, though what her heart was waiting on was beyond Moira. Wasn't he the kindest man she'd ever known? Had he not treated her with courtesy and respect since the day she'd claimed him? Against his will, aye, and certainly against his better judgment, but the care was there all the same. She wished to return his care in an equal measure, wished it with every cell in her being.

Stubborn Irish. Tom's words floated through her mind, bringing a smile to her lips. That's what she was, a stubborn Irishwoman if ever one had been born. Stubbornness had seen her through many a hard day, it had, and she should be grateful. Instead, she cursed her stubborn heart roundly, careful to recite the words under her breath, too low for Tom to hear.

They hadn't discussed the implications of the needing, though she was certain enough of the results. Her courage seemed to've deserted her. Each time she attempted to broach the subject, her mouth dried up and her heart beat double time and fear shriveled the words in her throat. He'd know soon enough, true, but she wished to share it with him now, while the wonder of it was new and fresh.

Tom's voice jolted Moira into the present. "...the Bones of the Just when you're digging around."

"I'll do that." James lifted a paper out of the box, frowned at it, and set it aside in one of the piles ranged around the table. "Any way I can look at the letter itself?"

"Sure. Ruanna's translated most of it. A couple of places might be names, a couple more she says are completely illegible,

175

but we could use the help on it, if you're willing."

"I'd love to take a crack at it. Archaic Hebrew's not one of my stronger languages, though."

"It's not one of my languages at all," Tom said, grinning. He raised his voice and said, "Hey, Rue. Do you have a copy of Begni's letter and your translation?"

She slid her chair back and stood. "I stuck them in your office. Be right back."

Tom and James drifted back into conversation, and Moira focused on the next scroll in her stack, a copy of intelligence gathered on the Shadow Enemy during the seventeenth century. She scanned through the painfully tiny handwriting written partially in a code she didn't recognize and gave up when Ruanna jogged into the room carrying the documents Tom had sent her after.

"Got 'em." She flattened them out on the table near Tom and James. "I'm pretty sure what we're calling Begni's letter is actually a translation of the original letter into Hebrew. No idea why that language was used when there were plenty others more well-understood."

Moira rose and moved around the table she was using, placing herself across the table from the trio examining the letter. A moment later, Phil situated himself beside her, casually bracing his forearms on the tabletop.

James pointed to the letter. "This section here. You've left it untranslated."

Ruanna shrugged. "Couldn't figure it out, though it might be a name."

"What are the letters?" Phil asked.

Ruanna shot him a sharp glance. "It's not that easy, Phil. Archaic Hebrew is an abjad. No written vowels. Plus, some of the letters have different meanings depending on where they're placed in the word. *And,* archaic Hebrew was originally written in another script entirely, while this, which I'm almost positive is a translation, was written in a stylized version of the Aramaic script, and that wasn't even a distinct script until a couple of centuries after Begni's letter was written."

James covered a smile with one hand.

Phil poked his tongue into his cheek and said, "Uh-huh."

Rue's cheeks flushed pink and she hunched her shoulders. "I told you. It's complicated."

"Humor me," he said. "I mean, what could it hurt? Maybe you'll jog a memory or something."

"Ok. Best guess, then." She exhaled slowly and rattled off the corresponding names for each letter.

James snagged a notebook and a pen and made her go through them again twice more. "I'll study these," he said, and lifted his own shoulders in a shrug. "Like Phil said, it couldn't hurt. It'd be better if we knew when Begni's letter was written, though, and maybe where."

Tom shook his head. "Are you kidding? We're still trying to figure out how the letter was added to the Archives in the first place."

"No, wait," Ruanna said. "There are clues in the text. Begni mentions an obscure battle between the People and the Shadow Enemy."

"What?" Tom rounded on her, eyes wide. "You didn't tell me that."

"I gave you the translation, didn't I?"

Moira hid a grin as she reached across the table and patted the back of Tom's hand. "There now, darling, she's forgotten you've not been among the People yer whole life and wouldn't know the significance of our history."

His eyebrows snapped into a vee over his brown-green eyes. "You've read the letter, too."

"No, I've scanned it, not studied it, and like yerself, I was looking for the obvious first." She patted his hand again and withdrew her own. "I'll study it more carefully and see what I can do about placing it for ye."

They each went back to their work. Moira settled into hers,

177

her mind caught more by how she could bring the subject of her likely pregnancy around to Tom than on their quest to locate the Sanctuary of the Seven Sisters.

SIXTEEN

TWO NIGHTS LATER, Tom and Moira sat together on the sofa watching a movie, her head resting on his shoulder, his hand covering hers. A typical date night for them. She had yet to agree to an actual night out. She'd barely consider going with him to The Omega, though she'd conceded that with India Furia and Councilmember Isolde rounded up and the remaining members of the Eternal Order apparently scattered, it was safe enough.

He dropped his head against the back of the sofa, only half his attention on the action playing out onscreen. How much safer could anybody be than in The Omega surrounded by a bunch of warriors, their weapons always at the ready? The only other place he felt safer was on the IECS campus itself, with its thick, protective walls and ever-alert guards.

Maybe she was afraid he'd kick her out, now that the threat presented by the Order was largely gone. He dropped a kiss to the top of her head and sighed. How could she still think he didn't want her, after everything they'd been through, especially now that she might be pregnant with his child?

Did she think that was his only reason for wanting her now?

The notion was so far from the truth it was laughable. In all his life, he'd never wanted a woman as much as he craved her, deeply, fiercely, with a consuming need to have her near burned

179

sharply into his heart. She filled every inch of his life with her vivid personality and mischievous smile. Every day, he crept a little closer to love. Every day, she gave him fewer and fewer reasons to hold himself away from that precipice.

She shifted beside him and brushed her cheek along his upper arm. "Are ye well, Thomas? Ye seem restless."

"I'm fine. When's the next time I can talk you into wearing those heels?"

She tilted her face to his, her smile coy and playful. "Oh, there's no talking there, darling. I'll wear them and gladly, if ye'll pet me accordingly."

His smile matched hers as a fist of heat slammed into his gut, bringing with it undiluted want and an urgent need to claim her as his own. "Whatever you want."

Her cell phone beeped. She snarled at it and snatched it off the table, flipping it open as she said, "Feckin' timing. Notice whenever we're here on the couch about to make love, me sister texts like she knows what we're up to."

"Guess that means we'll have to quit making out on the couch, huh."

Moira shot him a half grin. Her humor faded abruptly as she scrolled through Margaret's message. "Text Ruanna and see if she'll stay with ye, will ye? Maggie May has a lead on the Daughter that skewered me."

Tom's own humor drained away. "Not on your life, sweetheart. You're fresh from the needing and just now fully healed. I don't want you risking injury when you're still a little under the weather."

"Nonsense. I'm fit as a fiddle and raring to go." She dropped her phone on the table and stretched her way into a stand. "'Sides. Can't let the wound go unanswered. I've me reputation to think on."

Her tone was flippant enough to stir his irritation into anger. He stood slowly and stared down at her, his eyebrows furrowed, his arms crossed over his chest. "You're not going."

"Don't be ridiculous, Tom."

"I'm not the one being ridiculous here. Have you forgotten that you might be pregnant?"

Her eyes went flat and cold and hard as stone. "Not for a moment have I forgotten that, rest assured. I've still me duties to tend, though, and a mate to protect."

"A mate..." He scrubbed his hands hard over his face. "I can protect myself. Your duties can wait until you know whether or not you're pregnant or they can be passed off to somebody else. Jesus, Moira. You can't go off half-cocked right now, racing out of here on a damn whim, not in the shape you're in."

"Is that what ye think of me, Tom, that I give in to whimsy, that I've no consideration for me own state of body and mind?" She huffed out a breath and whirled, stalking out of the living room in long, angry strides. "Feckin' men. Shoulda chained ye when I had the chance and left ye there to serve me *whimsy*."

"I'd like to see you try."

She ignored the low threat in his voice and continued into the bedroom, him right behind her. He stood in the doorway and followed her movements with his gaze, her pajamas yanked off, fresh clothes yanked on with equal force, swift checks of her weapons. As he watched her, his concern resolved into decision. He stepped into the bedroom and slipped his own pajamas off, then rummaged through his clothes for dark, comfortable clothing.

"What in blazes are ye doing?" she barked.

"Going with you. I'd think that's obvious." He found a black UGA sweatshirt and pulled it on over a dark gray t-shirt. "Between your claiming me and your possible pregnancy, I think this situation calls for a team effort."

Her eyes narrowed into thin, blue slits. "When ye grow tits and become immortal, I'll consider letting ye accompany me on a mission. Until then, ye'll stay put under the care of a strong sword arm and be content with yer lot."

He slammed the drawer of his bureau shut. "I haven't been

content since the moment you walked into my life. What makes you think I'll start now?"

She flinched and her face paled. "Tom."

"No, I think you need to face reality here, Moira." He reached her in two strides and wrapped his hands around her upper arms, holding her gently in spite of the fury bouncing around inside him. "I'm not a man who can be tucked away and ignored when it's convenient for you, and I sure as hell won't stand by while you risk yourself and my child. I care about you, way more than I should considering that you'll never love me, but it's there all the same. How can you possibly expect me to let you go out there alone?"

"Tom." She stared at him for a long moment, then her hands came up and cupped his jaw. Her fingers stroked over the skin and her eyes met his, soft and sweet. "Ye must understand that I've done this sort of thing many, many times before. There's no danger of harm befalling me or the babe, should there be one. I swear it to ye."

"Then you should let me go with you. Please, Moira. Don't make me watch you walk out that door again, wondering if you'll ever come back."

"I'll come back, Tom. I will." She stood on tiptoes and touched her lips to his in a fleeting kiss. "And I'll text ye as soon as I'm done. Rebecca scolded me something fierce for not telling ye I was in hospital. I'll not make that mistake again with ye."

"That's not good enough."

But even as he said it, he knew there was nothing he could do to change her mind, no leverage he could hold over her to keep her safe. The only thing that might move her was a threat to leave and that would never work with her. Even if it weren't an empty threat, and it was, about as empty as a threat could get, the chances of her caring enough to take him seriously were nil.

His heart flipped in his chest and squeezed tight. She'd never love him enough to care one way or the other.

He sank onto the edge of the bed as a sick nausea rose in

his gut. Goddamn it. All this time, he'd fooled himself into believing he could hold himself back when his stupid heart had already taken the fall. He was in love with her, his wild Irish lover, and she was...

An immortal Daughter, destined to never know love.

Moira knelt in front of him and smoothed her hands over his hair. "What is it, Tom? Ye look as if a ghost snuck up on ye and said *boo.*"

He huffed out a laugh and leaned away from the warmth of her touch. He couldn't bear it, not now, not when every hope he'd ever had for a future with her had fallen into ruins at his feet. "You'd better go. Margaret's probably waiting for you."

She sat back on her haunches and eyed him. "Just like that, ye're giving in. Are ye out of arguments so soon?"

"Yeah, I guess I am. I think..." He choked on the word, inhaled sharply, cleared his throat around the tightness strangling him. "I think you should go."

"Ye're not acquiescing, are ye." She rolled back on her heels and pushed herself into a stand, her expression shuttered. "Will I be welcome back, then?"

He jerked his gaze away from her and rubbed his hands down his thighs. As if he could ever find the will to turn her away. "You'll do what you want, regardless of my feelings. Isn't that the way this works? You Daughter, me stupid man."

She hissed in breath. "I never thought ye were stupid, Thomas, not once. Ye've a keen intelligence, sharp and focused, but yer insistence in this matter is pure foolishness. Why can't ye trust me to know me way about things?"

"Because the last time you went out, you didn't come back." The harshly spoken words fell between them. Tom lowered his voice, softening it as much as he could around the fear grinding its way down his chest. "You nearly died."

"Not even close," she retorted, "and then, I had ye to pull me through. With our mating just around the corner and the possibility of a babe, do ye really think I'll allow death to claim me?"

Tom snapped his mouth shut, refusing to voice another doubt.

She stooped and kissed his forehead. "I'll be back before ye know it, I promise."

Her footsteps swished softly across the carpet, the outer door opened and shut. Tom sat on the bed, his heart numb, his mind blank. The future stretched before him, years and years of him sitting on the sidelines watching her risk herself, worrying every single time if she'd make it back in one piece, if at all, and he snapped. He was in love with her. That didn't mean he had to watch her try to kill herself.

He grabbed his overnight bag and stuffed a change of clothes and some toiletries inside, pulled his rarely used handgun out of the lockbox under the bed and tucked it among his clothes. He didn't bother with a note. What was the use? She'd likely be gone all night anyway, and frankly, he needed the space.

He grabbed his keys and a jacket, locked the apartment, and jogged down the stairs, away from the heartache awaiting him in the tiny apartment he called home.

MOIRA JOGGED OUT of Tom's apartment building, her mind focused on her meeting with Margaret. She slid into her Miata, cranked it, and called her sister while she waited for the motor to warm.

Margaret answered on the first ring. "Took you long enough."

"Sorry." Moira tucked the phone between her ear and her shoulder and rubbed her chilled hands together. Feckin' cold. "Had to talk Tom outta going with me."

"Pulled his pecker out, did he. Well, he's a man. It's bound to happen occasionally."

Moira ignored the sardonic tone and the swipe at her impending submission. Ki willing, it would happen before the babe she was certain she carried was born so the lass would never have to deal with the downside of the People's curse.

She shifted into gear and eased out of the parking lot, then sped through the twisting turns of the roads off of the IECS campus at a speed that would make Rebecca's hair whiten. "Will ye finally tell me who skewered me leg or do I have to beat it out of you?"

"Darling sister, remember who taught you to fight."

Moira snickered. How quickly the elderly forgot. "That'd be our mother, Maggie May."

A long-suffering sigh drifted through the phone's tinny audio. "Why do you insist on referring to me by that infernal nickname?"

"Because ye won't see reason," Moira retorted. "Now give over the name before I think of worse."

"Fine. It was that whelp Vivien Long."

Moira's grip loosened on the Miata's steering wheel. The car drifted across the double yellow line. She yanked it into the proper lane and snapped her jaw shut around a ripe curse. "What is she, a quarter century old? Feck's sake, she's still wet behind the ears."

"Got the jump on you, didn't she?"

"Because she hid behind a feckin' door, the cowardly cur. Why in blazes didn't ye tell me who she was in the first place?"

"And get on Tom's bad side when you went roaring off after her, still half wounded? You may not care for your lover's opinion, but I certainly don't want to be wary of him slipping something noxious into my food for the next forty-odd years."

A twinge of guilt twisted its way through Moira's heart. Doing one's duty wasn't ignoring your lover's opinion. It was...duty. And honor. And feck's sake, it wasn't like she wouldn't be home before he woke in the morning. Beating some sense into a whippersnapper like young Long would hardly raise a sweat. Moira pressed her lips into a thin line and scowled at the strip of road illuminated by the Miata's headlights. She'd be sure to tell Tom that, too, soon as she returned home and snuggled down beside his lovely warmth.

"Tom's not one to visit harm upon family, kaetyrm." Though he'd scolded *her* often enough. "I'm on me way to meet ye."

She hung up as soon as Margaret said goodbye and punched out a text to Ruanna, glancing between the road and her phone in irregular intervals. Another hour to Margaret's position outside Long's home, half an hour at most to run the chit down and exact revenge, and another hour, maybe an hour and a half for the journey home. A slow smile curled Moira's mouth. Midnight would see her back to Tom. If he was willing, she'd spend the rest of the night soothing his hurt.

Moira turned off of Highway 76 onto Highway 441 leading to Gainesville, passing through the sparse late night traffic speeding along the streets in Clayton. Her mind drifted as she drove, onto the house she and Tom would buy. Had to contact a real estate agent soon. Wouldn't it be nice to settle in before the babe came? If he was of a mind, they could pick a point halfway between her family and his, still close enough to the IECS for the commute to be bearable.

Her phone beeped as she crossed the dam spanning the Tallulah River. She glanced at it and frowned. What could Ruanna want? Moira tapped the message with her thumb, opening it, and her breath left her in a rush.

Tom gone, apartment empty, car gone. Please advise.

She eased into the center turn lane, brought the Miata to a stop, and flipped on the hazard lights. Tom was gone. No, it couldn't be. She'd just left him, safe and sound in the apartment. He knew Ruanna was coming to watch over him, knew Moira would be back as quickly as she could, and he'd, what? Ventured into the night alone and unprotected?

No, not entirely. He would've taken his handgun. Surely he would've, knowing there was a slim chance he could still be a target for the Order and other unsavory characters, but where

186

would he have gone?

Her heart tripped over itself, then banged against her sternum in a hard, rapid beat. She rested her forehead against the steering wheel, praying for calm. Had he left her after all? Even after their disagreement, he hadn't seemed that angry. Resigned, maybe, but that was to be expected. A Daughter had her duty. The sooner her mate understood that, the better.

Tom had understood. Hadn't he?

Moira cleared the tightness clogging her throat and texted Ruanna, asking her to check The Omega, then called Margaret. "Tom's gone," she said without preamble. "Ruanna said his apartment's empty and his car's gone."

"I'm on my way."

"No, don't. I'll search for him." Moira dragged in a slow breath, releasing it in a near whistle. "Round up Vivien Long, if you can. She might have info on the Order. We need all the help we can get there."

A long silence fell between them. At last, Margaret said, "It's not like you to turn the other cheek, kaetyrm."

"I know. He..." A tear trickled down Moira's cheek, startling her. She swiped it away with an impatient flick of her fingers. "Tom wanted me to stay home and let someone else chase me attacker down. Suppose he'll be happy now that I'm leaving it to ye."

"If he's gone, something that small won't bring him much happiness," Margaret said gently. "Are you sure?"

"Aye, as sure as I ever am. Tom is... I could love him, Margaret, truly love him. Already halfway there, truth be told." Moira's laugh was small and hollow. "And I'm probably preggers."

"So I'm to be an aunt again. Well, I suppose he's good for something, then, even if he is a man."

Moira laughed, this one looser, if not quite full. "Oh, he's good for quite a bit, once ye tunnel under his native reserve. I'd best see to him now. Pray he's merely run to The Omega for a gargle."

"May Ki keep him, and you. Call if you need me."

"Will do."

Moira ended the call and dropped the phone into the passenger's seat. He was ok. A pint at The Omega was nothing, and she'd told him it was safe enough. He wouldn't have remembered to wait for Rue and Phil. Surely that's all that had happened. He'd needed some fresh air and driven out to The Omega on a whim. Ruanna would text any moment with the news that Tom was kicking up his heels, contemplating life while he sipped a jar of the stout he favored.

The reassurance didn't settle well in Moira's heart. She flipped off the hazards and did a u-turn in the middle of 441, heading back toward Tellowee, her voice a quiet litany of prayers offered to the Lady Ki.

SEVENTEEN

THE ROAD LEADING out of Tellowee dead-ended on Highway 76. Tom stopped his car and stared at the large green sign on the other side of the road, its shiny white letters helpfully giving distances and directions to what passed for civilization in rural Appalachia. Clayton was to his left, Hiawassee to his right. Neither of the small towns held much interest to him right then. What would he do, pick one, drive to it, and then what? Where would he go? He'd given up his apartment in Atlanta when he'd taken the job at the IECS. Friends he had a-plenty, but none he wanted to bother, and his mother and brother would be in bed by the time he made it there.

He dropped his head back against his seat's headrest and blew out a weary sigh. The impetus that had driven him out of the apartment drained slowly away. Moira was what she was. He'd known that going into the relationship, accepted it even knowing he shouldn't. Goddamn it. Why had his idiotic heart chosen a woman so rash and reckless she had no care for her own child, let alone for the man who loved her? Her wit and humor and innate beauty didn't make up for that, not by a long shot, not when he'd needed her to listen to reason, not when he'd needed *her*.

A car shot by on 76, its headlights bouncing across the sign. Clayton or Hiawassee or parts beyond. He could go, forget

189

Moira, abandon the child she might carry, and regret it for the rest of his life. Or he could stay and try to get her to see reason one final time, maybe find a way to work with her until after the baby was born.

For a moment, he was tempted to turn left and never look back. His gaze was drawn to the road, ink black under the moonless sky, the asphalt a ribbon of futures possible. Even without a recommendation from Rebecca, he could work anywhere. He had the credentials, both academic and published, and he had the connections. What he wouldn't have was a heart. It would always belong to her, always, and there wasn't a damn thing he could do about it. Leaving her wouldn't change that, but it would fill that empty space with enough regret to last a thousand lifetimes.

So leaving was out, even for just a night. He glanced both ways, then cut a hard right and eased his Prius out onto the highway, angling back and forth until he was turned completely around. He wasn't ready to go home just yet. The thought of being cooped up alone in his empty apartment held absolutely no appeal. On impulse, he swung the Prius onto the side street leading to Naomi's and parked in her driveway. A few minutes later, he stood on her stoop, hands tucked into the pockets of his jeans as the brisk night air seeped through his clothing, chilling his skin.

He stared at the door, raised a hand, dropped it to his side. What was he doing here? If Moira found out, it would kill her, and then she'd kill him, probably literally. As mad as he was at her, it wasn't right for him to see Naomi on the sly, even if she was just a friend. Moira didn't understand that, though, never had, and that was his fault for pursuing the other Daughter. He pinched the bridge of his nose and stifled the bitter laugh pushing its way through the hurt and anger twisted into a seething knot in his chest. This entire mess was his fault from start to finish, though how he could've stopped the train wreck that was his life at the moment, he hadn't a clue.

Moira's enmity toward Naomi he could remedy, at least in part. He pivoted and stepped lightly onto the path leading back to his car. Behind him, the door opened and a soft voice called, "Tom? What are you doing here?"

He turned slowly, not at all sorry to've gotten caught. Naomi stood in the doorway dressed in a long-sleeved knit shirt and fleecy pajama bottoms with her fine hair pulled into a messy knot on top of her head. Right then, it hit him why he'd pulled into her driveway. He'd needed a friendly ear. He'd needed somebody to help him find a way to deal with Moira before her intransigence drove them apart for good.

"Hey, Naomi. You have a minute?"

She smiled and stepped back, opening the door wide. "For you, I have several. Come on in."

The knot in his chest unwound a fraction. He slid into her house behind her, grateful she hadn't kicked him to the curb, and glanced around. They were standing on the edge of an oddly-shaped great room. A full kitchen with gleaming black appliances and long mottled-brown, granite counters occupied the area to the right, separated from the remaining space by an island with tall chairs set under its lip. A rack holding copper-bottomed pots hung above the island surrounding track lighting positioned to illuminate the island when lit.

A sturdy wooden table sat parallel to a wall adjacent to the kitchen, its polished surface adorned by a crystal vase full of daisies. That wall was cattycorner to the rest of the room. A sitting area composed of a comfortable looking sofa upholstered in a nubby, deep red fabric with a matching arm chair and a black leather recliner was arranged facing a rock fireplace with an insert. A fire crackled cheerily within, throwing warmth into the room and light onto the hardwood floor. Bookcases scattered along the walls held photographs, knick-knacks, and books of all shapes and sizes. It was a cozy space in spite of the tall ceiling and open floor plan.

"This is nice," he said.

"I forgot you'd never been inside." Naomi smiled and gestured toward the sitting area. "Let's sit by the fire. I can hardly resist building one, even with central heating."

"There's nothing like a fire on a cold night," Tom agreed. His own parents had always kept one going in the winter, as much for the comfort as to save propane and keep him and his brother occupied splitting wood. "If you're in the middle of something, I can go."

"Not at all, Tom. You're always welcome." She sat on one end of the sofa, curled her legs up under her, and tucked her hands between her thighs. "I suppose Moira's driving you to distraction."

Tom sank onto the other end of the sofa and braced his forearms against his knees. "Something like that."

"What has she done that's sent you fleeing before her?"

The slightly mocking tone eased the knot in his chest another inch. "She's out chasing the person who stabbed her a while back."

"She's a Daughter. A wound like that calls for vengeance."

"When she might be pregnant?"

Naomi's gaze slipped away from his and narrowed on the fire. "She went through her needing?"

"Last week. It was..."

He exhaled a shaky breath, completely unsurprised by the throb of heat pulsing low in his gut and Tom Junior stirring beneath the fly of his jeans. Moira's needing had been the most erotic experience of his life. No matter what he'd done, she'd demanded more, pressing him into trying things he'd never tried before simply to satisfy her need to have him inside her. She'd exhausted him, exhausted them both, and still, she'd *needed* and he'd been more than happy to comply with that urgency

"Not like normal sex," Naomi said, and Tom nodded. That was putting it mildly.

"She went out tonight knowing she might be pregnant and I just snapped, I guess. What kind of woman risks herself at a time

192

like that? Would you?"

"That depends on the situation."

He glanced at her, surprised. "Seriously?"

She opened her mouth, then pressed her lips tightly together. "Duty is beaten into a Daughter from the time she's born to the time death delivers her to the Lady Ki. If the need were great, I'd go, even knowing I risked my child's life with my own. Some things simply must be done whether one wishes to do them or not."

"And this?" he asked softly. "Would you have gone out pursuing a woman who'd already gotten the better of you?"

"It's not that simple, Tom. It's not," she said when he cut a hot glare at her. "Among the People, Daughters live and die by their reputations. As long as you're with Moira, no one with any sense will bother you. She's too hot-headed, too eager to strike a killing blow. If she leaves this attack unanswered, her reputation could slip, putting you and your child at risk."

He slumped into the sofa and ran his fingers over its nubby fabric. "You honestly think she weighed her options rationally?"

"No," Naomi admitted. "I think she acted instinctively, as any woman in her situation would."

"Even you?" He shook his head and stared up at the beams crisscrossing the ceiling. "I'm sorry, Naomi, but I can't see you acting that way."

"Perhaps not. Then again, I don't have the reputation Moira does. Don't get me wrong. No one messes with me, but my name doesn't make my enemies quake in their boots, either."

He rolled his head along the top of the sofa and met her gaze. "I have a hard time believing a woman as sweet as you has enemies."

"Everyone does," she said mildly, though her dark eyes sparked with humor and a small smile curved her lips. She leaned forward and gripped his arm, her smile fading. "Don't do anything rash, Tom. You have a chance here, a real chance at a love so deep and lasting, it will fill your heart for the rest of your days. Don't throw that away simply because Moira doesn't know how to bend."

"You know, it sounds like you're trying to persuade me to stay with her." He cupped his hand over hers, rubbing gently. "Am I that easy to forget?"

"Not at all. In fact, if I thought it would do any good, I'd tempt you away from her." She slipped her hand out from under his and settled into the sofa with a sigh. "Your heart's long gone, though, and I'd rather take my chances on a man who has a place for me in his life."

"And Moira takes up too much of mine." And would for a long time to come, even if she left him as he always feared she would, someday when age had stolen his strength and dulled her need for him. "I tried to get my brother to meet a Daughter. Maybe it's a good thing he's still hung up on his wife. I'd hate for him to have to go through this."

"We're not all like Moira, headstrong and rash in our dealings." She hesitated, then said, "He's not dating?"

"Who, Mike?" Tom shook his head. "Naw. Says he's not ready yet."

"Oh." She ran a light hand over the cushion beside her, her gaze following its movements back and forth. "How are his children? Are they out of their braces yet?"

He glanced sharply at her, studying her casual interest and the gentle sweeps of her hand along the fabric. Daughters loved children, no matter who their parents were, but this seemed like more. Mischief mingled with a deep-seated need to see his brother happy again. "Not yet. Maybe in the spring, Mike said. Josh grew another two inches since school started."

She nodded, though her eyes remained fixed on her hand. "I suppose he's playing basketball, then."

"Not this year. Band. Maybe next year, though." Tom reached forward and wrapped his hand around her socked feet, layered one over the other. "Why didn't you tell me you were interested in Mike?"

She huffed out a laugh. "I was happy with the brother I had. Besides, I've never even met him."

"But you've seen pictures and I talk about him and the kids all the time." He waggled his eyebrows and grinned. "What was that you said about sexual compatibility?"

Color crept into her cheeks and her eyes snapped up to meet his. "Tom, really."

"It's a valid point." And a pertinent one, as he'd found out the hard way with Naomi. As much as he'd wanted to, he'd never felt the spark for her that roared to life whenever he was within spitting distance of Moira. "Don't throw away a chance to meet a good man just because we dated."

"I could hardly turn down the opportunity," she said in a voice caught halfway between exasperation and humor. "And with that settled, I think it's time for hot cocoa."

"None for me, thanks." Tom stood and stuffed his hands into his pockets. "I appreciate the ear, though. I guess I needed to talk it out more than I thought."

"We all need a friendly shoulder. Mine is always here for you." She unfolded her legs and rose gracefully. "Though I doubt Moira will allow you to take advantage of it often."

"Or not at all," he said, but the words were tinged with laughter instead of the bitterness holding him in its sway since Moira had left. "Can I take a rain check on the cocoa?"

Naomi tilted her head to the side, regarding him steadily. "You're always taking rain checks. That should've been my first hint that you weren't that interested."

"Oh, I was interested. Moira snagged me first, is all." He dropped a kiss to her forehead and eased back. "Think about what I said. Mike needs to put the past behind him. I can't think of a better woman to help him do that."

"I'll think about it," she said simply, and he let it go at that. All he could do was make the offer. It was up to her to act on it.

They chatted for a few minutes more, about the Archives and her daughter Kara, whose due date was right around the corner. If the knot in his chest hadn't completely loosened thanks to her patient counsel, at least it no longer threatened to burst. He slipped into his Prius, cranked the engine, and let it warm before shifting into gear and heading home. When Moira got home, he'd be waiting for her, arguments at the ready, and hoped she'd be willing to reconsider the boundaries of their relationship, and her responsibilities to the child he prayed she carried.

MOIRA DROVE HOME as quickly as she could, pushing the speed limit to a near breaking point. Her mind whirled uselessly, refusing to settle on a solid course of action. He had to be ok, that's all there was to it. He'd done some foolishly male thing and left home without telling anybody, that was all, but he was ok.

Her hands tightened on the steering wheel as she rolled to a screeching stop at the traffic light marking the intersection of Highways 76 and 441. Why hadn't Rue texted her back yet? Jaysus. It took less than ten minutes to go from the apartment to The Omega, and that at a quick jog. And how long to check inside? Even tonight on the last day of the traditional workweek, with the bar filled with People and outsiders alike, he'd still be one of the few men in the room and not at all hard to spot.

The light turned green. Moira gritted her teeth and controlled her lead foot, turning into the connector at a relatively moderate pace. Some twenty minutes later, she cut the wheels of the Miata into a less sedate turn onto the road leading to Tellowee. Her phone beeped. She eased off the gas and snatched it out of the seat, punching open Ruanna's text with her thumb.

Found him, it read. *135 Beecham, Tellowee.*

"One thirty-five Beecham," Moira murmured, prodding her scattered brain for the reason behind the address' familiarity. She pulled off the road into the opening of a side street and texted back. *Got him. Thanks.*

A few minutes later, she turned onto Beecham Street and

spotted Tom's Prius in the driveway of a brick-sided ranch with a well-tended front yard. Something shifted in her head and a hard fist of nausea punched at her gut. This was Naomi's house. That's why the address had seemed familiar, because it was *hers*. Tom had come here, to the woman he'd almost chosen over Moira, to a woman who was far better suited to the life he'd wanted than she had ever been.

She stared dully at the soft light seeping through the curtained window. Why had he come here of all places? Had he sought out the tenderness of another woman's embrace as solace for his bruised ego? Was he even now making love to Naomi, his mouth tasting her skin, his hands seeking the spots that would bring her the most pleasure?

Bile burned its way swiftly up Moira's esophagus. She swallowed it down through shallow breaths. Tears pricked at her eyes and she shook her head. No, it wasn't staying down. She fumbled with the handle of the driver's side door, pushed it open, and emptied her stomach onto the pavement outside her car, retching in silent heaves fed by the sorrow ripping through her chest. He'd left her. Ki's mercy, he'd left her and fled straight into the arms of another woman.

And she'd pushed him there as surely as a raging forest fire drove wildlife before it, the smoke and heat and roar of the flames a terrifying impetus for movement.

She searched for a napkin with trembling hands, wiped her face clean, spat the last of the sick onto the pavement. Well, there was nothing for it, then. Oh, she could mop the floor with Naomi as she'd threatened to before, but what good would it do? Tom had chosen and in that choosing, Moira had lost him.

The thought echoed in her head as she executed a k-turn and drove unthinkingly to his apartment. *I've lost me Tom*, a small voice said, *lost me Tom, lost me Tom.*

She made it inside the tiny home they'd begun to make without remembering one jot of the drive there, and that was as far as she could go. Her legs gave out just inside the door. She dropped to her hands and knees on the carpeted floor, put her back to the wall, and sat there, too numb to process the reality of his betrayal.

Hours passed or maybe a few scant minutes. A key in the lock startled her out of the hazy numbness engulfing her. The door opened, the lights flipped on, and she raised a hand, warding off its brightness.

"Jesus, Moira, what's wrong?" Tom knelt beside her, his hands gentle as he brushed the wetness from her cheeks. "Are you hurt?"

A bitter laugh escaped her raw, parched throat. Hurt was one word for what he'd done to her. Devastation might be a better one.

He scooped her up in his arms and stood, grunting as he lifted her weight high against his chest. A light floral fragrance tickled her nose and she gagged. That was Naomi's perfume. He'd really done it, then, and here was the proof. She should've been livid, should've kicked and screamed and railed at him for cheating on her. Instead, she lay like a lump, ensconced in the strength of his arms, her temper failing her for the first time in a century.

Tom nudged the bathroom door open and set her gently on the closed toilet seat. She shut her eyes and slumped there, unable to face his perfidy. The heater whirred to life. Water splashed in the sink. His fingers tilted her face up and a warm cloth chafed gently across her skin, cleansing it.

The sharp slap of wet cloth hitting tile sounded a moment before Tom's hands smoothed her hair back. "Did you find the woman who hurt you?"

It took her a minute to understand what he was asking and a minute more to formulate a coherent response. "Margaret found her."

"And you took care of it?"

"No," she said flatly. "Rue texted me, told me you were missing."

"Shit." His breath puffed across her damp face. "I forgot all about that."

Of course, he had. In his rush to reunite with the fair Naomi, he'd likely forgotten he lived in a small town that was easy to canvass and twice as quick with gossip. Word of his straying had probably already reached Rebecca by now, spread by gleeful lips all too eager to witness the fall of the mighty Moira Firebrand.

"I'm sorry," he continued. "I didn't mean to worry you."

Her eyes popped open and the sharp retort gathering on her tongue died a flaming death. His expression held genuine remorse and his hands were so tender as he ranged them over her hair and shoulders and arms, the tears rose again. She sniffed them away and fixed her gaze on the corner of the counter.

He pressed a soft kiss to her forehead. "You're chilled to the bone. Let me get you into a hot shower, then bed. A nice, long rest will do us both good. We can talk through everything in the morning when it's not so fresh in our minds."

"Ye wish to..." Her throat choked on the words, refusing them as surely as her mind refused the reality of his actions. She cleared her throat and tried again. "Ye still want me?"

His laugh was short and nearly humorless. "I never stopped."

She sat still while he worked her clothes off over limp limbs. He bundled her hair into a knot on the back of her head, secured it with a barrette, and cut the water on, letting it warm as he shimmied out of his own clothing. Moments later, he guided her under the streaming water, turning her back to it as he wrapped his arms around her.

She buried her nose in his chest, reveling in the male scent of him, in the smoothness of his skin under the crisp hairs scattered over his firm muscles. This might be the last time she'd have the pleasure of holding him so close and she wanted to savor it, wanted to fill herself with him and everything he was before he abandoned her for...

Moira sniffed again and wild relief flooded through her, shunting aside the misery. That was his scent on his skin and his alone. It was his tangy soap she smelled, not the floral stuff Naomi squirted all over herself every blessed morning. Near hysterical laughter bubbled up. "Ye didn't cheat on me."

"What?" He drew away and gaped at her. "I'd never do that."

"Ye were there, Tom. I saw yer car in her driveway..."

His glare cut her off in mid-word. "I needed a friend and she's the closest one I have here next to you. Hell, Moira. Pretty much all we talked about *was* you."

She dropped her gaze to his chest. "Oh."

"Yes, oh. I was this close to leaving you." He sucked in a breath, blew it out in one harsh puff of air. "I nearly did, but I just...couldn't. I stopped by her house on my way back through, on impulse really, and we talked, that's it. You have to believe me."

"I do," she whispered.

"Really." His voice was flat and hard and so far from accepting her answer, a shiver of dread ran down her spine. "That'd be a first."

"I do, Tom. For one, yer smell's all yer own, and for another, yer word's good. If ye say all ye did was talk, I believe ye, though I'm sorry ye felt the need to run to her instead of waiting for me to return and soothe yer hurt."

"Hunh."

He snagged the soap and bathed her without uttering another word, and for the first time since she'd met him, her presence had no apparent effect on his body. They finished bathing and dried quickly, the silence stretching between them muted by the fall of water into the tub and then nothing.

After, he tucked her into bed, secured the apartment, and slid in behind her, spooning her smaller body with his larger one. His steadfast loyalty should've comforted her. If not that, then she should've found a large measure of relief in his presence. She stared blankly into the darkened room as his breaths deepened and his arm relaxed where it draped over her waist. The knot of emotion strangling her wasn't in any way relief and it comforted her not one whit.

EIGHTEEN

SOMETHING woke Tom from a deep sleep.

He struggled to place it through the groggy fog enveloping his brain. The apartment was quiet and dark. No moonlight streamed through the curtains. James always complained about the streetlights flooding the campus, but those were on the other side of the building and never bothered Tom.

Moira inhaled sharply and rolled, fitting herself firmly into the cradle of his arms, her back to his front. He brushed his cheek over her hair. She'd looked awful when he'd come home, as if she'd been crying for hours, and her skin had been so colorless, for a moment he'd panicked, thinking she'd injured herself again and had lost too much blood to make it to the hospital on her own.

What he wouldn't give for her to never risk herself again.

It was bound to happen sooner or later, though, and it wasn't right for him to stifle her sense of duty or her need to protect herself and the family they were making. His talk with Naomi had pounded that lesson home. If he could just get Moira to wait until after the baby was born...

Her breath hitched on a sharp inhale. "Hannah," she said, her voice a hoarse whisper.

The fog lifted abruptly. Tom raised himself on one elbow and fumbled for the bedside lamp's switch. Light flooded the room, illuminating Moira's flushed skin.

Her hands knotted into white-knuckled fists in the blankets. "No," she said. "No, baby, don't."

A nightmare. He sat up and pushed the covers away, searching through his woefully limited medical knowledge for a way to help her. Was he supposed to try to wake her or was he supposed to let her work through the nightmare on her own?

She grunted as her body jerked, throwing her flat, and her back arched off the mattress. Her chest heaved with each breath and sweat broke out along her skin. Her face twisted into a raw grimace he'd seen one time too many after her leg had been slashed nearly to the bone.

He placed a firm hand on her arm. "Moira, sweetheart? Wake up. You're having a nightmare."

She sank into the mattress and her head rolled along her pillow. "Get away, Siobhan. Run, baby. *Run.*"

Her voice broke on the desperate plea. A tear streaked out of the corner of one tightly closed eye, and Tom decided that was enough. Whatever she was dreaming about, whatever was running through her mind, it needed to end now. "Wake up, Moira. Come on, now. Wake up for me."

She grabbed her leg and screamed, the piercing cry dwindling into harsh, racking sobs. "Hannah. Me Hannah. No. No! *Siobhan!*"

Clarity struck Tom with the force of a boulder. Hannah and Siobhan were her daughters, and Moira was dreaming about their deaths. He breathed around the horror filling him. She hadn't talked about them at all after the one time he'd asked her, and he hadn't found the nerve to push her, hadn't been able to force that pain on her again. Maybe he should've. He stared helplessly at her thrashing body. Maybe if he had, he'd know what to do now when her mind appeared to be lost in a hell she'd obviously witnessed.

Her body jerked once more before stilling. "Tom?"

He scooted closer and gathered her into his arms. "I'm

here, sweetheart. I'm here."

"Tom?" Her hands groped along his body and she shuddered. "So much blood."

Fear squeezed his chest in a fierce, unshakable grip. *Shit.* She was still trapped wherever her mind had taken her. "There's no blood," he said, his voice shaky. He cleared his throat, tightened his hold on her. "Time to wake up, sweetheart."

"No, there's..." She shook her head in frantic twists and her fingernails dug into his chest, cutting the skin. "Don't, Tom. *No!* Not...not..."

She placed her hands flat on his chest and shoved him, hard. "Get off, get off, *get off.*"

He rolled away from her, heart pounding, muscles aching from the force of her push, and slid off the bed onto the carpeted floor. His phone. Rebecca would know what to do, maybe Margaret. He fumbled along the nightstand, cursed long and low under his breath. He'd left it in the friggin' living room next to his glasses. Why in God's name was the damn thing never near when he needed it?

Moira sat straight up in the bed on a low gasp. Her eyes popped open, staring unfocused at the nightmare playing out in her mind. "I'm sorry, Tom, so sorry. I never told ye. Me heart."

She slumped limply onto the bed, her chest barely rising with each shallow breath. He scrambled his way onto the bed and searched for the pulse in her wrist, and heaved a relieved sigh at the steady throb. What the hell? Siobhan and Hannah he could understand, but what had *he* been doing in that nightmare?

He scrubbed a weary hand over his face. There was nothing he could do other than take care of her and pray the nightmare was over. In the morning, he'd draw her out, even if it meant going toe to toe with her. Some things were too important to ignore. Reliving your children's deaths was one of them.

A shiver ran over his skin. He pulled the covers up and tucked them carefully around her now peaceful form, padded into the living room and flipped the thermostat up a notch. They had a lot to hash out tomorrow, a lot that needed sorting, and for once, she would by golly listen to him.

THE NEXT MORNING, Moira woke slowly. Her muscles ached from head to toe and a low throb pounded in her temple. She grimaced and rubbed at it with numb fingers. Daughters never got sick and rarely suffered the aftereffects of any trouble they'd found the night before. What had she done to deserve stiff joints and what felt like the beginnings of the nasty hangovers her mortal friends were always going on about?

A warm arm slipped around her waist and pulled her into Tom's chest. She relaxed into him, closing her eyes against the brightening morning light. He was still here. Thank the Lady Ki.

"You're awake," he said.

"I am." She twisted around and risked opening a single eye. His face was haggard and pale, the laugh lines around his eyes and mouth deepened into dark grooves. "What's wrong?"

"Nothing. I..." His mouth pressed into a thin line. "It was a long night."

Her heart clenched into a tight ball of fear in her chest. She rolled onto her side away from him and cupped a hand over her eyes. "Do we have to talk about this now?"

"Yes," he said, and his voice was so hard, so firm, dread shivered down her spine. "You had a nightmare, something about Siobhan and Hannah."

The dread morphed into full-blown panic. She shifted in the bed, sat up next to him, and cupped a hand over his shoulder, searching his face for the damage she was sure she'd done. "Did I harm ye?"

"A little." He covered her hand and attempted a smile that faded as soon as it touched his mouth. "You watched them die, didn't you."

"I did, and I suppose ye want the whole of it now."

"I'd like that very much," he said softly. He opened his arms

205

and drew her down beside him, holding her close as his hand stroked over her hair and down her back, over and over again, comforting her in a way no man ever had before. "You told me once that they died in a pointless war."

"Aye, they did." She buried her face in his chest. His heart thumped under her cheek, *boom, boom*, and she measured its steady pace with each of her breaths. "Or rather, in a battle in the middle of a long, drawn out conflict over who could control the land, the English interlopers or the Irish who'd bled for her. Hannah was sixteen, barely into her womanhood, and she'd followed in her mother's footsteps. Hot-headed, she was, and spoiling for a fight."

"She must've been something," Tom murmured.

"She was. Beautiful as they come, was Hannah. Had a voice like a songbird, so sweet and pure and clear, but she never used it, not like she should've."

Her voice trailed into a thin silence. His hand stilled on her spine. "What happened?"

She huffed out a laugh. "What always happens in Ireland. The Irish Republican Brotherhood had been planning an uprising for months as yet another bloody attempt to force the English out. Hannah favored a young man, a member of the Óglaigh na hÉireann, the Volunteers, a forerunner of Ireland's modern military forces. She disguised herself and tagged along after him a time too many, and the next thing I knew, the three of us were in the middle of a feckin' war zone."

"The Easter Rising," he guessed.

She nodded. "One in a long line of many such rebellions. When her young man caught word of the rising, Hannah was determined to fight, and because she was so young, Siobhan and I went with her. Had a mind to protect her or some such. Never turns out well, does it."

"I guess that depends on the perspective. If I could protect you from this hurt, I'd do it in a heartbeat."

Her heart melted into a puddle. "Oh, Tom. There's no

protecting a mother's heart from the pain of a child's loss."

"Doesn't stop me from wanting to." He pressed a tender kiss to her forehead. "So Hannah acted impetuously, as her mother often does, and dragged you and Siobhan into the rebellion."

"That's the short of it. The longer tale is a bit bloodier. We were trapped in an alley, pinned down by English snipers on one side and the rebels on the other." A shaky breath shuddered out of her. "Guns drawn, heads down, taking what little cover we could find. We crouched together while a hailstorm of bullets and the Goddess knows what rained down all around us, mostly from the English. They had field artillery, ye know. Bloody Brits. We were discussing possible escape routes when Hannah's young man ran by the end of the alley with a gang of other bucks. She sprinted off, fast as a hare."

Moira swallowed the helpless fury. Useless to wish Hannah had listened when the deed was done and the past long written in stone. "A bullet caught her in the chest as soon as she stepped into the open. Siobhan and I raced after her, and I was hit." Her hand inched down to the place on her thigh where the bullet had torn through skin and muscle before lodging in her femur. Long healed. Never forgotten. "I went down, and in the doing, happened to glance 'round at what should've been our protected backside. They were gone and we were sunk. I told Siobhan to save herself. Me, I'm too tough to die, that's what I told her."

"No one's that tough, Moira, not even an ornery immortal Daughter."

The edge of humor in his voice eased some of the hurt filling her. "So ye claim, but I survived to tell the tale and me daughters didn't."

"You tried to save them, though."

"I did. Siobhan reached Hannah and pulled her into what little protection the alley afforded while I crawled toward them, dragging me leg along. I heard the boom of the artillery. I swear to ye, Tom, I watched it hit the street not ten feet from where me daughters were, Hannah cradled in Siobhan's lap. Siobhan was watching me, and I was watching the shell, praying it was a dud even as the feckin' thing exploded and ripped through the only two people I'd ever loved enough to..."

She choked on a sob, sniffed back the tears gathering in her eyes. "They were gone in a flash. The explosion loosened the side of one of the buildings and a chunk of it landed on me legs."

"Jesus," he breathed.

"I lived, though I don't know the whys or hows. I woke up weeks later in hospital, chained to a feckin' bed, interrogated as soon as I came around. What was I doing in that alley? Was I part of the Rising? Who else was with me? That sort of thing." She snorted. "As if I'd give out that kind of information to the feckin' English. Me legs were mangled, but they were healing. Soon as they had, I escaped and made me way to the other end of Ireland. Hid meself away and only came out when the People needed me. I had nothing to live for, not with me daughters dead and buried, and I couldn't stand the thought of leading another astray."

He squeezed her gently. "Moira the Reluctant."

"And before that I was a firebrand. Headstrong. Stubborn. Always itching for a fight and never afraid to speak out for what I thought was right and just." She shook her head and bit back the shame clawing at her heart. "Me father was a rebel, I was a rebel, and me daughters died because I didn't know well enough to teach them otherwise."

He was silent for a long moment. "Do you really think you could've stopped Hannah from running down that alley?"

"I could've kept her from being there at all," she retorted, her voice as hard as stone. "Rebecca wished me to relocate to the States closer to her. Jerusha was still young then, not three full years past sixty, and Charlotte wasn't much older, but no. I stayed stubbornly fixed to the country of me birth, following as recklessly in me father's footsteps as Hannah did in mine. It was me fault they died that day. Now ye know the truth of what I am."

"What is it you're supposed to be?" he asked gently.

She sat up and pushed away from him off the bed, turning her back so he couldn't see the hateful truth shining as sure as sin from her eyes. "Not the kind of woman ye want to raise yer daughter, Thomas. When she's born, I'll turn her care over to yer kinder hands and ye'll make certain she's not a thing like her mother."

"Moira, sweetheart. Don't say that."

"I speak only what truth I know. Ye'll do right by her, where I'd bring her nothing but pain. I've known it for the longest time. Much as I'd like it to be different, I'm not a fit parent, nor am I a fit lover." She forced herself to walk away from him, forced her limbs to move around a bone deep, aching sorrow. She paused at the bathroom's door and said, "I'll take care of ye, Tom. Never fear I'll leave ye absent what ye need for living, but don't rely on me for the softer things. Those were burnt out of me long ago."

She stepped into the bathroom and shut the door behind herself with trembling hands, not risking a peek at where he lay on the bed. What a fool she was, to think she could have him. She rubbed a hand over her chest where the softer emotions she'd claimed were absent wavered and throbbed. A bitter laugh escaped her throat. Two lies to the same man. She loved him so much, had fallen so quickly under his gentle charm. What was she to do now, with him too kind to push her away and another daughter taking root in her womb?

Hard as she searched for an answer, it eluded her, haunting her long after she'd finished preparing for the day ahead.

209

NINETEEN

TOM ROLLED onto his back and slung a forearm across his eyes. That had not gone the way he'd hoped. Then again, what had he expected? Moira was the most unpredictable woman he knew. Normally, he enjoyed her mercurial nature. It kept him on his toes and made her unexpected humor all the more attractive. Today, though, it was irritating. How had they gone from her telling him about her daughters to her essentially telling him it was over between them?

So much for smoothing over their argument.

He wasn't ready to give up on her, not by a long shot, no matter what she said. Surely she wouldn't have stuck by him if she didn't have feelings for him, especially when she thought he'd turned to another woman.

Which he hadn't, exactly. Seeking advice from a friend wasn't cheating. Yes, he should've waited for Moira to come back and hashed it out with her, or if he'd really needed to talk, he should've tracked down James or Phil or even George. Instead, he'd chosen to sort everything out with the woman Moira thought he still wanted.

Tom ran his hands through his hair. Yup, he was an idiot.

The shower turned on in the bathroom. He grimaced at the tightly closed bathroom door. Idiots didn't deserve to slip into the shower with the women they loved, and Moira hadn't exactly acted like she wanted him around.

Breakfast, then. *That* he could handle without screwing up.

He slipped into a pair of loose pajama bottoms and a sweatshirt and padded barefoot into the living room. He scooped up his phone on the way by the table and checked it one-handed while he filled the coffeemaker with water. Two missed calls and a text from Naomi. He thumbed the text up.

May have something. Meet me at the Archives.?

He checked the text's time against the coffeemaker's settings. She'd texted over an hour ago. What was so urgent that it had to be taken care of early on a Saturday morning?

Moira walked into the kitchen dressed in fresh pajamas, her skin glowing, her hair still wet, and poked her head into the fridge. "I can cook this morning, if ye like."

"I've got it."

She peered at him over her shoulder, her eyes narrowed into blue slits. "Ye're only saying that so ye can sneak green food onto me plate."

"Would I do that?"

"Aye, ye would." She closed the fridge's door and leaned against it. "What have ye planned for today?"

He glared down at his phone. "Well, I didn't have a damn thing planned outside of spending time with you."

"And then?"

"Naomi texted."

She crossed her arms over her chest. "I see."

"It's not what you think, Moira." He eyed her neutral expression and bit back a sigh. "She wants to meet at the Archives. Says she may have something."

"Did she, now?" She cocked an eyebrow. "Is that some kind of new slang for *I want to fuck ye blind?*"

"Funny."

Moira's wide mouth twitched into a half-grin. "What does the fair Naomi have?"

"No idea, honest." He dropped the phone onto the counter and leaned back, mirroring Moira's pose. "While we're on the subject of Naomi, I wanted to apologize for going to see her. It was totally innocent, but I can see how you'd think I was turning to her and away from you."

"Yer word last night was enough, Thomas."

"Was it?" he asked softly. "Prove it, then."

Her eyes widened as she gaped at him. "How in blazes am I supposed to prove a thing like that other than telling ye?"

"For starters, you can come over here and greet me the way an almost-wife greets her almost-husband," he said mildly.

Her jaws snapped shut. "Are ye playing me?"

"Never." He held his arms out to her and waited patiently while her expression shifted from wary to hopeful to acceptance. She stepped over, as carefully as if she were stepping through a minefield, and slid her arms around his waist, resting her head on his chest over the steady beat of his heart. He gathered her close and rubbed his chin along the top of her head. "That's more like it."

She *mmmd* out a laugh and the knot of tension gathered in his gut loosened and disappeared. The urge to tell her how he felt bubbled up in its place. He choked it down with a resigned sigh. Better to wait until she was ready to hear it or at least until she'd gotten over this sudden need she had to distance herself from him.

"I want to work this out," he murmured. "You and me and the baby, the claiming. I want to build a life with you. Don't you want that?"

She rubbed her cheek against his chest. "I do, Tom. More than ye can ever understand."

"Try me."

"I claimed ye, didn't I?"

"Maybe I want more." He cupped the back of her head, holding her as close as he could, enjoying the simple feel of her body pressed to his. "Maybe I want true love and a happy ever after."

"I told ye not to expect the softer things from me, Tom."

"Don't tell me you don't care for me," he warned. "I'll know you're lying."

"I don't, not as I should." Her sigh warmed his chest through the thin cloth of his sweatshirt. "I care as much as I can, though, and I promise, it's no small measure."

"I want more. I want you to care for me so much, you'll never be able to leave me. I want you to stick around and help me raise our daughter, and if God or the Lady Ki or whoever's out there blesses us with more children, I want you to be there for that, too. You said you'd never leave me wanting, that you'd never let me go without the things I need."

"I did," she said, her voice small and muffled.

"I need you."

"Tom."

"I do, Moira, so much." He brushed a kiss over the top of her head. "Just think about it, ok?"

She huffed out a small laugh. "I could hardly do elsewise."

He let her go and fixed breakfast, leaving out any questionable green foods, and coaxed her into laughter as they ate. After, he texted Naomi, arranged a meeting time, and hurried through his morning ablutions, driven by curiosity as much as anything. By the time he was finished, Moira was ready. He found her on the living room couch, scowling down at her phone.

"What's wrong, sweetheart?"

"Margaret..." Her mouth twisted into a grimace. "It's nothing, Thomas. A minor glitch is all."

He sighed, but let it go. Rome wasn't built in a day. Insisting on her opening up to him overnight would only drive a wedge between them.

A few minutes later, they were out the door walking hand in hand toward the Archives, bundled up in jackets and hats and gloves to ward off the late fall chill. They passed through security and made their way to the central research room. Naomi stood at one of the long wooden tables, sorting through two archival boxes. She glanced up as they approached and called out a friendly greeting.

"Feckin' morning people," Moira muttered. "Always so damn cheerful."

"Be nice," Tom said.

"I know, I know, she's yer blasted friend. Wouldn'ta been if I'd got here first, mind ye."

He grinned and slung an arm around her shoulders. "I love that sharp tongue of yours. Come on, sweetheart. Let's see what Naomi's got for us."

She marched toward the table, carrying him along in her wake. "Spillfeite."

Naomi nodded coolly. "I see the lovebirds have made up."

"If y'all can't play nice, I'll make you both stand in the corner." Tom jerked his chin at the boxes. "What's up?"

"I was thinking about what you said last night, about Begni's letter?"

Moira stuffed her hands in the pockets of her cords. "Would this be before or after ye were talking about me?"

"After," Tom said firmly. "Now behave or no make up sex."

Moira shot an appalled glare at him, then pressed her mouth into a thin line.

Naomi cleared her throat and glanced down, a small smile gracing her mouth. "This box holds material we received about three years before you joined us, Tom, not long after I took over. The items were smuggled out of Turkey by a Daughter working at the Konya Archaeological Museum. Apparently, she ran across a storage box full of what she thought was correspondence and immediately recognized a key phrase." She inhaled deeply. "The Bones of the Just."

"And ye've been sitting on this the whole time?" Moira asked.

Naomi shook her head. "It just clicked last night when Tom

mentioned that Ruanna was having a hard time deciphering the copy of Begni's letter. *Deciphering.*" She glanced between them, then threw her hands up. "It's a code, a cipher. That's why Ruanna couldn't translate all of it."

Tom rubbed a finger over his chin and glanced at Moira. "She wondered why it was written in archaic Hebrew."

"Aye," Moira said. "Made a big deal over that one phrase, as I recall."

"I'll ask her about it. James, too." Tom turned back to Naomi. "So, what's so exciting about these boxes?"

"Oh, quite a bit." Naomi flipped through the files holding the unknown Daughter's smuggling efforts, stuck a placeholder in between two, and pulled one out with a triumphant flourish. "I think this contains the reply to Begni's letter or is part of a series of correspondence between her and another, and I think somewhere in here, there might even be a key to the cipher, if that's what we're dealing with."

Moira gaped at her. "Ye're feckin' kidding me."

Naomi grinned. "Not a bit."

"Holy Mother of God," Tom said. "How did you figure that out?"

"I didn't. The Daughter who smuggled this material out of Turkey included a note that she'd tried to translate some of the correspondence, but couldn't. She speculated that they were in code and noted that one was written to Begni regarding the Bones of the Just."

"It can't be that easy," Moira said.

"Nothing ever is." Naomi opened the folder and smoothed it flat, keeping her hands well away from the ancient paper. "Care to have a go at it?"

Moira leaned closer and frowned. "It's the same feckin' gibberish Ruanna was drooling over."

Tom sighed. "Hebrew?"

"Possibly," Naomi hedged. "I never had it translated, relying instead on the notes sent along with this material for cataloging

215

purposes. But, I never forgot it. Some things nag."

Moira slid a rueful glance at Tom. "Don't I know it."

He slid a hand around her waist and squeezed gently. "You're not getting out of eating green things, sweetheart, no matter how much you complain." To Naomi, he said, "This is a fantastic find."

"I wish I'd connected it with your work here earlier." Naomi shook her head, sending blonde curls swinging around her shoulders. "And that I'd cataloged it better. Perhaps you would've found it already if I had."

"You remembered it now. That's what's important."

"So what now?" Moira asked. "Call Ruanna and have her translate it?"

"Nope," Tom said with a grin. "It's Saturday and I want to spend time with my fiancée. This can wait until Monday."

"Slacker," Moira muttered.

"Pragmatist," he countered. "Let's get this to my office and lock it up. Meet us here first thing Monday morning, Naomi?"

Naomi flipped the file closed and returned it to it's place in the storage box. "Oh, no, Tom. You don't need my help."

"Aye, we do." Moira reached out and snagged one of the boxes, sliding it across the table with a steady heave. "Once Ruanna's done, we might have some other clues to follow up on and yer knowledge of recent acquisitions could come in handy."

"Easier than sorting through the blasted catalog," Tom agreed. "Besides, we miss you around here."

Moira sputtered out a laugh. "Speak for yerself, Thomas."

Naomi smiled. "Some things never change, do they?"

And some things changed a lot. Tom eased the box out of Moira's arms and hefted it against his chest as Naomi lifted the other one and followed him and Moira to his office. Just a few months earlier, he'd been blind-sided by Moira's beauty and sharp temper, and now, he enjoyed having them as an everyday part of his life. He listened to her and Naomi's discussion of the possibilities contained within the two boxes they carried and pondered the many possibilities he'd been blessed with since meeting his wild Irishwoman.

AT SUNDOWN, Rebecca dressed in dark clothing and kissed Robert goodbye. An errand, she said, and knew even as she uttered the half-truth that he wouldn't accept it at face value. He'd known her too long and knew when not to pry. She'd tell him. Of course, she would, but not yet, not until she'd fully come to terms with the vision the Woman had given her.

Tellowee was draped in the frigid darkness of early December when Rebecca stepped into her back yard. She tugged on a black knit cap, tucked her too-light hair under it, stuffed her hands into thin, leather gloves. The security lights flashed on as soon as she walked onto the patio. She ignored them as she continued across the yard through the gate in the wooden fence surrounding it and across the street into the poorly lit communal playground.

She kept her pace casual, a Daughter out taking a nighttime stroll, sorting out her thoughts. Nothing suspicious. Nothing to earn a second glance, not in a town where half the younger residents were sneaking into the homes of the other half for good-natured fun or good-natured sex, depending on the ages of those involved. She veered toward the edge of the woods on the other side of the playground, then melted into its shadows.

When she judged her distance at halfway through, she veered again and circled around, laying down several paths along the well-worn trails should anyone dare follow her. An hour into her journey, she was satisfied with the misdirection she'd given. She stepped off the path onto a thick carpet of pine needles and launched herself upward, catching a low-hanging tree limb.

The branch was thick and sturdy. She pulled herself onto it and balanced lightly at its base while she studied the trees around her. Thin moonlight filtered into the upper branches of the tree, providing just enough light for her to make out a path from the one she'd claimed to the next one over. She climbed up, scooted out onto another limb, and swung herself into the next tree.

A memory rose, of Bobby playing Tarzan among these same trees, and Rebecca smiled. Little monkey. He'd always loved the woods, loved playing warrior in them long before Indigo broke his heart and, in trying to outrun the pain, he'd become one.

The smile faded as Rebecca progressed steadily through the tightly-packed woods and finally dropped down twenty feet behind her target. She studied the small, unassuming house with its unadorned yard. It sat on the outskirts of Tellowee, its lot surrounded by the forest she stood in. One interior light was on, shining through the room's lone window like a beacon against the night. A figure was outlined in the window, rocking back and forth with its head down. Rebecca peered carefully around the house and the sides of the yard. Nothing stirred in the night's black depths.

She made her way with carefully placed steps to the back door and knocked softly. It opened a bare slit, revealing a slice of a young woman wearing a black turtleneck and jeans. Her dark hair was twisted into thin braids swinging loosely around her unlined mocha skin.

"The hour grows late," Rebecca said, her voice a scant whisper. "Is your charge well?"

The woman nodded. "She sleeps quietly, safe within my family's embrace."

"Allow me entrance, sister, so that I may also watch over her."

The woman swung the door wide and stepped back, waiting until Rebecca entered before closing the door firmly and locking it. "Is something wrong, Director?"

Rebecca slid her cap off and tucked it into a pocket of her jacket. "Nothing out of the ordinary, Luna. I had a sudden urge to visit the Oracle."

"She's resting. Hasn't moved an inch all day." Luna turned

218

and led the way through the minimal kitchen into a carpeted hallway flanked by stark, white walls. "We've tried everything. Singing, reading, talking to her. Yesterday, MaryJean and Honor set up a small table in there and tried to get the Oracle to play poker with them."

"Did it work?"

Luna snorted. "What do you think?"

"I'm sure it didn't hurt to try." It was at least as creative as any of the other methods they'd used to wake her, in times past and present. The only thing that had worked so far was James whispering in the sleeping woman's ear. Somehow, Rebecca didn't think Maya would appreciate having him try that again.

Luna poked her head into the only lit room, startling the Handmaiden reading in the rocking chair into dropping her book. "Director's here. Take the back, will you?"

Luna moved on without waiting for a reply. One door down, she opened the door and jerked her chin at the two Handmaidens seated on either side. "Director needs a mo."

The two women rose silently and filed out between Luna and Rebecca, murmuring a polite greeting to Rebecca as they passed. She slipped inside and sank wearily into one of the vacated chairs, ignoring the door closing quietly behind her.

The Oracle lay on her back, her eyes closed, her olive-toned face peaceful as she slept. The Handmaidens had washed her hair earlier and spread it out behind her in a dark fan of midnight curls. One of the Handmaidens would braid it later and tuck it out of the way. Another would apply henna to the Oracle's fingertips or paint designs across her hands, and yet another would give her a pedi.

Rebecca had fulfilled her duty in the same manner when she was young, well before bottled nail polish was even a glimmer of a possibility. She'd tended the Oracle's body, watched over it with the keen eye of a warrior, and sat many hours by the woman's side talking herself hoarse in the faint hope of gaining a single response.

It had never happened, not once.

She leaned forward and laid a hand over the Oracle's still one where it rested on the bed alongside her thigh. "This might be my last visit. The Woman came to me not long ago and warned me that my time among the People is nearly at its end. I wanted so much to see you awaken, wanted so much to know who you were."

A bitter ache rose, clogging Rebecca's throat with useless tears. She swallowed them down. Tears were an indulgence she couldn't afford, not now when the Prophecy was so close to being fulfilled. Not now when the People were about to lose one of their strongest leaders and she had yet to train another to take her place.

That would change soon, but for tonight, she needed the comfort of the woman who'd been one of the People's most enduring legacies. They had so little they could cling to as the world changed continually around them, as it ever did. Soon, though, perhaps the People could truly be free of the curse holding them forever apart from the remainder of humanity.

Rebecca let her hand fall away and tucked it into her lap next to her other hand. "We're sifting through the Archives, searching for Sanctuary's location. The Bones of the Just. That's the only clue we have right now. I suppose it will have to do."

She continued talking, outlining the changes to her family, the hopes she held for the future, and for the People. She talked until her voice thinned and her throat dried, until the bitterness hounding her since the Woman's visit drained steadily away. When her heart emptied itself of words, she stood and pressed a gentle kiss to the Oracle's forehead.

"There's so much to do still, so many preparations to make. *The Shadow approaches.* If the Woman had been more specific, I'd know what to prepare for." Rebecca sighed and eased away from the bed and the woman it held. "I hope you awaken soon. The People need you. They need what knowledge you hold of our past. Please, I..."

The futility of her need halted the plea. Even if the Oracle woke, Dr. Phillips said the chances of her being mentally undamaged were slim. After all those centuries spent resting in a coma, first in the grotto where she'd been found long before Rebecca's birth, and then wherever she could be hidden and protected, and finally here, in Tellowee; after all that time, her mind was certain to've withered, even if her body had not. The Oracle couldn't help the People. That remained to those who were yet among the living.

Rebecca smoothed her hair back and rubbed the nape of her neck as she made her way to the door. A soft hiss came from the bed. She turned and searched the room for the noise's origins. The sound came again, from near the head of the Oracle's bed. Rebecca peeked under it, found not even a dust bunny, and levered herself into a stand, frowning as she tried to place the sound.

The woman's lips parted on a soft gasp and her eyes flew open.

Rebecca froze in place, one hand clutching the edge of the footboard, the other clenched into a fist at her side.

"Gulnar?" The Oracle blinked rapidly and her dark eyes darted around the room, landing on Rebecca. "Gulnar nadji?" she demanded. "Aza nadji olnena?"

The last word trailed off as the Oracle's eyes rolled back and she arched off the mattress, her body shaking violently.

Rebecca leapt forward and caught the Oracle as she twisted perilously close to the edge of the bed. "Handmaidens!"

Luna burst into the room followed by two Handmaidens, pushing Rebecca out of the way. They braced themselves along the edge of the bed, blocking Rebecca's view. Two other Handmaidens rushed in. Rebecca slipped out, leaving them as much room as they needed. She placed a hand over her racing heart and breathed deeply, willing herself to find calm.

The Oracle had awakened, if only for a moment, and she'd spoken. Clearly, concisely, and in a language that seemed achingly familiar, though Rebecca couldn't place it for the life of her. She waited in the hallway out of the way, listening intently to the Handmaidens' quiet conversation as they cared for the Oracle, hoping against hope that the woman was fine.

A few minutes later, Luna staggered into the open doorway, her face pasty under the natural dark tones of her skin. "She's awake. Seizure wore her out, but she's really awake."

A smile bloomed across Rebecca's face. "Blessed be Ki."

"Yeah," Luna said faintly. "Many, many blessings."

"We've waited so long." Rebecca grasped the other Daughter's shoulder and shook her lightly, spreading some of the happiness zinging through her. "May I see her?"

"Yeah, sure." Luna slumped against the doorframe with a small laugh. "Holy Mother, Director. Never thought I'd live to see this day."

"Nor did I," Rebecca said, and she stepped back into the room holding one of the People's greatest hopes.

LESS THAN THREE WEEKS 'til Christmas and The Omega was hopping. Tom picked at the label of his Duck Rabbit Stout as he glanced around the room, taking in the nearly shoulder to shoulder crowd pressed into the bar's main area. He and Moira had dropped by after supper, hoping for a little relaxation after a long day spent working. She'd made her way to the bar where Sig was leaning, promising to come back after grabbing a bottled water, and had apparently become engrossed in the pre-season college basketball game playing on the overhead television.

He'd wanted to spend time with her, true, but he was just as happy to sit across the bar and catch glimpses through the crowd of her moods swinging back and forth according to how well her team was doing. She slapped her mug down on the bar and wiggled her butt in what he secretly thought of as her happy dance. He sipped his stout, hiding a grin. Now, there was true poetry in motion.

James leaned back in his chair and threaded his fingers together over his stomach. "So, Naomi came through for you, huh."

"Maybe in a big way, though I wish to God she'd waited until Monday to tell me. Do you know, she and Moira dragged me back in to work this afternoon so we could sort through those damn boxes?" Tom shook his head and ignored James' snicker. "Could be good we did, though. There were a couple of things Naomi had forgotten about. A relatively recent translation of Begni's letter, for one."

James' eyebrows shot up. "You're kidding."

"Not a bit. Wish we'd had that two months ago. Problem is, that same section Ruanna tried to translate? The person who did the other translation couldn't figure it out either."

"So it might really be a code then. Too bad there's no key."

"Naomi thinks we can use all those boxes of papers to maybe reconstruct the key." Tom lifted his beer bottle and tilted the top toward James. "That'd be your area, though. Me, I'm still searching for clues to Sanctuary."

James snagged his bottle of beer and took a sip. "No luck, huh?"

"None a'tall. The closest we've come yet is Begni's letter and now the boxes Naomi remembered." Tom slumped into his chair. "It seems like I'm missing something important and it's frustrating as hell. I just don't know what else we can do at this point."

The heavy beat of an alternative metal song ended and a dreamy ballad came on. The lights dimmed in the bar. James and Tom grinned at each other.

"That'd be our cue." James set his beer on the table and stood. "You grabbing Moira?"

Tom risked a glance at her. She was wiggling again, God help him. Tom Junior chose that moment to perk up. "Maybe in a minute."

"Save my beer."

James left the table, threading his way through the crowd angling its way onto the dance floor, and Tom turned his attention back to Moira. The people around her shifted, hiding her from view. He glanced up at the TV. Looked like halftime was coming up. He'd catch her then, see if she wanted to dance. Seemed like a perfect way to segue into the evening's end. A little dancing at their favorite bar, her pressed close against him, his hand on her waist under her sweater, and maybe a kiss or two to set the stage. Then later, it'd be just him and her making love all night long.

He scrubbed his hands down his thighs as his stomach twisted into a knot. Stupid to be nervous when they'd had sex so many times before. This time, though, it was a little different. This time, he knew he loved her. God, he hoped she was beginning to love him, too, at least a little.

The crowd parted and Tom sighed. Moira was standing toe to toe with Sigrid, arguing over who knew what. *Again.* Will pulled his wooden bat out and tapped it on the bar, and a couple of people glanced around, then turned back to their conversations. Business as usual. Tom shook his head and pushed himself out of his chair. Time to go break that up.

A light hand fell on his shoulder and he glanced around. The Daughter with spiky green hair who'd ridden with him and Moira the night of Bobby's kidnapping stood just behind Tom. He turned, facing her, and mustered a friendly smile. "Hey! Long time no see."

The slight smile stretching her bow mouth barely stirred her cold features. "Not quite three weeks. You've been busy."

"Ah, yeah, sort of." Tom rubbed a hand across his nape. The hairs on the back of his neck tingled. Maybe Moira was watching him. He peeked over his shoulder. She'd turned back to the bar and was watching the game again, and he was stuck making polite conversation with a woman he'd met once and whose name he didn't even know. "So, how've you been?"

"Very well, thank you, though I'm about to be much better."

Her hand flashed down and up in a smooth blur. A sharp prick in Tom's side startled him and he flinched.

The Daughter's smile turned deadly. "Come quietly and no one will be hurt."

He jerked away from her instinctively and was hauled back by her firm grip. He shook his arm, trying to dislodge her hand, and earned a sharp poke in his side. "What the hell?"

"Come quietly," the Daughter repeated, "and no one else will be harmed, including your hellcat of a girlfriend. Glance slowly around and wave at the nice woman facing us."

Tom eased his way around, all too aware of the Daughter's knife pricking into his side. A vaguely familiar Asian Daughter was leaning against the bar next to Moira, her oval face impassive. She met Tom's gaze and nodded. He faced the green-haired Daughter. "And?"

"That's the woman who'll kill Moira if you don't come with me now."

The blood rushed from Tom's head. He swayed and caught the back of his chair, steadying himself. Moira, dead, when he'd just found her? A memory pushed to the forefront of his mind, of her lying on a hospital bed, her skin pale, her leg covered in blood. He swallowed down the bile clogging his throat. "Ok, all right. I'll come with you. Just leave her alone."

The Daughter's smile widened. "Good boy."

She led him from the bar, her smile firmly in place, her hand wrapped like a steel band around his arm. He did exactly what she asked him to, when she asked him to do it, following her outside into the crisp air toward the parking lot. What did she want? And why him, a middle-aged archivist who...

His thoughts skidded to a halt. He'd posed exactly that question to Moira the night her brother was kidnapped. What was it she'd said, that he could be a target *because* he was an archivist and might know something about the People that others didn't?

Surely that wasn't right, though.

The Daughter led him to his car. She prodded him into unlocking it and sliding into the driver's seat while she took the back and held the knife between the front seats, jabbing it into his side in an unneeded reminder of who was in charge.

A warm trickle of liquid slid down his side under his shirt. "What do you want?"

"Start the car. Drive one block toward the IECS' main gate and stop in the street. We're picking somebody up."

His mind raced through an array of possibilities. Maybe Moira had seen him leave. Her image popped into his head as he'd last seen her. No, she'd been watching the game and hadn't noticed him leaving, and even if she did and tried to follow, that other Daughter would stop her, wouldn't she? Moira could probably take her, but by the time she'd mopped up that mess, he'd be long gone.

He eased out of the parking lot onto the main road. One block later, he brought the Prius to a stop in the middle of the street. A Daughter of medium height with her glossy sable hair pulled into a perky ponytail opened the passenger's side door and slid in. "Well, hello, lover boy." She twisted around in the seat toward the green-haired Daughter. "Any problems?"

"Not a one. Tommy boy came along quietly once I threatened his mate."

The brunette snorted. "Moira the Reluctant. Wish I'd finished her off the day she came after that useless brother of hers."

Tom's hands tightened on the steering wheel. Well, shit. Margaret hadn't caught the woman who'd attacked Moira and it was entirely his fault. Why had he distracted her away from the chase? Why hadn't he understood her need for vengeance? Why the fuck hadn't he insisted on going along? Next time, he would and that was all there was to it. She'd just have to get used to the idea of a man standing by her side.

If there was a next time.

The brunette leaned forward and traced her fingers along

the inside of Tom's thigh. "I'm itching to give you a matching scar, lover boy. Maybe I'll nick an artery this time and rob that shrill-tempered Irish shrew of another love."

"Viv." The green-haired Daughter's voice was flat and sharp. "We don't have time for your games."

"There's always time for games, darling Hadria."

Hadria snorted and flopped into the back seat, taking the knife with her. Tom's side burned where it had dug into his skin.

"Now, Thomas," Viv said, her voice as peppy as her ponytail, "we need to get into the Archives, so you'll be driving us right along if you ever want to see that witch you're banging again, 'k?"

Tom's chaotic thoughts latched onto a flaw in her plan. "I can't get you into the IECS. You have to have an ID. I have to sign for you. Who's going to believe I'm traveling alone at night with two strange Daughters, especially since everybody knows I'm with Moira?"

Viv grinned. "Everybody'll believe it, all right. After your little visit to Naomi Spillfeite's house last night while the cat was away chasing after *moi*, I made sure to spread the rumor far and wide that you had a little some-some going on the side."

Tom stifled a groan.

"We almost had you last night," Hadria added. "Would've nabbed you on your way out of town if you hadn't turned around and poked your dick in the German."

"Too many eyes," Viv said, her pretty face twisting into a mocking frown. "So many people looking for you last night, Tom. Were you a naughty boy? Do you need a *spanking*?"

"Behave, Viv." Hadria kneed the back of Tom's seat. "Drive. We'll take care of getting ourselves in."

So much for that. Tom drove, winding down the darkened street as silence fell inside the car. He turned into the short driveway fro the IECS' main gate and stopped beside the guard shack, rolling down his window as he did.

Andrea stepped up beside the car and leaned close to the

open window, a friendly smile on her face. "Hey, Tom. You're out late."

"Not quite as late as I intended," he muttered.

Viv eased forward. "Moira asked us to escort him home. Something about a game she was watching and Tom needed his rest?"

Andrea's smile dipped a fraction and Tom's hopes soared. Surely Andrea knew Moira well enough to know she'd never let him go anywhere with two strange women. Surely.

"Is that so." Andrea's expression settled into the hard mask of a guard doing her duty. She peered into the backseat, eyed Hadria for a moment, then straightened. "Regs say you're supposed to sign in here."

Viv graced Andrea with a dimpled smile. "We'll go straight there and back, promise. It'll take five minutes, ten tops."

Andrea nodded. "If it were anybody else, I'd have to see your IDs, but since you're with Tom and Moira sent you, I'll let you pass."

He forced a stiff smile onto his face. This was probably the only time Andrea had ever made an exception to a rule, and it was the one time he needed her to be a stickler. "Thanks, Andrea. See you tomorrow."

She stepped away from the car and waved him through. The gate popped open and slid away from the road, and Tom drove through, his hope of wiggling his way out of the mess he was in dimming with every inch he drove away from Moira.

TWENTY

MOIRA SCOWLED at the tele hanging over the bar and sipped the water Tom had insisted she switch to in case she was preggers. Feckin' water for cripes' sake, as if a blasted ale would harm the babe. Her mate needed a strong lesson on a Daughter's physiology, and she woulda given it to him, too, if he hadn't gotten that determined look in his eyes.

She snorted and swigged another sip of the tasteless fluid. Thomas Fairfax had her wrapped around his little finger. If he so much as twitched, she melted at his feet like a simpering schoolgirl. Useless, it was. What kind of Daughter allowed a man to dictate her actions? Not her, that was who.

Will finished drawing a pint and set it down in front of Sig. Moira ignored the people jostling her and slapped her palm on the top of the bar. "Oy there, Will. Draw me one, there's a good lad."

Will's handsome face creased into a dimpled grin. "Tom said you'd ask and made me promise on my mother's sword that I wouldn't serve you a drop of alcohol until the baby's born or you find out you're not pregnant."

"When did Thomas have time to advise ye on such matters?"

"It's called a phone, Moira."

She shot a narrow-eyed glare at him. "And ye listened to

him over yer own cousin?"

"I'm not getting in the middle of a domestic squabble."

"Domestic..." She huffed out a laugh. "Feck's sake, Will. I'm the Daughter here."

"And he's a concerned mortal who's head over heels in love with you."

Her hands tightened around the bottle and nerves kicked up a flutter low in her gut. "Ye really think so?"

Will braced his forearms on the bar and leaned close to her. "It's pretty obvious. His eyes follow you wherever you go, have for months. Right now, he's sitting over there staring at you with a half-witted smile on his face."

She forced her eyes down to the bar, suppressing the urge to peek over her shoulder and see that for herself. "Is he, now."

"And then there's the fact that he hasn't killed you yet." Will shrugged easily. His green eyes glinted in the dim overhead lighting. "Me? I woulda kicked you out the first time you pulled that high-handed, Daughter-knows-best crap with me."

"Oh, go on with ye then," Moira said, grinning. "Find another to pick on before I remind ye how to treat yer elders."

He straightened, matching her grin with one of his own, and swung around at a call for more beer from a Daughter standing at the other end of the bar.

Moira sipped her water, grimacing at its blandness. She should've known Tom would think of an ale's effect on the babe. She'd be right sure to tell him her body metabolized the alcohol long before it could hit her womb, though she doubted that would sway him.

And when he didn't listen to reason, she'd grit her teeth and not say another blasted word about it. Better for him not to worry, not over a trifle like the occasional pint or three.

Sig elbowed Moira casually as she lifted her mug to her mouth. "Tom," she said behind its rim, her voice barely audible above the noise of the crowd and the song on the jukebox.

Just as casually, Moira turned, putting her back to the bar in time to see Tom slip out the front door, followed closely by a green-haired Daughter.

Moira's breath caught in her chest. What was Tom doing with Hadria Vulpa? And what had possessed him to step outside without telling Moira first? Hadn't she drilled it into his head yet that he was never to leave the shelter of her protection?

A dull object prodded Moira's side. She risked a glance to her right and earned a harder prod.

"Don't," a low voice beside her said. "She's only borrowing him. As long as he cooperates, he'll be fine."

Moira stared at the door, tuning out the dwindling murmur of the crowd and the sappy love song on the jukebox. She narrowed her focus to the Daughter holding a gun at her side, well below where anyone would see it, and struggled to place the voice, the hint of an Asian accent, the pressure of the barrel stuck in her back, anything that might signal a weakness or give her a clue to the other woman's identity. She hadn't been paying attention to her surroundings. Why the fuck hadn't she paid attention? "He's my mate. I'm duty-bound to go after him."

"Not if you want to live."

"Oy there, girlie. Have ye an original threat or must I make up me own?"

The barrel dug sharply into Moira's side. Make up her own it was. She slung her right arm back in a swift, short swing. It hit the gun and knocked it with a clang against the side of the bar. The area around them fell quiet and the press of the crowd eased away. The other Daughter inhaled sharply and pushed her arm in front of Moira's, bringing it up in a solid, backward elbow thrust, smacking Moira hard in the chest. The breath whooshed out of her. She caught the other Daughter's arm with one hand and elbowed her in the side twice in rapid succession.

Sig back stepped away from the bar. "Need help?"

"I got it," Moira gritted out.

The other Daughter yanked on the arm Moira held, jerking her forward. Moira stepped into the motion and pivoted around, swinging the other Daughter in a wide circle, scattering the crowd around them.

One Daughter held up her mug of beer and scowled. "Watch it."

"Sorry," Moira muttered. She grabbed the other Daughter's glossy black hair and pulled her forward away from the beer, letting go in the middle of the pull. Shame to waste a good pint.

The other Daughter rolled away from Moira, landing in a crouch. "Why do you never do anything the easy way?"

Moira grinned as recognition hit. "Well, if it isn't the sacred Snow Beast."

"Would you stop calling me that?"

A wooden bat tapped on the bar and Will said, "You know the rules. No fighting in the bar."

"She's taken Tom." Moira kept her eyes on the Daughter crouching eight feet away. Min Li Snow Dragon was not a Daughter you turned your back on, not if you wanted to live long. She also wasn't known for working well with others. What was she doing colluding with Hadria to kidnap a mortal? "Why is that?"

Min Li smiled, softening the brittle set of her features with genuine humor. She stood slowly and shook her hair back over her shoulders. "You expect me to just tell you?"

Moira lifted one shoulder, dropping it on a sigh. "Sure, and why not?"

"It's not my secret to share."

"It's a secret that'll get you killed."

"Not by your sword, Moira Firebrand." Min Li rested a hand on the hilt of the dagger strapped to her thigh. "My role here is done. A favor repaid, a debt wiped clean. The answer to your question lies not within me."

Moira rolled her eyes. "Feck's sake, Min Li. For once, can't ye give a straight answer instead of spewing that mystical Far East bullshite."

"What's the fun in that?" Min Li slid one foot backwards,

her gaze fixed on Moira. "I trust you'll not retaliate against me and mine for delaying you long enough for your lover to serve his purpose."

"Ye'll trust no such thing, unless ye're a bigger fool than I thought," Moira retorted. "The only reason I haven't wiped the floor with ye is because ye likely know where Tom is."

Min Li raised a single, black eyebrow and eased back another step, parting the crowd behind her. "I know where he's headed, true. Then again, so do you."

"The Archives," Moira said flatly. Damn it, hadn't she warned him?

Min Li nodded solemnly. "It's not the where that should worry you, Moira, but the who. Can you guess who waits for Tom in the place where history lies?"

Cold fear gripped Moira's heart. "The Eternal Order."

"More precisely, the one you let get away." Min Li tutted and walked slowly backwards into the narrow aisle bracketed by curious onlookers. "A shame you allowed love to subsume duty."

"A shame you backed the wrong Daughter."

"Not quite." Min Li bowed slightly, her dark eyes unblinking. "Please give your mother my regards."

Moira nodded. "I'll be seeing ye, Min Li."

"Not if I can help it."

Min Li whirled and jogged through the door. Moira yanked her cell phone out and punched in the number for the Archives' security. Her gaze met Sig's as the number connected and rang, and her heart, so calm during the confrontation with the Dragon, wobbled and throbbed in her chest. The Eternal Order had Tom. If so much as a single hair on his head was bruised, someone would pay dearly.

THE IECS CAMPUS was empty, its streets brightly lit by the security lights dotted at even intervals along the sidewalks. Tom drove cautiously through, his erratically whirling mind torn between scrambling for a way to delay the two Daughters and worry over Moira. She'd been fine when he'd left. Sig was there. The other Daughter would protect her, and if not her then Will or Maya or one of Phil's women.

He parked outside the Archives and got out, not bothering to run. He was fast, or fast enough for a forty-year-old man, but he was no Daughter. They'd catch him before he could make the entrance. No telling what they'd do to him for trying to escape, and he needed to be hale and whole if he was going to have a real chance at surviving whatever these two had in store for him.

They escorted him into the Archives, pausing at the guard station near the entrance. It was manned by a single guard dressed in black from head to toe, her pale blonde hair twisted into a severe bun at the nape of her neck. She rose as they approached and nodded at Tom. "You're here late, Dr. Fairfax."

He managed a small smile and signed the log-in sheet. "Just a little work, Marilyn. It won't take long."

"Of course, sir." Marilyn tapped the sheet with one long finger. "Friends, too."

Tom dutifully signed them in and waited to one side while Marilyn handed Hadria and Vivien visitors badges. They clipped the badges onto their shirts as if they weren't in the process of kidnapping him for nefarious purposes. A routine visit to the Archives. He pinched the bridge of his nose and bit back a sigh. God. What had he gotten himself into?

They fell into step beside him, their booted footsteps echoing in the concrete hallways. Once they rounded the corner and passed out of sight of the guard station, Hadria and Vivien jerked the badges off and dropped them on the floor near the wall.

"Tracking chips," Hadria murmured. "Yours, too."

Tom dug his wallet out of his back pocket and handed her his clipless ID. "We're in the middle of a granite mountain surrounded by concrete."

"They still work pretty damn well short range." She dropped

his ID next to the visitors badges and wrapped a firm hand around his upper arm. "Come on. They're right behind us."

He glanced over his shoulder. "No, they're not."

"Are, too." Vivien grabbed his other arm and tugged him into a walk, her expression as flat as Hadria's. "They're herding us, probably hoping to pin us down inside the Archives."

"Lucky for us, we know the way out."

Tom glanced at Hadria. "Through the front door."

She barked out a soft laugh. "Daughters never, ever build only one way in and out of a building."

"We're in a feckin' concreted-over cave system," he enunciated slowly, and winced. Damn it. He was picking up Moira's bad habits.

"Exactly. Now shut up."

He snapped his mouth closed and lengthened his strides. The Daughters set a fast pace through the tunnels, pulling him between them as they followed the twisting turns toward his office. Not once did Tom see another soul. Try as he might, he couldn't hear anybody behind them, either.

Hadria jerked him to a stop at his office door. "Make it quick, Fairfax. Viv, go take a look-see."

Tom pulled his keys out and fumbled for the right one, selected it and inserted it into the lock, his head turned partially toward Vivien jogging to the end of the corridor they'd just walked down. She stopped at the juncture and carefully peered around the corner. A moment later, she ducked back and pressed herself flat against the wall, nodding slightly.

"Stop lollygagging." Hadria pushed his hands out of the way and unlocked the door. "We have three minutes at the most and a lot of ground to cover."

She opened the door and shoved him inside, slipping past him in efficient strides. She scooted around the side of his desk and rifled through the precisely labeled files held within the two boxes Naomi had set there that afternoon before they'd abandoned work for a meal.

Tom straightened and faced Hadria. "You didn't really need me to get in here, did you?"

"Sure, we did." She pulled out a file, extracted a single sheet of paper, and rolled it into a tight cylinder. "You make a good hostage."

"Jesus Christ." He exhaled slowly around the anger boiling up from his gut. "You kidnapped me so you could have a hostage?"

"No. You're here to deflect attention away from me." She extracted another file and flipped through it quickly, shoving it out of the way in favor of a third file. "Where's Vivien?"

Tom sidestepped to the door and peeked out. Vivien had her back turned to him as she peered around the corner. Hadria snapped her fingers once, drawing Tom's attention. She mimed shutting the door, then beckoned him over.

"What the hell are you doing?" he asked.

"Saving your bacon. The Order heard you were getting close to finding Sanctuary. We were supposed to take you the same night Bobby Upton was kidnapped." She glanced up, a cold smile fixed to her mouth. "Moira held you too tightly."

Thank God she had. He raked a hand over his hair. "I don't know anything, I swear."

She tapped a finger to her forehead. "You've seen too much."

"I haven't seen a damn thing."

"Really? Hmm." Hadria came around the end of the desk and slapped the rolled paper into his palm. "What's this?"

He unrolled it and stared down at the typescript. "The second translation of Begni's letter. We just discovered this today."

"And it's important because...?"

He shrugged. "It mentions the Bones of the Just."

She shook her head. "This isn't the one you need anyway."

He froze. "You know something."

"Oh, yes, lots," she agreed mildly. "The point here isn't

what I know, Tom. It's what *you* know. Why is this letter important?"

"I honest to God don't know."

The door swung open and Vivien stepped inside. "There's a force of half a dozen Daughters at the end of the far corridor. They're moving down now."

"Moira?" Hadria asked.

A slow smile curled the corners of Vivien's lips into a sneer. "No sign of her."

Tom's stomach clenched. Was that good or bad? Had she escaped the Daughter at The Omega or had she been killed coming after him?

Hadria leaned over the desk and grabbed the papers out of the third file. "I have what we need."

Vivien yanked the letter out of Tom's hand and shoved him toward the door. "Come on, lover boy. Time for a quick getaway."

"Oh, no," he said. "I'm not going a step farther."

"To the exit and then you can sull up." Hadria gripped his arm and dragged him into the corridor. A shout rang out at the far end. "No time for arguing."

He yanked his arm, grimacing when her grip tightened. "I'd say now's the perfect time for arguing."

Vivien's hand lashed out and a sharp stab of pain radiated through Tom's thigh. He glanced down. A short, olive green hilt stuck out of his jeans. Blood seeped up around the knife's blade. He pressed a hand to it, only dimly aware of Hadria cursing low and long under her breath and Vivien's triumphant smile glowing brightly from her pretty face.

He sank to the floor and collapsed onto his side. His muscles throbbed painfully around the knife's blade, soaking his fingers with his own blood after every pulse. Moira. Sweet God. He'd just found her, her and the baby. He'd just found them.

He closed his eyes as rough hands pushed him onto his back. A long *whish* sounded and a moment later, more hands

237

were on his thigh, tightening a band around his upper leg above the cut. Sharp taps fell on his cheeks. He opened his eyes and fixed blurred vision on Hadria's face floating over his own.

"Keep your eyes open and a hand pressed tight to that wound. Don't pull the blade out. Do you understand?"

He nodded, tried to over the buzz in his head and the agony radiating away from the knife lodged in his leg.

Hadria tapped his cheek again. "I need you to focus."

"Focus," he repeated. "Am."

"Good." She leaned down and placed her lips against his ear, her voice so low he could barely hear it. "Count your way down. Remember that."

She pushed herself away from him and rose slowly, her hands spread wide as she backed away from him. "I had no hand in this."

"Ye're the one that feckin' kidnapped him, Hadria," Moira called, and Tom sagged against the floor. She was there. His Moira was there. At least he'd get to say goodbye.

"Not for harm. This I swear."

Hadria pivoted and raced down the corridor, followed by what sounded to him like a herd of elephants. Footsteps stumbled to a stop beside him. Moira dropped to her knees and ran her hands over him in frantic strokes.

"Tom. Blessed Goddess." She pressed her forehead to his. "Sweet Thomas."

He closed his eyes, welcoming the numbness creeping over him. It deadened the pain, drowned out the fierce sorrow welling up within him. "Moira." A cough worked its way out of his lungs and he gasped his way through it. "Go."

"I'm not leaving ye, Tom."

He rolled his head along the floor in a weak shake. She wasn't the one leaving. He was. Couldn't she see that? "Love you. Much."

"Oh, Tom. Oh, my precious Tom."

Her voice sounded oddly tight, as if she were crying. It

would be ok, he wanted to say. She'd be fine, her and the baby. He tried to lift his hand, tried to hold her one last time. The numbness surged forward and swept him into a darkness so deep, no light remained to guide him back to his heart.

TWENTY-ONE

WITHIN THREE MINUTES of Tom falling under Vivien's knife, two on-duty security guards had retrieved a rolling gurney from a nearby storage closet. Moira knelt beside him, pressing her hands against the wound in a useless effort to staunch the dribble of blood seeping out around the knife's blade. Hadria had used her own belt as a tourniquet. Why the fuck wasn't it working?

Hard arms came around her chest, pinning her arms to her sides, and dragged her away from Tom. Moira screamed and bucked, struggling to break free. "Let me help him! Feck's sake, let me help me mate!"

"Shh, now." Sig's quiet shush blew gently against the side of Moira's face. "The guards are wrapping his leg. An ambulance is on the way. You need to calm down and let them do their job."

Moira sagged into Sig's hold. The two guards knelt beside Tom, one to either side. Their hands moved swiftly as they wrapped gauze around his thigh, anchoring the knife in place. The moment it was secured, they lifted him gently between them and placed him on the gurney, buckling him to it with long straps.

Sig released Moira, pushed herself into a stand, and pulled Moira up. They set off at a jog behind the guards pushing Tom toward the Archives' entrance. Moira's heart pounded hard in her chest. He was so pale, so absolutely still, and he'd lost so much blood.

Why had Vivien stabbed him? There was no sane reason to. He held so much more value alive than dead. He could've fed the Order information for years, if they'd needed it. Stupid to risk killing him, not only for the information lost, but for the enemy made. Surely Vivien knew Moira would never rest until his injury or, Ki forbid, his death was avenged in the most excruciatingly painful way possible.

And it would be painful, Moira vowed as she burst out of the Archives into the night. Vivien Long would pay for what she'd done, even if Moira couldn't claim the debt with her own hands.

An ambulance was waiting in the parking area, its lights strobing through the darkness. Two paramedics, one a burly man in his early twenties, the other a slender woman pushing forty, stood at the rear beside the open doors. The guards rolled the gurney to a stop and stepped back, answering rapid questions as they were asked before fading out of the way. The paramedics lifted Tom into the ambulance. The male paramedic climbed in behind him and began preparing an IV drip. The female turned to the Daughters gathering around the emergency vehicle.

Sig nudged Moira. "This is his mate."

Moira stumbled and swayed. The paramedic beckoned her forward with an urgent wave, and Moira found the strength to scramble inside the ambulance. The doors slammed shut behind her. A moment later, the sirens roared to life and the ambulance eased out of the Archives' parking area.

Moira dragged herself onto the padded bench placed along one side of the interior. Her vision blurred unaccountably. She swiped the back of her hand across her eyes and discovered tears. Feck's sake. Daughters didn't cry, not over a mere man.

Only, nothing about Tom was *mere*, not his masculinity or his heart, not his intellect or his patience, not the love he'd expressed so haltingly as he lay on the cold concrete, his life's blood spilling from him in slow gurgles.

He loved her.

She pressed a trembling hand to her own heart over the love raging inside herself. Funny that so many men had said those words to her, but none had ever touched her as deeply as Tom's.

The ambulance eased to a stop, the doors were flung open. Moira pressed herself into the side of the interior as Tom was lifted out and rolled through the entrance to the county hospital's Emergency Room. She followed at a slower pace. They wouldn't let her stay with him. Likely he'd need surgery.

She sank onto a chair in the lobby and dropped her head into her hands. *Please Ki, let his arteries be intact. Please let him live.*

The chair beside her creaked. A soft hand fell on her back and a low, male voice said, "Your mother's on her way."

Moira reached blindly toward her step-father and latched onto his knee. "Robert. Thank the Goddess."

"Sigrid called and told me to rally the troops. What happened?"

"The Order kidnapped Tom. One of the kidnappers stabbed him in the thigh."

"And she's still alive?"

Moira huffed out a laugh, swallowed down the hysteria bubbling up behind it. "She fled and I... I couldn't leave him lying there in a puddle of his own blood. Sweet Goddess, Robert, there was so much blood."

"There, now. He'll be fine once Doc Phillips sews him up."

"He has to be."

They sat there for what felt like hours as nurses ambled up and down the corridors and family and friends trickled in, gathering around Moira and Robert in globs and clusters. Rebecca squeezed her way through the crowd and carved out a space to sit beside Moira. She was dressed from head to toe in black.

"Ye shouldn't have interrupted yer mission," Moira murmured.

"Family first." Rebecca draped an arm around Moira and

pulled her close, rocking her gently. "Sigrid briefed me on what happened. Any news on Tom yet?"

"None a'tall. They're taking their bloody sweet time."

"They're doing their job, darling. Don't begrudge them using what time they need to heal him."

Moira sniffed back a sob and buried her face in Rebecca's neck. "Oh, Mum. Ye should've seen him. He was near as pale as the floor and so blessed still. Why did she have to stab him? What purpose could hurting him possibly serve?"

"Who knows what motivates the Order?" Rebecca smoothed a tender hand over Moira's hair. "I have a call in to Naomi. Hopefully she can help us figure out what was taken so we can at least know why he was targeted."

They fell into a stiff silence. Around them, people shifted and murmured quietly amongst themselves, and the hospital's business continued on. Moira retreated into her mind, shutting out the announcements crackling through the overhead speaker and the speculation running rife amongst the waiting crowd.

Finally, after an interminable age, Ethan Phillips strode through the group dressed in fresh scrubs, his handsome face set in weary lines under his close-cropped auburn hair. He squatted in front of Moira and Rebecca. "I thought I asked you to take better care of your family, Director."

Rebecca grasped the doctor's bare forearm and smiled gently. "I'm afraid there's no help for that, Ethan. They find trouble whether I wish them to or not. How's Tom?"

"Holding his own. The knife nicked his femur. Thankfully it didn't hit any arteries, but he lost a lot of blood."

"Can we see him?" Moira asked.

"I'll have a nurse come get you as soon as he's settled into a room." Ethan tapped a curled finger to Moira's chin. "And you'll take the other bed and get some rest. Doctor's orders."

"I'll not leave him."

Ethan rose and cupped one capable hand over Moira's shoulder. "He's sedated right now. It wouldn't hurt to hold his hand, though, or just sit with him. People always underestimate the good having loved ones around can do."

"Thank you, Doc." The words squeezed their way past the worry constricting Moira's throat. Ethan nodded and left, and she slumped into the hard plastic chair, resigned to another long wait.

BY THE TIME TOM had been deposited in a regular room, Moira's nerves had stretched to the breaking point. She followed the nurse to his room, took one look at the sweat dotting his face, and snapped at the young mortal to fetch soap, hot water, and a washcloth.

Rebecca perched in a padded chair at the end of Tom's bed and regarded Moira with a calm, steady gaze. "There's no need to raise your voice, darling."

"Look at him." Moira smoothed a hand over his brow and finger combed his hair away from his face. "He's in pain. Why'd they not give him some feckin' drugs?"

"I'm sure they have."

"Well, it's not good enough."

Rebecca leaned forward, her expression tightening into a hard mask. "Moira, darling, I love you, but you will not speak to me in that tone of voice."

Moira dropped her forehead to Tom's and clenched her eyelids shut. "Sorry, Mum. I'm worried, is all."

"As are we all. When will you avenge this strike against you and yours?"

"Tom wouldn't want me to."

"Hmm."

"He fusses when I risk meself."

"Are you certain?"

Moira straightened and speared her mother with an incredulous stare. "Reckon I oughta know when he fusses. Feckin' hard to miss, it is."

The corners of Rebecca's mouth twitched. "I'm sure it is.

244

Are you certain he's not fussing because he sees the risk as needless? Have you tried explaining to him why you avenge injuries such as this?"

"I told him I was duty-bound..."

"Duty." Rebecca's back hit the chair with a thump as she reclined into it. "If you told him you risk yourself out of love for him, what would he say?"

"He'd not wish me to risk meself for him."

"Would he want you to do it for you?"

Moira tangled her fingers in his hair, anchoring herself to the man who'd brought reason into her life, and love. "He might, if he thought there was no other way. Tom's more one for words, not violence."

Rebecca laughed. "If he wanted to avoid violence, perhaps he shouldn't have fallen in love with a Daughter."

A fraction of the worry melted away. "True."

The nurse returned with the supplies Moira had requested and left after dumping them on the nightstand beside Tom's bed. Moira ignored the girl's disgruntled glare and gently cleansed Tom's face. His chest rose and fell in even intervals beneath the hospital gown someone had clothed him in. Otherwise, he was still as the dead. She tugged the sheet up over his chest and pressed a kiss to his forehead, then dropped into a chair on his left side, opposite the IV needle inserted in his right hand.

"I know where she is," Rebecca said.

Moira clasped Tom's free hand between her own, chafing warmth into his chilled skin. There was only one person her mother could mean, the woman who'd done this to Tom, not long after she'd stabbed Moira in nearly the same place.

"Will you go after her?" Rebecca continued.

"Would you?"

"I would never have allowed her to leave the Archives alive. Then again, I'm not in the first throes of love."

The amused tone should've rankled Moira, would've if worry hadn't jammed everything else out. "He won't understand."

"Must I repeat myself, darling?" Rebecca leaned forward and caught Moira's gaze with her own. "He'll understand. Tom is no ignorant boy to be swayed by fear. Explain the whys to him once he awakens, but take care of the betrayer now while she's within easy reach. Don't allow her another opportunity to strike."

"Says me mum, the general."

"Some things never leave you."

Moira nodded. Hadn't she her own haunting burdens to bear? Pray Ki Tom would never be one of them. "Will ye watch over him?"

"As if he were my own."

Moira stood and kissed his still, still mouth. "I'll be back, Thomas, and when I return, ye'll heal apace and be whole again, do ye hear me?"

She slipped past her mother and out the door before she lost the will to leave him.

VIVIEN LONG was ensconced in a tarpaper shack on the outskirts of Tellowee. Moira sat in her car outside the rundown building and stared at the shadows passing to and fro in front of the lone curtained window. She counted three separate shadows, judging by height and mannerisms, though there were likely more people inside, probably members of the Eternal Order.

All traitors to the People.

She got out of the Miata and deliberately slammed the door. While she waited for a reaction, she did a cursory weapons check, then leaned against the hood of her car facing the shack. A deadly calm stole over her. Siobhan and Hannah, she'd never been able to avenge. By the time she'd woken in hospital, the evidence trail had been long gone. Here, though, she could make a difference. She could make certain no one was ever foolish enough to come after Tom again. In this small way, she could protect him. Surely he'd understand that.

A whoosh came from inside, followed by a crack and a low grunt. The front door creaked open and a slight figure stepped through, arms raised, face shrouded in shadow. "Hello, Moira."

"Hadria. Ye know why I've come."

"I do. Would it do any good to ask how you found us?"

"None a'tall."

"I suppose you want to kill me."

Moira shifted against the car and shrugged. "Ye saved him, though I'm none too happy ye put him in a bad situation to begin with."

"He was never supposed to be hurt. We needed to know what he'd found, that's all. You and I both know he's more useful alive." Hadria stepped forward and her face passed into the thin light cast by the moon glowing overhead. "She's being disciplined now. You're welcome to take a turn."

"If the injury had been done to me, aye, I'd wield the whip, but it wasn't. Tom is mortal and he's me mate. Even now, he lies in hospital recovering from a near fatal wound. Would ye allow such to go unanswered?"

Hadria's mouth pressed into a thin line. "You're putting me in an awkward position here, Moira. I can't risk exposing the rest of the Order just so you can have your revenge and I don't want to have to fight you."

"Then don't," Moira said bluntly. "Take yer leave through the back door along with the others. Send the girl out before ye go. I'll consider it just payment for kidnapping Tom and won't come after ye and yers in return."

"You're going to let known members of the Order go in exchange for one woman?"

"Aye, though if ye don't mind, I'd like to get on with it. Tom's not in the best shape and I'd rather not be away from him longer than needs must."

Hadria's hands dropped to her side and a cold smile blossomed on her face. "A better punishment, then. I need a moment."

"Make certain no one sneaks around behind me. I'll kill them as well and hunt the remainder of ye down. Ye know I'll never rest until ye're all dead and buried."

Hadria nodded and eased backward into the shadows surrounding the front door. She disappeared inside. A moment later, the door reopened and Vivien Long stepped out, one hand resting on the hilt of a dagger strapped to her thigh, the other scrubbing over her face. "I heard you're here to kill me."

"Something like that," Moira said. "Are ye well enough to fight?"

Vivien sputtered out a laugh. "They'd barely started when you pulled in. Three licks from a whip won't keep me from gutting you like a fish."

"Oy, girlie. Ye've a right big ego there."

"What, you think I'm scared?" Vivien gave a mock shudder, then bared her teeth at Moira in a malicious grin. "Not a chance. You've been hiding too long, Moira. You're rusty, old. Weak. A third grader on a sugar high could take you."

Genuine amusement curled through Moira. "Is that so?"

"I'm not the only one who thinks it."

"Ye'll be the last," Moira said flatly. "Are ye finished with yer aimless prattle or would ye like to boast a bit more to yer friends hiding in the shadows?"

Vivien jerked back and glanced around the yard. "They were supposed to leave."

"There now, girlie. Did ye really think they wouldn't wish to witness yer set-down, after ye broke their rules and injured a mortal? That's not how the Order works. If ye'd been paying attention, ye'd know this."

Vivien's expression hardened. She pulled the dagger out of its sheath and fell into a defensive stance, her free hand forward, the dagger held at the ready. "They'll witness your death, not mine, Reluctant. Prepare to meet An."

"I think not."

Moira drew her Glock from its holster, aimed, and pulled

the trigger in one fluid movement. The bullet caught Vivien in the stomach and rocked her back two steps. Her expression melted into a shocked gape as she staggered and sank to one knee. Moira walked forward, holstering the gun as she went, and yanked the knife Vivien had used on Tom out of a side pocket of her cargo pants.

Vivien pressed her hands to the gunshot wound. "You shot me."

"Aye, I did." Moira swung her free hand around and knocked the dagger from Vivien's loosened grasp. "The thing about us rusty Daughters is, we're a lazy bunch. We never exert ourselves if there's an easier way to solve a problem." Moira backhanded Vivien, knocking her to the ground. "My problem is twofold. Ye're to be punished for what ye did to me Tom, but ye need to suffer in a way that'll discourage others from coming after him."

Vivien coughed and stared up at Moira, her eyes wide. A thin stream of blood trickled out of one corner of her mouth. "You *cheated.*"

Moira knelt beside Vivien. "The thing ye seem to've forgotten, girlie, is the fact that ye cheated first. Now, if ye'll hold still a moment, I'll be getting on with it."

She vaulted forward and straddled Vivien's shins just below her knees, then brought the point of the knife down on the inside of the other Daughter's thigh, piercing through leather and skin in one sharp thrust. "Anatomy 101. The femoral artery is here."

A strangled cry erupted from Vivien. Her hips bucked, nearly unseating Moira, and one hand came up in a roundhouse punch that missed its target by inches. Moira curled her free hand into a fist and punched Vivien just below the gunshot wound. The breath whooshed out of the injured Daughter. She curled her hands around her stomach and curled her torso upward.

"Now, where was I? Right. The femoral artery." Moira sliced slowly down Vivien's thigh, laying it open to the night air.

Vivien screamed as blood spurted out of the cut, quickly soaking the ripped leather pants and the skin beneath, its hot, metallic scent drifting upward.

Moira swallowed the bile clogging her throat. Yup, she was definitely preggers. Tom would be ecstatic, though of a certainty, it made her duty that night a bit harder.

She sat back and examined her work. "Aye, that should do it. Suppose I should even them out." She yanked the knife out of Vivien's thigh, punched it into the other one, and worked the blade slowly along the skin, slicing through the underlying tissue and artery.

Vivien gasped. Her hands slid away from her stomach and her skin paled under the thin moonlight. "Ki..."

Moira leaned forward, her heart weary. "No, girlie," she murmured gently. "Ye'll not be blessed with that path."

She sat there for long moments, waiting for the life to drain out of Vivien, waiting for the misguided Daughter to still, and felt nothing beyond relief. Word of the brutal reprisal Moira had meted would spread far and wide among the People, and nobody would ever dare threaten Tom again.

The blood seeping out of the cuts and gunshot wound slowed to a trickle. Moira rocked back on her heels and stood. She walked around the blood-soaked earth and pressed two fingers to the pulse in Vivien's throat. No heartbeat thumped under her touch. She tossed the knife on top of the body and pitched her voice loud enough to be clearly heard. "This is what happens to those who challenge me. Let this lesson be learned well tonight."

From the shadows, soft voices answered. "Blessed be Ki."

"Blessed be Ki," Moira said. She stared down at Vivien's sightless eyes for a long moment, then turned on her heel and left. Tom needed her now, and she needed him more than she'd ever believed it possible to need a man.

TWENTY-TWO

A NIGHTMARE HELD Tom in its grip. The knife came down, striking him in the thigh, and he fell onto the hard floor. Moira called out for him. He struggled to keep her back, struggled to keep her safe.

"Moira," he murmured.

From a distance, a familiar voice said, "She's coming, Tom. Rest now."

He slid back into the fevered dream. The knife came down. He hit the floor. Moira's sweet voice called to him. Knife. Floor. Moira. Knife, floor...

Count your way down.

The dream shifted abruptly. Another woman knelt over him, her cold eyes drilling into his. *Count your way down. Remember that.*

He glanced down, expecting to see a knife buried deep in his leg, but it was gone. Begni's letter was in his hand. Moira took it from him and read it, her wide mouth tilted into a smile. *I sometimes forget ye're not of the People, Tom.* The Bones of the Just shall forever lie in sacred slumber. Why hadn't Rue translated all of it?

This isn't the one you need anyway.

The thought broke into the dream, cutting it short. Tom fought his way to awareness through hazy layers of pain and

251

fatigue, and opened his eyes. The room was darkened by curtains pulled over the windows. He glanced toward them. Pain stabbed through his head and he winced. God above, his head hurt. What the hell had he done to it?

A gentle hand captured his. "You're awake."

Tom grunted. "Not..." His voice croaked out, barely escaping his dry mouth. He cleared his throat and tried again. "Not really."

"How do you feel?"

"Run over by a train."

"You lost a lot of blood."

"Moira?"

"Did Moira stab you? No, darling. She's out hunting down the woman who did this to you."

He sighed and rolled his head carefully toward the voice. "Good."

Rebecca leaned into his line of sight and came into focus. "I told her you'd say that. She seemed to think you'd disagree with her enacting vengeance."

"Not..." *This time*, he wanted to say, but his parched throat had finally had enough. "Water," he whispered, and gratefully sipped it through the straw Rebecca pressed to his lips. It slipped down his throat, soothing the scratchiness.

"Rest now. Save your strength. Moira will be back soon. By the Lady, you'll need every bit of it to deal with her."

Tom shook his head and immediately regretted it as a throbbing pain crashed through his temples. "Begni's letter. Ruanna. Need them."

"That can wait..."

"No. Need them."

Rebecca's hand tightened on his. "All right. I'll arrange for the letter and Ruanna to be here, but only if you promise to rest now."

"Will," he managed, and slumped into the mattress. "Need Moira."

"I know, darling. She'll be here soon."

Tom drifted off, barely aware of Rebecca's quietly placed phone calls or the nurse coming in and adjusting the drip of his IV. Moira had been right all along, though not in the way she'd thought. The answer had been under their noses the whole time and now he had the key to unlocking it.

MOIRA DROPPED BY Tom's apartment, showered, and changed into clean clothes on her way to the hospital. She'd done what she had to, but that didn't mean she wanted him to see her spattered with blood. He'd worry and he'd fuss, and he was too weak for either.

She texted her mother with a quick *deed done*. And good riddance, though Rebecca might be none too happy Moira had let the other members of the Order go. Ah, well. That wasn't her job. If Rebecca wanted them tracked, she most certainly knew how to do it.

Moira secured the apartment, then slipped quickly into her car and started it. She allowed herself to dwell on what she should've considered when Rebecca told her where to find Vivien. How had her mother come by that information?

She mulled it over during the short drive between the IECS campus and the county hospital. As the director of the IECS and the unofficial head of the People's efforts to protect their settlements in the US, Rebecca was privy to information ordinary Daughters weren't. Still, knowing the location of a rogue element like the Order and not doing anything to stop them? That didn't quite strike true. Moira shrugged one shoulder and turned into the hospital's parking lot. As she always had, she'd trust her mother knew what she was doing and worry about keeping her own family in order.

The hospital was quiet in the pre-dawn dark. Moira jiggled the lock on a side entrance and snuck past the nurses on duty. Visitors weren't allowed to come and go at night, though that had never stopped the People from seeing to their injured kin.

When she slipped into Tom's room, Rebecca was seated in a chair at his bedside, her gaze fixed on him. She looked up and smiled as Moira quietly shut the door. "There you are."

"Sorry I took so long. Me clothes weren't fit to wear once I was done."

"She's dead, then."

Moira nodded and ran her palms down her thighs over the clean jeans she'd changed into. "Vivien Long will never bother another again, though I let the other members of the Order go in exchange for her."

Rebecca's blue eyes glittered. "They can be found again, when the time is right."

"Good, then. How is he?"

"Resting. He woke an hour ago and demanded to see Begni's letter and Ruanna."

Moira's eyebrows shot up. "Did he, now."

"It could be the sedatives talking, but I'm taking no chances. Ruanna and James will be here by noon along with a copy of the letter." Rebecca rose into a full body stretch. "He asked for you."

Moira's gaze drifted to the even rise and fall of Tom's chest, to the peaceful expression on his thin face. "Ye told him I'd return soon?"

"I did, and now, I'm leaving guard duty to you." Rebecca brushed a kiss over Moira's cheek. "I'll be back after breakfast. Call if you need me."

"I will." Moira turned and followed her mother's progress toward the door. "Thank ye for watching over him."

Rebecca smiled faintly. "He's soon to be my son. How could I not guard him as such?"

She left as quietly as Moira had entered. Moira dropped into the chair her mother had vacated and gathered his fingers between her two hands, stroking warmth into them. He was safe now. No matter what happened, he'd always be safe. She scooted the chair closer to his bed and rested her head in the crook of her arm. A little rest, now that she'd done what she could to protect him, and on the morrow, she'd care for him as a woman cared for the man she loved.

His fingers wiggled in her hand, jerking her awake. She glanced at the light filtering through the curtains, then at her watch. She must've dozed, though she could've sworn she hadn't.

It was gonna be a long pregnancy.

Tom shifted on the bed. A low groan grunted out of him. "Moira?"

She stood and smoothed a hand over his forehead. "I'm here, love."

"Missed you." He *mmmd* and turned his head toward her, blinking up at her with clear, brown-green eyes. "I really have to pee."

She snorted out a laugh and dropped her forehead to his. "Sweet Thomas. Let me get a nurse."

"Mm-unh. If a woman has to see my naked penis, it's gonna be you." He levered himself up onto an elbow and grimaced. "Groggy."

"Let me help, ye stubborn man."

She hitched his arm over her shoulder and aided him to the bathroom and back, urging him into slow, careful steps, taking as much of his weight as she could. After, he dropped onto the narrow hospital bed with a tired sigh. "That really hurt, but God, I feel so much better."

"Ye should've let me get the nurse."

"What you can do is climb up here with me."

"Are ye feckin' crazy? Ye've a near mortal wound, Tom. The last thing ye need is a woman curled up next to ye."

He leveled a determined stare at her. "I will always need you near. Now, either climb up here with me or I'm crawling into the chair with you."

"Tom..."

"Moira," he countered evenly. He scooted carefully to the edge of the bed and held his arm out. "We need to talk before

Nurse Ratched comes in and ups the meds in my IV."

She stared down at him, torn between exasperation and need, and finally gave in. What would it hurt to lay next to him for a few minutes? As soon as he was out, she'd take the chair again and he'd be none the wiser. She eased onto the bed and stretched out beside him, her legs straight, her head on his chest.

He curved his arm around her shoulders and brushed his face against the top of her head. "I love you."

Though he'd said it earlier, she couldn't quiet believe it. Rather than hurt him with a denial, she held her tongue.

"I know you care for me," he continued. "I know you still want to claim me, but this changes everything, sweetheart. Lying there in the hallway with that knife stuck in my leg? I thought I was dying. I thought I'd never see you again, never get to hold you. Never get to know the baby, if there is one, and it was the most awful feeling."

"Hush now, Tom. Ye need yer rest."

"Not until I get this out." He shifted beneath her and rubbed a slow hand over her arm. "I knew I loved you the night you went after her. I should've told you then and I was too much of a coward. I'm telling you now, though, and I'm telling you something else, too. I'm never letting you go. I don't care if you never grow old. I don't care if you never submit and become mortal. You're stuck with me. We're getting married and you're living with me and you're helping me raise the baby." He yawned and when he spoke again, his words slurred together. "You set the terms when we became lovers. I'm changing the rules now, and you're gonna follow them whether you like it or not."

A hint of amusement curled through her. "Is that so? And I've no say in the matter?"

"None a'tall," he murmured. "Now say it so I can go to sleep."

"Say what?"

"Say you'll never leave me."

"Oh, Tom." She raised up and pressed a gentle kiss to him

256

mouth. "I never could."

"Good." His breaths evened out and his arm loosened around her. "Love you."

"I love you, too," she whispered. She closed her eyes and settled down beside him, her heart lighter than it had been in ages. He loved her and, contrary to every logical reason he had not to, he wanted to spend the rest of his life with her. She'd marry him, just as he'd said. She'd live with him and do as he asked because she loved him and trusting his judgment was all she could give him, all she could do until...

A sharp pain stabbed into the base of her skull. She hissed in a breath as the pain sparked outward, seeping rapidly into every nerve in her body. A shiver washed over her, and another, becoming a hard shudder. She rolled away from Tom and off the edge of the narrow bed, falling to the floor in a crashing heap. His voice, low and urgent, came from far above her, so far away. She lay on the floor as the pain ebbed and rebounded and her consciousness receded, her last thought a prayer of gratitude to the Lady Goddess that She had finally given Moira someone to love.

TWENTY-THREE

TOM'S GAZE drifted from the letter in his hand to where Moira rested on the other hospital bed in his room. As soon as she'd dropped off the side of his bed nearly six hours earlier, he'd fumbled for the call button and gotten a nurse in. She'd helped a groggy Moira into the other bed. Her offer to fetch Doc Phillips had been flatly rebuffed by Moira's insistence that a good rest was all she needed to cure what ailed her.

What kind of ailment sent a healthy woman into what had looked like seizures? How could rest be the best remedy for that?

Ruanna flipped a finger against the copy of Begni's letter he held. "Come on, Tom, don't keep us in suspense. What's so important it couldn't wait until you got out of the hospital?"

He rubbed stiff fingers over his forehead and adjusted his reading glasses. The cut in his leg throbbed and pinged every time he moved. No more meds, though, not for a while. They clouded his head too much. He had a funny feeling he'd need his wits about him long before his leg healed. "I think I know why you couldn't translate this one phrase."

James' eyebrows shot toward his hairline. "Do tell."

"Remember how Naomi said that maybe the letter was in code and how we might find the key in those boxes she retrieved?" Tom shot a curious look at Rebecca. "Where is she, anyway? I thought she'd be here by now."

Rebecca reclined in the chair placed at the end of his bed and crossed her legs. "She isn't answering her phone. I've sent someone to see why."

"That's not like Naomi."

"I'm sure she's fine." She nodded at the letter in his hand. "If you please?"

"Sure. Sorry." He shook off his worry over Naomi and concentrated on the indecipherable text Ruanna had helpfully highlighted in yellow. "I'm pretty sure Naomi was both right and wrong. The letter *is* in code, part of it is anyway, but the key is in the letter itself, in this very phrase right here."

Rebecca tilted her head and regarded him with cool blue eyes. "You figured this out while being stabbed and sewn back together?"

Tom pressed his lips together. He could give Hadria away, share what she'd told him, and possibly risk exposing her to whatever she'd been trying to cover up when she'd shanghaied him and dragged him into the Archives. He could do that or he could let it go. Sure, she'd put him in danger, but she'd also given him a huge clue on how to solve the puzzle that had been nagging at him for so long.

And she'd saved his life.

He fixed his gaze on the letter, avoiding the knowing look Rebecca directed his way. "Something like that. Now, this first letter. What's its place in the Hebrew alphabet?"

Ruanna squinted at the letter. "Tet. It's the ninth letter."

"Ok. Count from the end of the phrase to the ninth letter away from it. James, could you write this down?"

The three of them worked through the phrase, Ruanna counting the numerical values of each of the letters in the indecipherable phrase, James writing the corresponding letters in the text down on a blank page in a spiral notebook, and Tom keeping their place within Begni's letter. When they'd gone completely through the phrase and matched every letter in the key to its corresponding letter, they went through it one more time, checking their work.

Tom laid Begni's letter on his lap and ran a shaky hand over his face. Thank God they'd gotten through it so quickly. His strength was fading fast. All he really wanted to do was crawl into bed with Moira and sleep for a hundred years. "Can you decipher it, Rue?"

She took the notebook from Tom and frowned at the letters James had recorded. "This makes no sense. It's not anything I recognize as Hebrew."

"Shit." He closed his eyes, struggling to focus his thoughts around the bone deep weariness and the ache in his leg. "Ok, let's think this through. You said you thought this copy of Begni's letter had been translated from something else."

"Yes," she said slowly. "No idea what, though."

"What if we don't need to know?" James asked.

Rue glanced at him. "What do you mean?"

"Well, presumably, the idea was for someone to actually be able to read it, but the Daughters are a paranoid bunch. What if the unencoded code was still in code?"

"Was that supposed to make sense?" Rue asked.

Tom took his reading glasses off and rubbed wearily at his eyes. His thigh was beginning to hurt. Meds were probably wearing off. "No, I see where he's going with this. Daughters *are* paranoid. I bet Begni was worried this letter would fall into the wrong hands, so she translated it into Hebrew, right? What if she kept the answer, the message hidden inside the letter, in the original language as an extra layer of protection? What if it's not supposed to make sense in Hebrew because it's still in another language, maybe one her enemies wouldn't understand so easily?"

"The language of the People," Rebecca murmured. "Could it be?"

James handed Ruanna the pen. "Write down the sounds each letter stands for."

Ruanna inhaled sharply as she grasped the pen. "I guess it's worth a shot."

The pen scratched across the paper as she converted each letter symbol into its corresponding sound. After a moment, her hand grew still and her face paled. She scribbled something else, stared intently at the notebook, then staggered to the room's only other chair and dropped into it.

"What?" Tom asked.

Ruanna shook her head and passed the notebook to Rebecca, who looked it carefully over, her expression closed. After a long moment, Rebecca glanced at Tom and James, and said softly, "Kaetyren Ladognen. The City of the Sisters."

James crossed his arms over his chest as a slow grin spread over his face. "Tom, you son of a gun. You did it."

"I had a little help," Tom said faintly. "Tell me you know where that is."

Rebecca shook her head. "It's a near mythical place, an underground city supposedly used as a refuge some four or five millennia ago. It was eventually abandoned, though Daughters made pilgrimages for centuries after." Her eyes went wide. "The Oracle was found asleep there in a grotto, lying among the remains of the dead."

" 'Five shall there be in the City of the Sisters, and there the Bones of the Just shall forever lie in sacred slumber,'" Ruanna quoted. She scraped a hand over her braid. "What happened to the skeletons found with the Oracle?"

"I don't know." Rebecca slumped into the chair. "They can't all still be there, though. Councilmember Lydia identified one Sister's remains at a local nightclub a couple of months ago. Sigrid and George are testing those now."

"But the letter only mentions five sisters," Tom said. "What happened to the other two?"

"Lost in history, most likely," James said. "Where's the City of the Sisters supposed to be?"

"Turkey." Moira pushed herself off the bed, one hand held to her forehead. She swayed, then plopped back onto the bed,

261

sitting gingerly on its edge. "It's in bloody, feckin' Turkey."

"Naomi said Begni's letter was found in Turkey," Tom said.

Moira nodded, then winced. "We'll have to go, Tom."

"No, darling, you've done enough." Rebecca rose gracefully and moved across the room, settling onto the bed beside Moira. "I'll send Jerusha. She's familiar with the area and knows the languages and customs. In the meantime, you and Tom can continue searching for anything you can find on Sanctuary in the Archives' holdings."

"You mean this isn't it?" When she shook her head slightly, Tom dropped his head back against the bed's headboard. "Great. One puzzle solved and now you hand me another one."

A shaky laugh sputtered out of Moira. "Oy, Tom, yer life's full of problems of a sudden."

Not as many as he'd like it to be. He hadn't exactly convinced Moira to marry him yet, had he? And the throb in his leg was quickly morphing into a burning agony. "Not to be rude, but can we finish this up after I get out of the hospital?"

"First it's get here as quickly as we can, then it's go away, I'm done with you." Ruanna stood and tapped a soft hand against the end of the bed. "I'll bring Phil by for a good visit before supper."

"Thanks, Rue."

James held his hand out to Tom. "I'll come by tomorrow. Get some rest."

Tom shook James' hand. "I will, thanks."

James trailed Ruanna out of the room.

Rebecca hugged Moira with one arm. "I'll leave the two of you in peace for a while, though I'm only a phone call away if you need me."

"We'll be fine," Moira said. "Tend to the People's business. I've a keen yearning to know what awaits us in the lost city."

"We have to find it first, though I have a few ideas there." Rebecca stood and pressed a kiss to Moira's forehead, then touched light fingers to Tom's. "Rest. Heal. Take care of one another."

"We will," Tom said. He watched Rebecca leave, measuring her progress with impatient eyes. As soon as the door closed behind her, he turned to Moira, determined to ferret out of her exactly what had happened to knock her out for most of the morning.

AFTER REBECCA LEFT, the room fell into a silence broken only by the whoosh of heat rushing out of the vents and the hum of the overhead light. Moira met the hard gaze Tom shot her way.

"So," he said. "About this fainting thing."

Moira crossed her arms over her stomach. Her head was still spinning, though not as fiercely as it had when she'd woken flat on the floor with an unfamiliar nurse bending over her. "Wasn't fainting, exactly. More like losing me immortality."

His expression remained perfectly neutral, neither skeptical nor accepting, crossing into none of the expressions she'd expected to observe. Love, maybe, or joy. Even gratitude would've been welcome, but he just sat there, watching her fidget and squirm.

She forced her hands into fists, stilling their restless twitches. "I was praying to the Lady Ki, promising to follow where ye lead, it being the only thing I could give ye."

"And then you fell off the bed, knocked your noggin on the floor, had a few seizures..." He grimaced and ran a hand over the bandage covering his thigh. "I didn't know what to do for you."

"Nothing, Tom," she said gently. "We Daughters are a hardy lot, inside and out. When the Lady Ki blesses us by lifting the curse, some take it hard, others easy, but we're all grateful to no longer carry that burden."

"Are you?"

"Course, I am. Why would ye ask as if ye didn't know?"

He leaned his head against the headboard and closed his eyes. "I'm afraid to believe it's really true. I never thought you would, you know, never thought you could trust a man enough to love him."

She stepped carefully across the floor between the two hospital beds, pushing down the dizziness assailing her with an impatient thrust of her mind. A woman only had one shot at real love, she figured. She'd given it a stab a time or two and never had it stick, but this time she knew. *This* time was different. Her love was strong and true, else the curse could never have been broken.

His eyes popped open at the first scuff of her boot along the tiled floor. He held a hand out to her and welcomed her when she perched on the edge of his bed.

"Thomas, me love, ye must understand the hardness a Daughter's heart accumulates over the years." She ran a had down his forearm, so pleased to be near him her heart swelled to ten times its normal size and near burst in her chest. "We endure many hardships, many losses, some accidental, others deliberate, and it turns us from the sweet children we were into the scarred mess of battle-ready warriors."

A corner of his mouth curled upward. "I thought you were born a hellion."

"Hushit." She smiled and brushed her fingertips over his sweet mouth. "I thought ye might be the one who could break the curse the night we first danced."

His hand sought hers and held it in a tight grip. "And stupid me, I kept trying to deny the attraction. I was scared, Moira, so scared I'd give you my heart and you'd hand it back torn to shreds."

"Ye had a right to believe such. I've never loved a man before outside me family, and I've never loved a man as well as I love ye." She twined her fingers with his and stared down at the union she hoped to duplicate for the remainder of the lives Ki gave them. "Did ye mean all those things ye said, about living with me and raising the babe together and all?"

"I meant every single word."

"I'll never yield completely to ye. It's not in me nature."

264

"I'm not asking you to, exactly." He scooted himself higher in the bed, then tugged her against his chest. "I want to make a life with you, Moira. I don't think we can do that if you're running all over the world being a Daughter while I'm taking care of our family."

She smoothed her cheek over his chest through the thin hospital gown he wore. "And when duty calls me away?"

"I'll miss you so much and pray every day that you return safe and sound, but I won't begrudge your going, not if you have to go. Oh, sweetheart." He pressed a kiss to the top of her head and sighed. "We've both gone about this all wrong, each of us trying to be the one controlling our relationship, when all along we should've been working together. How about we try that now? How about we let go of all that fear and work on loving each other for a while?"

"As ye wish, sweet Thomas." She fiddled with his gown, ruching the paper thin fabric between her fingers. "Siobhan and Hannah would've adored ye. I wish they'd lived to meet ye."

"Me, too, sweetheart." He sighed into her hair. "I wish the past hadn't been so hard on you or that we'd met sooner so I could've helped you deal with it or carried some of the load for you. I love you so much."

Emotion clogged her throat, thickening her voice. "I love ye, too, Thomas. Ye must believe me."

"How could I ever deny it, when you're here next to me, showing me how much?" He hugged her tight. His gentle strength surrounded her, shoring up her own. "I don't know about you, but I'm tired of being cooped up in an apartment. Let's go house hunting next week."

She smiled and held him close, and they spoke softly of the future, of the home they would make and the children they would rear, of the love they would share through the long years ahead of them. The nurse came in and fiddled with Tom's IV. He drifted into sleep, and Moira not long after, both dreaming of the life they would build, together.

EPILOGUE

SNOW FLUTTERED GENTLY to the ground outside the windows of Lukas Alexiou's home. He relaxed into the chair at his desk and sipped the two fingers of bourbon he allowed himself each evening. His office was dark, deliberately so. Most of his home's residents thought him asleep on this brisk December night.

At times, it paid to encourage others in their beliefs, however misguided.

He stared into the night at the quietly drifting snow. If only his own thoughts were as peaceful, his own life. He rubbed a single fingertip over the ache gathering behind his forehead. Marco could be such a child at times. He, of all people, should have trusted Lukas' judgment. His brother should have loved him enough to understand why they could no longer attack the People openly.

Prudence demanded patience. Lukas possessed more than his share of each.

He sipped the bourbon, savoring its slow burn. Marco was no longer content to hide in the shadows of his elder brother's rule. He fomented rebellion among the troops and openly sought the counsel of their uncle, Pinico, who would not rest until he had plunged them into an out and out war with the People.

War was not the answer here. Clinging to the hatred bred by

the generations-long blood feud between his people and the Daughters' would only bring an end to them both. Why did his closest family refuse to see this?

A sound behind him alerted him to another's presence in the room. Lukas inched his hand under his chair to the handgun holstered beneath the seat.

"Leave that," a familiar, emotionless voice said.

He swiveled around, set his bourbon on his desk, and switched on the small lamp placed on one of its corners. Soft light flared, illuminating a spare circle of space. A woman stepped into the light, her masked face nearly obscured by the hooded coat she wore.

He rose and bowed. "Ankana."

The woman inclined her head in a single nod.

He curled his fingers around the edge of his desk, stilling their slight trembling. Hope rose, thick and sweet and so strong he could barely draw a breath around it. "Why have you come?"

"It is time."

That breath left his lungs in a rush. He sank slowly into his chair and stared at her, his mind racing, his heart tumbling beneath the emotions her simple words had roused. It had been so long. He had done so many things, terrible, necessary things, and now, they had all come to fruition. "I shall leave on the morrow."

"That is best." She slowly drew her gloves off, one at a time. They were black leather, thin, the palms slick from years of wear. "You are not yet ready, child."

Lukas stared at the narrow hands revealed by the gloves. Memory flashed through him, hard and fast and viciously painful, of those hands touching his forehead, forcing him to remember lives long dead. Each one ended in a brutal death, each one was him, and not, and each time, he bowed under the weight of a burden that was his alone to bear.

So much pain. So much suffering, endless centuries of it pressing against his mind, sloughing away sanity and reason.

The tremble begun in his hands spread to his arms, to the fluttering beat of his heart, overtaking him in a rapid surge of fear. He sat and clenched the arms of his chair tightly between stiff fingers and met Ankana's cool gaze behind the impersonal serenity of her flat, wooden mask. "I accept what you willingly offer."

She moved slowly around the end of the desk and knelt before him. "Such a good child. Fate shall be kind to you."

He bit back the bitter laugh rising through the fear. Fate had been unkind to him from the moment of his conception to the present and seemed to linger best on what harmed him most. It would be worth it, though. Some day, everything he and Ankana had been working toward would come to pass. He would have his reward; if not the love his heart craved, then surely an end to the misery he had endured for far too long.

Ankana raised her hands and cupped his face. Her skin was cool, smooth, and somehow as comforting as a mother's touch.

An image flashed into his mind accompanied by a ripple of discomfort. Seven women sat around a campfire, light and shadow flickering across their smiling faces. This was the way it always started, with the seven women and their shared joy.

Another image leapt into his mind, and the discomfort twisted into the first tendril of pain. A sleeping city, a strong moon shining down, a warm, desert breeze blowing across the land.

He panted through the steadily increasing agony, knowing what was coming, knowing he couldn't stop it, and dreading it all the same.

Seven women crept forward, spears raised, expressions fierce. They slid over walls and into homes, unchaining the women bound there, shoving their spears through the men's chests as they lay helpless in sleep.

In the city, a cry arose. Other voices joined in, raising a chorus of warning through the darkened homes. Men spilled out of their beds and onto the streets, the closest weapon they could find held aloft as if that alone would halt the justice raining down upon their heads.

Sweat broke out along Lukas' skin. Why did she always show him this first? He knew the legend, knew what had begun that day or on one very much like it. He knew the consequences of what those women had done, and still, Ankana dragged him through it over and over again, as if the memory were not already ingrained into his mind so deeply he could never forget.

A young warrior stirred from slumber and raced outside, a sturdy, fire-hardened spear in one hand. He fought against the crowd racing away from the melee, searching for the cause of the alarm, and came upon a scene that had haunted Lukas since the moment Ankana had shared it with him.

A woman lay on the ground, her dark eyes turned toward him, her life's blood slowly ebbing out of her through a wound in her side. The warrior dropped his spear to the bare dirt ground and held his hand over hers, pressing them both into her wound. "I'll get help," he murmured. A healer, someone, *anyone* who could staunch the flow of blood and save the woman lying there, her beautiful features contorted into a grimace. She whispered something so softly it was lost among the grunts and screams of the raging battle. He leaned closer, placing his ear next to the gentle curves of her lips, and listened intently as her broken voice recited words he had no hope of understanding.

Lukas closed his eyes. *Not this. Please not this,* he prayed, but the vision continued, unmindful of his plea.

A sharp pain erupted in the warrior's side. He touched a hand there and stared disbelievingly at the crimson liquid staining his fingers. The woman's lips ceased their movement and her eyes fixed on the sky above them. A second pain joined the first, this one higher in his chest, shoving him forcefully against the woman's prone body. The warrior grasped her fingers in his own and recited a litany to the goddess of death as a cold blackness crept around the edges of his awareness.

Lukas squeezed his eyelids as tightly together as he could,

panting through the pain filling him, made by wounds he'd never received. *Please let it be over. Please let that be the only one.*

That image faded and was replaced by another and another and another in a dizzying rush of time after time, captured in single moments scattered along history's meandering paths. Death, always death, rushing up to meet Lukas with the eagerness of a child awaiting Santa Claus on Christmas Eve, the Reaper's icy fingers flipping through the centuries as if they had taken only moments to live.

"No," Lukas murmured, unaware of his own voice over the scenes raging through his head and the tight fist of agony squeezing the breath from his lungs.

Again and again, he witnessed the deaths of men who somehow became him. Again and again, their fear and pain etched their way into his consciousness, shoved into his mind in wave after relentless wave of sound and fury.

He gritted his teeth against it, gritted his teeth against the scream rising in his throat. His fingers clawed into the chair's arms, bruising his skin as the past poured unceasingly over him.

"Only one remains," a woman's voice said, and the images ground to a halt.

A spear hung in the air, its sharpened point hovering ten feet away from Lukas' heart. He faced it as calmly as he could, uncertain what to do in the face of this new vision.

Ankana walked slowly out of the darkness into the sphere of light surrounding him and the spear. "This is your destiny, Shadow."

She rested a single fingertip on the butt end of the spear and pushed gently. Under the force of her touch, the spear spiraled slowly forward. Lukas' gaze fixed on the weapon. He tried to step aside, tried to force his limbs away from the spear's deadly trajectory. They were frozen in place, unmoving, no longer his to control. His heart leapt into a frantic beat as the spear came ever closer, moving faster and faster toward its target.

"This is the moment you were born to fulfill."

No, not this, never this. Had he not endured a hundred deaths in precisely this manner? Had he not earned a better death somewhere along the way, in the years of sacrifice since his thirteenth birthday, in the manner in which he had halted the war between himself and the People?

The spear leapt forward and thudded into his chest, slicing cleanly through flesh and bone and the fragile tissue of his heart. A raw scream burst from Lukas' throat, and in the vision, his life bled slowly away, taken by the hand that had promised to save him.

About the Author:
Lucy Varna lives in Georgia, surrounded by her large, extended family. Visit her online at:

www.lucyvarna.com
www.daughtersofthepeople.com

The Daughters of the People Series
Book 1: *The Prophecy*
Book 2: *Light's Bane*
Book 3: *The Enemy Within*
Book 3.5: *Tempered*
Book 4: *In All Things, Balance*

Look for *Say Yes* (A Sons of the People Novel) coming in April 2015 and *Sanctuary* (Daughters of the People, Book 5) coming soon!

Also by Lucy Varna, the Cullowhee Heritage Series
Book 1: *A Higher Purpose*
Book 2: *A Wicked Love*

The adventure continues...

Sanctuary (Daughters of the People, Book 5)
Jerusha Mankiller and Drew Martin continue the People's search
for Sanctuary and the Bones of the Just.

Available soon!

Future books in the series:

Book 6: *The Gathering Storm*
October 2015

Book 6.5: *Redemption*
February 2016

Book 7: *War's Last Refuge*
June 2016

Don't miss the first Sons of the People novel!

Single mom Sera Noland wasn't looking for love the day Levi
Ewart walked into her life, especially when her heart, and her
son's, had already endured enough hurt to last a lifetime.

Look for *Say Yes* (A Sons of the People Novel)
coming in April 2015.